BLOOD OF THE KEY

Part Two of The Berylian Key Trilogy

Book Two of the Pantracia Chronicles

Written by Amanda Muratoff & Kayla Mansur

www.Pantracia.com

ISBN: 978-1-7337011-2-9

First Edition: June 2019

This book is dedicated to our parents,
for all your love and support.

The Pantracia Chronicles:

Visit www.Pantracia.com to discover more.

Chapter 1

Winter, 2610 R.T. (recorded time)

Kin imagined his day progressing quite differently.

Every part of his screaming mind fought, urging him to pull away. But he couldn't. Alana's energies tightened around his, squeezing like a python against his attempts to access the Art. The pit of his stomach roiled as his mouth responded to hers, deepening the forced kiss.

Enveloping her slender form, Kin's fingers played at her waist.

Her dress hugged her hips in a traditional Aueric style. Sickly hot breath pressed against his lips, and it felt utterly wrong. She wasn't Amarie. Not the woman Kin loved.

He struggled, trying to think of Amarie instead. Imagining the way her deep, ocean-blue eyes could make him feel with only a glance, opposed to the disgust brought on by the toxic green of Alana's gaze.

Where is Amarie? he wondered.

Alana tasted bitter.

His desire for the auer woman in his youth had long mutated into an ugly rage. Raven hair tangled amongst his fingers, too thin to be Amarie's. Cold hands touched his jaw, eliciting chilling goosebumps along his skin.

His connection to the energies of Pantracia felt trapped beneath a layer of ice.

How could the power he'd traded his entire life for be so useless?

His thoughts drifted to memories of the temple where he'd met the creature he now called Master. Alana led an unwitting seventeen-year-old to *him* with the promise of great power.

Artless, Kin would never gain the affection of an auer like Alana. His childish dreams cursed his future, riddling it with storm clouds, now grown to a permanent monsoon.

The Master, who appeared a man as simple as Kin, demanded obedience in exchange for his gift. Greed thrived within the shadows the Master gave those who served him. He didn't lie about the power he'd endow, granting access to energies unlike any others in Pantracia. But the duration of service was never discussed.

Of course, at the cost of a piece of his soul, Kin should've known better than to think it anything shorter than the remainder of his life. No one could escape the Master's indelible mark. While it granted unquestionable power, the Master somehow controlled the source. He infested his servants, becoming a blight Kin could never rid himself of. Even if he tried, the Master could always trace the flow of energy to find him.

That knowledge assured Kin he always had access. Unlike him, Alana wasn't a Shade.

Kin's mind strained, his entire body shaking. Stinging pain erupted from the frozen brand on his forearm. His right arm regained control first, summoning the energies the geometric tattoo granted him.

Cold vines of black ink wrapped around his arm, grasping at the air. They licked over his flesh to purge Alana's hold. The shadow slithered across his chest, sinking into his veins to re-establish control.

Kin jerked away, gasping for breath. He caught a faint ripple of his power as it dove back into the tattoo, reasserting itself into the set of thirteen shapes. He leaned over, lightheaded, hands grasping his knees for support as he glared up at Alana.

She stepped back, her flat shoes scraping against the cobblestone garden path, her long amethyst skirt swishing at her ankles. Red lips stood out against the dark complexion of her face. Her cavernous eyes dug into him, pupils swollen as if human. The edge of her lip twitched, a tension showing either amusement or aggravation. Maybe both.

"Now, that wasn't so awful, was it, Kinronsilis?" Her voice grated against his ears. "It wasn't so long ago you craved affection from me."

Kin sucked in another breath, forcing his back to straighten. He delved into the well of energy nestled within him, where the Master's link connected. He needed to assure himself the connection was still there, even if he sometimes wished it wasn't.

The corrosion, like a void at the edge of his soul, still swelled with darkness.

A growl bubbled past Kin's tongue. "You bitch," he spat. His hand moved to his aching chest. It took more energy than he'd anticipated to break free of her. "What are you playing at?"

Alana merely smiled, her hands crossing over her abdomen as she lifted her chin.

The distant slam of a door somewhere within the estate broke the silence, followed by chattering voices.

"It's already done," Alana mused, her eyes hinting towards the hibernating ivy on the gated archway behind Kin.

He turned to see a cloud of dirt beyond it, as if someone had hastily left. Wisps of dust curled on themselves, drifting to settle with a sense of finality.

A rock plummeted to the pit of Kin's stomach, his mind whirling. *Amarie.*

His attention flashed back to the auer as her green-painted nails bit into the ink of his tattoo. A hiss escaped him, his arm twisting to her will. She looked as if she hardly exerted herself to yank Kin's back out of alignment. He hunched, his face forced lower than hers.

"Let her go, Kin," Alana snarled, her pearl-like teeth clenched together. "She's a distraction you don't need. I'd have thought you wouldn't need a reminder of what'll happen if you disobey."

Fear tickled his senses as Kin thought of the consequences. She knew his commitment to the Master was different from hers. Alana's loyalty was a choice, while Kin no longer had that luxury.

Using what strength he could muster, Kin ripped his arm from her grasp. "I'm not afraid of death." He squeezed his forearm to dampen the flow of blood her nails had caused. "I'm no longer the scared child you fed to that monster."

"Your recalcitrance will undo you," Alana warned. "It's not only death you should fear from him, *Sae'quonei*."

He grimaced at the old nickname, which meant 'little one' in the ancient Aueric tongue. It'd frustrated him as a teenager, but as a man, it was even more infuriating.

"You honestly lecture me? You warn *me* of the dangers of service? I'd never have known them if it weren't for your interference in my life," Kin said.

"Is this how you show gratitude?" Alana frowned, flicking her nails against her thumb. "How you thank the woman who saved you?"

"Of all the things to call yourself, and believe me, I can think of *many*, one of the last I would choose is *woman*," Kin sneered.

Alana's eyes flashed with anger, breaking through the calm demeanor she otherwise assumed.

If he could infuriate her, she might be distracted enough to lose control of her delicate hold she still had on his will. Then he could go after Amarie.

"You question my loyalty to that beast without taking the time to understand the truth," Kin hissed.

Unrestrained fury crossed Alana's features, and he wasn't given the chance to continue speaking.

Dizzying agony shot through him, forcing his head aside as the back of her hand struck him across his face. He paused to stretch his jaw, rubbing at the radiating pain.

"You're certainly not loyal if you think of him as a beast, you misled boy. That girl has clouded your mind and turned you into a fragment of the man you could've become. Tell me, Sae'quonei, why do you cling to her so tightly? Like a babe on the breast of his mother? She'll find the embrace of a true man. With a bed much warmer than yours."

Rage brushed away the pain, and he turned towards her. He held his stance in defiance. He'd cowered to her assumed authority too much before and couldn't back down now.

He forced a wicked smile, and her brows knitted together, scowling. "Jealous, Alana?" Kin asked, forcing a coy tone. "Did your confidence rise from the misguided infatuation of a young human boy who didn't know better? Or are you afraid? Terrified of what the shadow fiend will do to you if you lose your hold on his pawn to gain the throne of Feyor?"

Much to Kin's disappointment, Alana laughed coldly at him.

"What he'll do to you, soft one. What he'll do to *you*. Not me. I have no reason to feel jealous. I doubt she'll ever speak to you again. You're still mine," she said with satisfaction.

The faint echo of hooves faded into the distance, confirming her conclusion. They beat out of time, suggesting a second horse accompanied Viento. Another wicked smile crossed her lips, renewing the pounding ache in Kin's heart.

"Sounds as if she already has a new companion. Perhaps she'll forget you sooner than even I predicted." Her voice turned sinister. "Allowing you to return to more *pressing* matters. I urge you to remember your commitment to your master."

"Commitment." Kin spat the word. "You say it as if there's a choice when you know damned well there isn't." His knuckles popped as his fists clenched at his sides. "I've slaved dutifully for the past ten years. And contrary to your beliefs, I still serve his desires despite the yearning of the uninfected parts of my soul."

"You should take caution in your continued arrogance in denying his preeminence. He is your master, Sae'quonei. *You* chose to commit to him. *You* made the decision, as a selfish, greedy child. You, not I. Ten years is nothing but a drip—"

"Don't play innocent! You know the part you played in this charade," Kin yelled without intending to. "Ten years may be a blink of an eye for you, but it is far more to me. You played me—"

"Your human frailty is none of my concern. And don't humor me with talk of your soul." Her voice took on a low tone. "You have no soul. And he wasn't the one to take it from you. You're a disgrace to your family and are becoming an embarrassment to the Master with this nonsense talk. I expected more of you. He *demands* more of you."

An urgency to pursue Amarie encouraged Kin to depths he didn't previously believe himself capable of. "Are you really so afraid of him yourself? You continue to tiptoe and call him Master?" he asked. "Why are you so terrified to speak his true name? Uriel is no god—"

Kin promptly forgot his next words as a vice seized his throat, Alana's fingers sinking into his flesh like smoking-hot iron. Instinct gasped for breath, which didn't come. His hand clapped on her wrist, tearing at her frosty skin. The other went to his side for a sword carelessly left behind in the illusion of safety in his own home.

Alana's Aueric strength threw him to the ground, his head spinning as a raspy breath drew the oxygen he'd been denied. His vision blurred, straining to focus as she leaned towards him. The tips of her black hair brushed his cheek.

"Oh, Sae'quonei," she tutted, running her fingers along Kin's jaw. "It's time for a visit. You're overdue for a reminder of why you serve."

Blackness enveloped him, its origin unknown but encompassing. Fear lumbered in his chest, and he steeled himself against the dark.

Chapter 2

Running came easier than Amarie expected once Viento's hooves pounded beneath her. The old habit to flee, which she'd repressed with her desire to stay and attempt a life with Kin, reverberated through her with each pulse of her black Friesian's gallop.

She made her way south, followed by Talon. She wasn't entirely sure just how far they'd gone before she managed to force her power back into the tight little box which kept it hidden.

Viento slowed to a normal pace, and the harmless blue flames provoked by her emotions subsided.

She didn't know how to explain to Talon who she was. What she was. She felt terribly grateful when he didn't ask. How could he ever understand that she was the Berylian Key? According to thousands of years of storytelling, it wasn't supposed to be a person. No end existed to the well of natural energy she alone could access, unlike the source any other practitioner of the Art contained. Even Talon, with his natural ability and thousands of years of possible life as an auer, couldn't hold a candle to her potential.

Kin knew what she was, but he'd betrayed her. He tossed her aside, along with the love he claimed to have for her.

Amarie sought escape from the sour memories as they rode southeast.

The steady beat of hooves from Talon's Andalusian mare echoed behind her, and she glanced back at her uninvited companion.

Talon's Aueric features would catch any other woman's eye. His green eyes, so different than Kin's steel-blue human eyes, bore into her. He wore no cloak, the black sleeves of his light linen shirt flattened against his arms by the wind. A fitted deep green vest held the material to his chest.

How had it already been three days since leaving the Parnell estate? It didn't seem possible. Nights and days blended together. But they arrived at Meleasol, which her map confirmed was a three days' ride from Greg's Town. From Kin.

The pang of memory flashed through Amarie, the sight of Kin leaning against the door frame of the bedroom they'd shared for one brief night. The image created a sharp spike in her stomach, threatening her control. She swallowed, fighting to suppress her emotions.

The gravel roadway crunched as Talon brought his horse beside her and Viento.

Her headstrong, black Friesian sidestepped, sensitive to Amarie's emotions and still wary of their new traveling partner. Perhaps he had more sense than she did.

"We made good time," Talon said, his dulcet tone trying to be comforting despite the mundane words. At least he didn't ask if she was all right. He seemed to understand it was a question she didn't want to hear.

"Hopefully, the inn isn't full for the night," Amarie said. Her voice sounded as hollow as she felt. All she needed was time. Time to rewrite her brain and heart to be on the same page.

Fortunately, the inn had plenty of rooms and space in their stable. During the previous nights of travel, Talon and Amarie camped under the stars. She expected him to complain about the hard ground, but he'd remained silent.

Talon slept those nights. Amarie mostly laid awake, tormented by her thoughts and regrets.

She found herself standing alone in her rented room as the sun dipped low on the western horizon. Watching the slow descent that signaled the end of the day, her gaze shifted to the roll of the hills beside the glowing orb of light. Looking back in the direction from which they'd come, her heart stung but she shook it off with a roll of her shoulders.

Averting her eyes, she took only one step from the window before she heard a gentle rap at her door. Muscles stiff, she paused. She didn't feel keen on seeing Talon.

"It's Talon," he said through the door. "I brought you dinner."

"I'm not hungry," she responded with half-hearted insistence.

"Amarie," he said after a pause. With a heave of a sigh on his breath, he continued. "You need to eat something. I'm staying here until you do."

Her usual response would have been to laugh at him and let him sit out in the hallway as a mere test of his determination. But she didn't have the spirit to embark on a playful dance of will. Her feet silently took her to the doorway, where she opened the wooden door to reveal his face.

Why are you still here? she wondered. *I can manage alone.*

Talon stood, his ebony hair in a loose ponytail at the nape of his neck, with a small wooden tray in his hands. It bore a bowl of what she guessed was stew, with a hunk of bread beside it.

"I'm not hungry," she repeated.

"I understand," Talon said, his voice strangely firm. "But you still need to eat. You expended a lot of energy the other day, and it's going to take a toll if you continue starving yourself."

No, it won't, she thought, not having explained to him that the azure fire drained no energy. Amarie gingerly took the tray from him and placed it down on a nearby table.

He looked disappointed by her refusal but didn't budge from her doorway.

"Maybe later," she offered.

Talon's jaw flexed. Clearly unaccustomed to the obstinate quality she was prone to, it was only a matter of time before he lost all patience and left.

She'd gotten used to his company over their three days traveling together and couldn't quite decide if she'd regret his departure.

"Perhaps a walk, then?" he asked.

He hadn't let her out of his sight for most of their journey thus far, and she supposed staying in two separate rooms wouldn't dissuade him from keeping on with his surveillance.

His expression was difficult to read while he waited for her response. A part of her wanted to close the door, while the other wanted to seek comfort in the company of the man who kept her from doing something remarkably stupid. Like confronting Kin. Or Alana.

Against her better judgment, she nodded. She didn't bother to bring any of her usual weapons outside, feeling lost to their purpose.

Not the most friendly of places, Pantracia held many dangers. Neither city nor wilderness offered true safety, but wild animals usually had the intelligence to steer clear. People rarely had such sense. By sticking together, they formed a less attractive target to city thugs, but a good fight seemed appealing.

Curious glances followed Talon instead of her in a welcome change.

Amarie didn't try to find her voice as Talon led her up a street towards the edge of the city, then down an uneven path following a dried-up stream. The smooth rocks of the small riverbed waited patiently for the rains and melting snow which would come with the change of season. Beyond, loomed the forest, dense against the purple twilight horizon of the east.

Monstrous pines offered a preview of the terrain they ventured towards. The trees would only grow larger the farther east they journeyed. The pines and cypresses of Aidensar's legendary forest grew as wide as houses and as tall as mountains.

Amarie swore the air was warmer than it had been near the estate and let her cloak fall loose around her. The temperature would continue to rise as they made their way farther into the rainforests of Aidensar, which rarely saw snow even in the depth of winter.

As he looked towards the darkening sky, Talon's eyes shone with flecks of starlight reflecting against the gem of his iris.

"Talon," she started, finding his name oddly comfortable. "Why are you still here? Not that I don't...appreciate your concern, but I've been alone before." She looked up at him. If this had been a different time in a different life, she might have found a certain serenity in the moment.

His striking features and blind dedication to her well-being would have been enticing, along with his patient demeanor.

"I suspect that may be true," Talon said, offering a reassuring smile. "And I don't doubt your ability to be alone, but it doesn't mean you should be." He looked away from her towards the shadows of the tree line ahead.

The towering silhouettes blocked the moonbeams in the distance. Foreboding darkness engulfed the trunks, any remnants of the sun's light long gone.

"Besides," Talon said after the pause. "It may seem strange, but I feel a responsibility to you. After telling you the things I did."

His words forced her to think of Kin and what Talon had told her about him. Kin had never outright lied, at least not about himself. He'd claimed honorable purposes for his pursuit of a Berylian Key Shard. But he *served*, rather than worked for, someone. According to Talon, he had no control over his own will.

But he did lie about Alana, revealing Kin had played Amarie from the beginning. He swore to protect her, hold her, as he'd never done with the auer. She'd believed it until she saw them together.

She shook her head, staring at her boot as she twisted her toe in the dirt.

Instead of being alone, Talon stood beside her, claiming he felt responsibility for her.

Responsibility. How quaint.

"Well I suppose that's every woman's dream," she commented dryly. "To be endured over some misplaced sense of obligation."

Talon tilted his head, lips pursed. After a moment, he smiled and crossed his arms, looking back towards the trees. "I don't believe *endured* is the right word," he said. "Though if it helps you deal with the pain you're feeling, I'm happy to fill any role necessary."

His words echoed in her mind and brought a surprising smirk to her lips.

Any role necessary?

Amarie let out a sigh to suppress the threatening sarcastic humor. "None of this is your fault. You don't owe me just because you were the one to tell me the truth. I'll be fine without you, and I'm sure you have better places to be." She looked ahead at the impending darkness of the denser tree line.

"Quite the contrary," Talon said. "I don't have any other place to be. I'd intended to stay at the estate for some time. Catch up with my sister. But now I have a distinct distaste for her company."

During her time in Eralas, Amarie never encountered an auer with the empathy Talon displayed. It was curious, but likely due to the distance he maintained from his people. How long had it been since he visited his homelands? She'd suspected Talon was a *rejanai* like his sister, an auer banished from Eralas.

Her feet stilled, and she turned to face him. "Surely, there are many places you could go that don't involve coddling the heartbroken." She attempted a smile but felt her resolve falter when the softness of his gaze threatened her composure.

"Is that how you see my presence here? Coddling?" Talon asked. "I don't. Rather, I'm spending time to ensure you're strong enough to protect yourself should the need arise. In some ways, I know more about the dangers you face than you do."

She looked down with a shake of her head. "I'm strong enough," she said with a steadier voice than she expected.

"Are you certain?" he asked. "Are you truly certain?" His gentle tone came with a touch to her wrist.

No.

Forcing her gaze to move, she looked at his hand on her skin. The deep tan of his complexion stood against the lighter tone of hers.

"You don't understand the danger you subject yourself to by being around me," she whispered, not daring her voice to speak any louder.

His grip tightened before he released her, offering a smile. "I'm familiar with danger," he assured, matching her tone. "I already walk with precarious weight on my shoulders and don't fear more. I chose to follow you, remember? I'm aware you hold a power. A power I suspect Kin knows of. But I also offer knowledge of Kin's Art and the creature he serves."

Talon underestimated the threat she posed, but she resisted the urge to argue with the auer over information she loathed providing him. But he was right, Kin was intimately aware of the significance of her power. She wondered how long it would be before he shared her secret with another.

"You're intent on aiding me, then?" she asked. As much as she wanted to trust Talon, a part of her wondered if this was just another act of manipulation.

Talon's gaze pierced hers, unrelenting. Auer weren't particularly known for stubbornness, but this one had the trait.

"If you want to be alone, I'll depart at your request," Talon said, shifting uncomfortably. "I won't force my company on you. But I'm determined to do what good I may still accomplish in my life."

Although tempted by the offer, she couldn't deny the comfort the budding friendship provided her. It was something different. A distraction.

She held his gaze this time, trying to hear his words for what they were. He wanted to do some good, and it made her wonder what he desired redemption for.

Another man with a dark past?

The hint of a smirk touched the corners of her mouth. "You'll just force food on me," she said.

He laughed, a gentle sound rolling over his lips. "Perhaps," he agreed with a shrug. "Eventually you may finally concede to its necessity. Like the rest of Pantracia."

She turned in the same direction as before and watched him as they started to walk. "Perhaps you're right." She let out a deep exhale, enjoying the fresh scent of the pines.

"Where are you planning to travel from here?" Talon asked.

"Away," she said. "Somewhere warmer, hopefully. Central Aidensar, or Helgath." She contemplated. "When the winter thaws, Ziona might be a good option for me as well." She didn't assume Talon would still be with her by then, but she was beginning to come to terms with the need to make plans and continue her life without Kin.

"There's nowhere you consider home?" Talon asked.

"Not anymore," she said. "Olsa was my home once, but I have no desire to return."

He had an ability to draw the truth from her.

"I understand." Talon nodded. "If you do intend to travel farther into Aidensar, then I'm even more determined to stay by your side. You don't strike me as someone to join a caravan, and I've heard the tales of danger associated with traveling this part of the world alone. Regardless of power, someone will need to watch over you while you sleep."

"Caravans aren't for me," she agreed. "It certainly wouldn't hurt to have an ally." She'd encountered wild situations before in these woods. Another person on her side could make all the difference.

"We leave in the morning then?" Talon asked. "Towns make me anxious. Too many eyes seem to focus on the out-of-place auer." He sounded irritated in a way she hadn't heard before.

His discomfort in being stared at was familiar to her. Five years ago, while seeking refuge from Helgath, she'd ventured to the island of Eralas to uncover more information about the Berylian Key. Humans were as uncommon on their lands as an auer was amongst humans.

"Getting back to the wild is fine by me," she said. "It's been nice not having curious eyes on me for a change." She smiled.

"Yet another reason to keep me around, I suppose," Talon said playfully, but his expression remained grim. "Though if you ask me, you're the far more interesting one of us. I'm a typical auer in many ways. But you, I suspect, are far from an average human."

His unclear meaning caused another wave of doubt regarding his reason for staying. Eyeing him, she tried to decipher the motivations fueling him.

"You've kept your suspicions to yourself so far, has that been difficult?" she asked teasingly. A solace filled her as they stepped into the looming shadows of the dense woods.

"I wouldn't consider it so," Talon said more seriously with a glance her way. "Of course, rushing to conclusions is not something typical of my heritage. We're blessed with plenty of time to work things out. Has it been making you anxious?"

"No," she answered quickly. "On the contrary, it's been a relief not have to lie to you." She let out a short laugh, surprising herself with the honesty.

"Then I'm glad. I'd rather not make you feel the need to lie. I haven't done so to you and plan to continue in such a fashion. I have the time and patience to wait."

She felt herself nodding in agreement to his words, having experienced enough secrecy. "We have that in common," she admitted, noting the gentle rise of Talon's eyebrow at the implication. It was another aspect of her self-proclaimed curse she hadn't shared with Kin. And one she still tried to wrap her head around. She never knew her mother's exact age, but Amarie remembered she always looked young and jubilant.

The book she'd stolen from the Great Library of Capul ten months ago hinted at the potential for agelessness. The first edition volume, written in the original Aueric, theorized what would happen to the power of the Berylian Key if it was absorbed into a living host rather than the crystal which housed it before. Eternal life was only one of the few reasons it was sought after so feverishly.

It was all theory, and the Berylian Key could not fully prevent death. Her mother had died when Amarie was only six.

"I'd prefer not to lie or mislead you either, and so far, I haven't," Amarie said. "However, trust isn't something I can afford to give. Especially since my last confidant was undeserving."

The gleam in his eye when he looked at her spoke for him. His hand came to firmly grip her bicep, halting her walk so she would have to look at him.

"Trust is earned," Talon agreed. "I don't believe I deserve it yet but hope I might as our relationship progresses. I'll give you no reason to feel otherwise. I've experienced enough deception in my life already." He squeezed her arm before his grip loosened to a tender touch.

Staring into his spring-green eyes, Amarie couldn't have agreed more. Grateful for his understanding and patience, she smiled. "Then I won't deceive you," she promised, both to herself and to him. If he asked something of her, and she wasn't ready to share, she'd simply inform him she needed more time.

No lies, not from her lips. Not this time.

Chapter 3

Only vaguely aware of himself, pressure from the energies around Kin blinded him and made breathing difficult. He passed the time by focusing on each inhale, hoping to force his way free of the black.

Days passed. Something in his mind told him it had been so long, even if it only felt like hours since his exchange with Alana in the garden of his childhood home. The trek Alana forced him on surely took them farther from Amarie.

His stomach twisted at the thought of Amarie while trying to decipher where he was. The air felt impossibly thick, his body hovering in perfect darkness. His skin itched, like his mother's thick winter curtains when he'd wrapped himself in them as a child. But unlike woolen material, this didn't warm him. It frostily nipped at the deepest corners of his being.

It all abruptly ceased when someone grabbed the curtains and tugged, spinning him wildly free from the depths. His eyes burned, refusing to focus. The skin of his knees stung, torn by the broken marble he landed on. With his palms pressed against the cold surface, Kin tried to force his body upright.

A wave of warmth touched his cheek, emanating from a bonfire Kin loathed. The abandoned temple smelt of blood and death.

Kin caught Alana's scent, like cut roses left without water for too long, directly behind him. As he found his footing, he turned to face her. A gale of winter wind howled through the broken front door, whipping her hair forward to dance like tendrils of shadow that would be coming soon. The chill penetrated Kin's thin tunic, and his hands instinctively wrapped around his shoulders.

Her darkened eyes narrowed, lips in a thin line. She hardly reacted while Kin shivered. She no longer wore the dress she'd been in before, but her new attire offered little additional warmth. A blood red chemise fell off the edge of her shoulders, exposing her smooth bare skin. The sleeves tightened at her wrists, but slits allowed the firelight to shimmer against her tanned arms. A tight-fitting grey corset accentuated her narrow hips. Leather breeches, skin tight and laced along the sides met knee-high boots, which looked barely used.

Before he could speak, she threw the bundle in her hands to Kin. His fingers closed on the familiar material of his cloak. Unfurling it, he wrapped it around his shoulders. He didn't offer her thanks as he buttoned it at his shoulder, where it attached to cover his chest. She certainly didn't deserve it considering where she'd brought him.

Avoiding looking at the fire, he examined the shape of his shadow beside Alana's. They stretched, creature-like, along the floor towards the far broken archway.

He'd been in the main hall enough times to know it was exactly forty-eight paces from where he stood to the door. There were twenty-two decrepit benches swallowed by the vegetation fighting to reclaim the human structure dug into the side of the Dykul mountains. The altars, in small semi-circle alcoves, were completely overgrown with branches of trees once carefully preened as avatars for the goddesses of the Wild and the Harvest. Nothing remained of Nicosa Domon and her order here, only the rampant battle for reclamation by her wild twin sister Allara Saen.

Amarie's face appeared in his mind, granting him distraction from his dismal surroundings. The perfect curve of her lower lip pinched between her teeth. The locks of her deep-auburn hair falling from her ponytail and demanding to be caressed from her lovely face.

The swirl of color within her eyes, the blues of the sea and darkening twilight sky. Beneath the blue was the flicker of more, which he saw only when he held her in his arms, when their breath mingled, and she shared her energy with him. Tangled in passion, her irises welcomed the onset of sunset pinks and purples.

The same colors shone inside the shard his thumb traced inside the pocket of his cloak. Its hard, crystalline surface bit into his flesh and urged his mind to clear all thoughts of Amarie. He couldn't think of her now.

A sickening pulse of the corrosive tumor within his soul brought terror Kin couldn't prevent no matter how he tried. It rumbled deep in his gut, ever constant. It surged for a single horrible instant, and he swallowed, trying to control the nausea as shadows at his feet rippled.

Turning towards the back wall beyond the bonfire, framed with a tangled curtain of leafless ivy, Kin watched the Master approach.

He appeared nothing more than a man, with thick light-brown hair cut short at the sides of his head. Eyes like Amarie's glared in disappointment, the more turbulent sea of blue flecked with onyx and dirty gold. His strong hand scratched at the dense, neatly-trimmed beard framing a smile. He revealed the slightest bit of his white teeth as he stepped around the firepit.

Finely crafted and fitted clothing confirmed his wealthy appearance. His hand sported a gaudy ring, too large and golden to define anything but nobility. But of what house, what country, was unclear. Not that it mattered. With his power, he could certainly be whoever he damned well pleased.

"Kinronsilis." The Master's voice sounded eerily soft, eliciting a shiver down Kin's spine.

He tried not to flinch as the Master stepped forward, the shadow behind him rolled casually off the back fresco to follow. It danced unnaturally with his movements, passing unhindered over beams of orange sunset still peeking into the temple.

Kin averted his gaze, stooping to a respectful bow with his closed fist pressed to his chest. He held the Berylian Key shard tight within his grip, hiding it from the Master's view. The only way out of this situation was to hand it over. Kin would've drawn out his task as long as he could to allow himself time to be with Amarie, to find a way to have a relationship with her. Nothing mattered more than her. But Alana forced his hand.

As the Master's eyes slid past Kin to Alana, the pressure on his chest lessened, and he stood straight. He suspiciously watched the shadows behind his Master. In his peripheral vision, the ragged hem of someone's skirt caught his attention. He studied the well-worn work boots beneath the dirtied brown-orange hem. A black cloak was pushed back from it, equally worn.

Other than being his senior Shade by a few years, Kin couldn't recall anything about Trist. Her fit body had only the slightest curve at her hips with a black sash tied tightly around her waist. Blonde hair, with thick streaks of white twisted through it, lay braided over her shoulder. Her cheeks no longer held the tautness of youth, and her musty hazel eyes were framed with wrinkles like Kin's mother's.

She gave a simple nod of acknowledgment to Kin, which he returned. Another Shade's presence while he reported to the Master made his stomach knot.

The Master walked past him, focused on Alana. When his arm coiled around her waist to draw her close and kiss her, Kin's distaste for the woman surged. The wave of nausea came again with the little whimper from Alana's chest, her nails dragging with a bone-chilling scrape over the rough tunic covering Uriel's chest.

Kin swallowed a mouthful of bile, forcing himself to count the lumps of vegetation over the old benches again and try to block out the wet sounds of their affection.

"Alana," the Master purred with another pleased groan from her lips. "What have you brought me?"

"Doubt and distrust, My Lord," Alana crooned, the glow of her eye shifting to Kin. "I thought it best for Kinronsilis to be reminded of his duty."

A low growl rumbled from the Master as his fingers slipped away from Alana's waist, and his shadow pulsed at his feet.

Kin set his jaw, biting down on the side of his tongue to encourage his own self-control and remain upright rather than obey instinct to cower in the corner.

Trist's boots shuffled on the altar floor; even she wasn't immune to the aura ebbing through the air around them.

"Oh, Kin," the Master said as if speaking to a child.

So close, Kin could clearly see the tiny obsidian shards within his eyes. Uriel's eyes. A name Kin knew better than to speak aloud.

Uriel is no god, Kin reminded himself.

"Has your loyalty faltered? I hoped your previous task would discourage such behavior," Uriel said.

Kin recalled the terrified face of Bellamy, a young Shade he'd been tasked with bringing before the Master after attempting to flee service. Kin left Bellamy to die, to be torn apart by Uriel's will, on the very step Kin stood on.

"No, Master," Kin whispered, surprised his voice worked. "It hasn't. Alana speaks of things she doesn't know the truth of."

Alana frowned in the corner of his vision.

"Oh?" Uriel asked, glancing at Alana as her knuckles grasped the side of her breeches. "Then your task is progressing?"

"Master, it's done," Kin said. The sharp corners of the shard bit into his skin as he squeezed his fist tighter. He sought joy in making Alana look like a fool, using the pleasure to push back the fear raging in him.

"Done?" Uriel gave Alana another quizzical look, then walked between Kin and the firepit onto uneven, broken steps. "Alana, explain, please," he said with a misleading tone of civility.

"Lord, I have reason to believe Kin is drifting from service and if he truly has completed his task, it raises even more questions," she said as she walked forward.

Kin sidestepped from her hand before she could shove his shoulder aside.

She gave him another flash of anger.

Uriel's eyes narrowed, and his shadow grew unnaturally larger to encompass both Alana and Kin. A terrifying silence followed, the uneasy sound of Kin and Alana seeking strained breaths while within the shadow, echoing alongside the crackle of the fire.

"Give it to me," Uriel growled, the pools of his eyes moving to Kin. "The shard." He outstretched his palm.

Kin shuffled forward with an inhale and released the crystal from his grip. It stuck to the indentations of his skin briefly, before plopping into Uriel's hand.

The firelight flickered over it, radiating within the veins of purple and blue seeded through the opalescent semi-transparent stone.

Uriel took it between his thumb and forefinger to hold it to the light.

It glinted as the fear of Uriel realizing the truth crept into Kin, freezing his veins. The Master could never discover the shard was useless. That seeking them was futile. Kin steeled himself with a forced inhale, fueling his resolve with the determination to keep the truth of the Berylian Key's power secret.

The black shadow cast around Uriel twisted, snaking forward, and growing darker. It folded on itself, coalescing into an inky vine curling through the air. The tendril crawled up Uriel's tunic and over his arm to wrap around the shard. It gobbled up the object before oozing back and leaving Uriel's hand empty. The shadow dissolved back into the one Uriel's form casted, disappearing as if it had never been.

"Tell me, Kinronsilis," Uriel said, his body turned sideways. "Did you come across Ormon while you were completing your task?"

Shock surged through Kin, and everything in his mind tackled the emotion before it could surface on his face. He kept his expression even and his breath the same as he considered the name. He hoped he looked thoughtful rather than guilty.

He most certainly had encountered his fellow Shade. They'd pursued the same task.

Ormon somehow traced the presence of a Berylian Key shard to Amarie. He confronted Kin in the deep forests just south of the border to Feyor. Duty and fear insisted he should tell Uriel the truth.

It's not too late, a nasty voice at the back of his head urged. He could still spill it all to his Master. *Come clean and confess. Tell him about Amarie and the truth of the Berylian Key.*

Uriel would be so pleased with the new information Kin brought, he'd forgive the part Kin played in Ormon's death. He was dead with one of Amarie's crossbow bolts through his throat.

"I did not," Kin lied, mere moments after he was asked the question, crushing the internal voice suggesting otherwise.

"Pity," Uriel said. "I'd hoped you might have some further knowledge of his death." He scratched at the underside of his beard again, heaving an exaggerated sigh.

Kin resisted the urge to gulp.

"Now, Alana." Uriel's attention turned back to the auer, whose spine straightened at her name. He beckoned a hand to her, and she obeyed, climbing the steps to him.

She rose her chin as his hand moved to touch it, gliding over the curve of her neck.

"Tell me more about Kin's disobedience, my dear."

Alana's eyes fluttered towards Kin's and then Trist. They stayed there for a moment before they returned to the Master's. "I will, My Lord," she whispered seductively as her lips curled. "But not here. I think it's better we discuss this in private." She tugged at the bottom of his tunic, color rising in her cheeks. She leaned her body closer to Uriel's.

He didn't move, but his eyes swam with desire; the only human-like response Kin had seen in him.

"Very well." Uriel's voice grew deeper. His head angled towards the back of the temple, looking at Trist. "If Kinronsilis knows no more of Ormon, then you must act on the information you already have. Pursue and complete your task," Uriel commanded.

The woman bowed deeply. The end of her braid nearly touched the ground as it draped over her shoulder. Trist pulled her cloak to cover her simple buttoned dress and lifted the hood over her head.

"At your will, Master," she whispered, her voice tender and misplaced within one capable of what she was. She stepped back and, with a wither of vine, faded into the shadows of the wall.

Pursue? Did Trist know who killed Ormon? The knot in Kin's stomach pulled tighter.

"As for you." Uriel's gaze turned to him, forcing Kin to refocus from the shadows Trist disappeared into.

He hoped he hid the fear in his eyes.

"I need some time to contemplate where your skills may be best placed. And Alana has some things to tell me." Uriel eyed Kin, something in his gaze hinting he already knew much more than Kin wanted him to. "You will wait before I grant you your next task."

A searing pain shot through Kin, radiating from the tattoo on his right arm. He couldn't stifle the yelp of pain as he tore at his sleeve, and his fingers moved to the burning flesh. The geometric lines of ink swirled in tendrils around his arm, digging like worms into his flesh as if it were fresh dirt.

The inverted triangle closest to his elbow folded in on itself until it became part of the original line traced down the center, his skin raw as if the mark had just been cut from his flesh. The change signaled a demotion, drowning him in dread.

Whatever Alana said had costed him. He completed his task and should have gained a new symbol of his power, not lost one.

Biting his tongue, he controlled a retort at the decision, but his eyes must have said it.

"It's temporary," Uriel said, raising a hand to close on the motes of shadow rising through the air from Kin's arm. "Based on Alana's news. I'll call you when the time for your next task has come. And do try not to dally before you return?" A demand disguised as a request.

The pain in his arm subsided, and Kin stood straighter before giving another feigned respectful bow. "At your will, Master," he said quietly, successfully containing the instinct to growl it.

Chapter 4

Lynthenai's hooves beat rhythmically with Viento's on the worn roadway weaving through the Aidensar forest. Outside of Meleasol, the trees evolved from their already large sizes into ancient behemoths of a forgotten world.

Aidensar reminded Talon of Eralas in many ways, which brought a bittersweet comfort. The pines were as wide as city streets, stretching out of sight towards the sky. Sprinkled amongst them were oaks and cypress of equal grandeur, blessed from a time in which the ley lines fed directly into them, rather than its current spread in a fine net across the land.

Talon was far too young to remember such a time, but when he was a child, he'd been told the stories. The trees and ruins his people left on the mainland of Pantracia were forgotten by the humans who controlled them now.

Amarie led the way, a habit quickly formed at the beginning of their travels together.

Talon didn't mind, comfortable with following. He used the time instead to lavish himself with the energies of the forest around him, bathing in the solace it brought to his auer blood.

The birds were boisterous this time of year, so many having migrated to these woods from the parts of Pantracia affected by the snows of Nymaera's winters.

They'd agreed to head east, farther into Aidensar and away from

Delkest. Busy trade routes became their standard path, lessening the lingering danger the forests of Aidensar possessed. But bandits and grygurr didn't always stay away from the main roads.

Talon hoped for the former rather than the latter if they were to encounter trouble.

Humanoid beasts of questionable origin, grygurr possessed strange, feline appearances and behaviors. Far more intelligent than animals, the vicious scavengers organized in packs and encampments throughout the areas untouched by human populations.

As midday came, their custom of stopping to eat and rest the horses persisted. Patting Viento on the neck, Amarie pushed him off to graze after she retrieved their lunch from the packs on his saddle. She kept her sword at her side, which Talon deemed a reasonable choice. Her demeanor appeared more relaxed around him after their shared walk a few days before.

He ventured to believe she might come to trust him.

Her rapturous blue eyes demanded a certain softness from him, a patience and kindness he wasn't accustomed to displaying. At times during their rides, he found himself admiring the way the sunlight played off her dark hair, catching the red tones and reminding him of smoldering embers. Her features were fine and well-shaped with a softness in her chin which complemented the defined curve of her jaw. The fullness of her pink lips constantly threatened to distract him from his purpose of friendship and were unlike the sharp angles and thin mouths typical of auer women.

Talon's curiosity about Amarie went beyond her beauty and even beyond whatever mysterious power she held. Protective instincts weren't common for him, but they'd surfaced more rapidly than he could have anticipated upon realizing Kin's involvement with her.

"If we continue at this pace, we should be to Elyier in a little more than a week," Talon commented, seeking conversation to distract him from his thoughts.

Amarie lifted her gaze to meet his and flashed a smile which appeared more genuine than the day before. "That's good. I've never felt compelled to linger longer than necessary in these woods," she replied, walking to him and offering the parchment of fresh fruit.

Talon took it, resting it in the palm of his hand for them to pick from. He popped a grape into his mouth. "That's because you're smarter than most." He smirked. "There's a reason all of the villages near here are built in the branches and off the ground."

"They make you feel small, don't they?" Amarie asked while gazing at the trees. She continued as he glanced upwards. "This place makes me uneasy, too many opportunities for disaster. Am I right in assuming you're able to protect yourself if the need arises?" Her hand idly touched the pommel of her short sword.

"Little late to be asking, isn't it?" Talon teased, as he looked back at her.

"Too late is when grygurr overtake our camp, and I ignore you while you get your delicate auer ass handed to you," she quipped.

A soft laugh rippled through his chest. It was a pleasant feeling he didn't experience often enough. "I'll have to be more careful about my self-deprecating comments regarding my ass in the future." Talon smiled, remembering his joke outside the Parnell estate. "Especially if you're going to make a habit of remembering them. But yes, I am perfectly capable of defending myself. You may absolutely ignore me. And may I assume the same for you?"

She looked sideways at him. "Yes, you're welcome to ignore me. I can handle myself."

Good, he thought. His skill in the Art wasn't often used to protect others. The depth of her power, mostly unknown to him except for a brief display, appeared enough to defend herself. Now, if he could only figure out why she still bothered with the blade at her side.

Talon questioned his ability to completely ignore Amarie in the event they did encounter trouble. He tried to focus on the relief he felt that her mood seemed to be recovering and wondered if she truly felt the same mental healing she portrayed on the outside.

"Then I pity whatever poor grygurr thinks we might be easy targets," he said.

A distinct possibility reigned that grygurr would avoid them. Rumor suggested they often kept away from auer, which was rooted deep in the myths interlocking their people. He doubted Amarie knew the stories, since they weren't common knowledge, but he wasn't keen on sharing. Of course, if she asked, he'd answer. As he would with any of her questions. There were too many things she needed to know with her connection to Kinronsilis.

"Have you fought them before?" Amarie asked as she leaned against a tree.

"Honestly, no," Talon admitted. "Never had reason to before, but I've heard plenty of stories about their fighting techniques, and they don't worry me. Have you encountered them?"

"Twice," she admitted. "And I'd rather not go for a third." She crossed her arms loosely in front of her chest. "I daresay the tactics you've heard are true, and then some. They're smart and difficult to overpower."

Talon rewrapped the parchment of food. "Makes you wonder why anyone even bothers to travel through their territory." He caught up to Viento enough to stuff the food away in Amarie's bags. "Of course, we're a pair of those fools. There are greater things in Pantracia to fear than grygurr, though."

Her gaze darkened. "Don't I know it," she agreed with an even, unreadable tone.

No matter how he danced around it, things would always come back to the topic he feared discussing with her. He grimaced, watching massive pine needles crunch beneath his boot.

"I'm not referring to Kin, if that's what you're thinking," Amarie offered, voice marginally lighter as she clarified.

Even with Talon actively trying to avoid the topic, his name came up anyway.

Talon looked at her and forced a shrug. He didn't want to continue to tiptoe around the subject, it just made things uncomfortable. "I didn't think of him specifically either," he said. "I was thinking more specifically of his order. Shades. Another creature of legend like the grygurr, though a bit less common. You're either extremely lucky or unfortunate to have encountered both in your short lifetime."

Her eyes remained on him, the deep blue holding less hurt than in the days before. "I would go with the latter, in this case," she confirmed, and he couldn't blame her.

Amarie's lack of surprise at the term Shade hinted that she'd heard it before and had connected it with Kin. Humans used bedtime tales to explain the mysterious patches of death that appeared in villages and otherwise lush landscapes. Few knew the truth. Shades were depicted as ghostly monsters, unnatural creatures who drained areas of life for no apparent reason. But they always had a task.

Talon grew serious, crossing his arms over his chest. "You do know you can ask, right?" he urged, looking into her determined ocean-blue eyes. "Anything you want to know, you can ask me."

Amarie appeared to debate internally for a few moments, her eyes studying him a way that examined his very soul. Had she looked at Kin the same way when they first met?

"Yes, I know I can ask." Her gaze fell to the forest floor. "I just haven't been sure if I want to know. Kin knows some sensitive information and, since he is a Shade, I fear what consequences might follow. Can you tell me of the one he serves?" she asked, voice barely reaching him.

Her inquiry caught him by surprise, despite his invitation. He took in a breath as his mind rushed with images from his experiences with Kin which he was still piecing together himself.

"I can't pretend to know everything," Talon admitted. "The web of secrecy around the being who all Shades serve is dense and purposely so. I don't know its true name, only what they call it—Master. Most of my information is inferred through what I know of Kin and his service. My sister always made it explicitly clear that I wasn't to speak to her about it. She denied having any knowledge at all for many years."

Amarie fell silent again for several moments, her gaze distant. He wasn't even entirely sure she was listening to him, so he hesitated.

Her irises flicked back to him, and she shook her head. "I can't explain the predicament I'm in without sharing the same information Kin knows. It leaves me in a precarious position. I don't know how to seek answers without explaining," she said, choosing her words with care. "Kin could easily exploit his knowledge. I'd be an asset to his Master. If all you say is true, he'll pass this information along to the one he serves, yes?"

Talon felt an unfamiliar anxiousness tighten in his stomach.

"Should I be expecting an army of Shades to come for me?" she asked, with a vulnerability she hadn't previously shown him.

Talon's breath caught in his throat. The strange overwhelming instinct to embrace her, comfort her, was unlike him. His heart thudded, mind buzzing, as he resisted the inclination.

"It's possible," he admitted somberly. "From what I understand, Shades are essentially servants. I have deduced that they receive a single task at a time, and all their attention is focused on completing it. Through the completion of these duties, they earn favor with the Master, and he grants them further power. Shades of longer service are more powerful, typically, because they have completed more tasks. There is no room for moral reservations. Whether a Shade agrees or disagrees with what they are bid to do, they must complete it or suffer consequences.

"Kin expressed a clear distaste for his first several tasks, but greed and compulsion were enough to dissolve his conscience," Talon concluded.

"Doesn't he have a will of his own?" Amarie asked.

"In a sense, he does. But it is deeply corrupted by the desire for self-preservation and advancement. I don't pretend to know the man he has become after ten years of service. From my understanding, most of the Shades who served before him are no more. He's one of the oldest. I believed the corruption would kill him, but he has yet to burn through. Instead, the destruction follows him and creates children's tales."

"What were his tasks?"

"I only know the details of a fraction of them, but they suggest the Master is quite keen on amassing power. It's strange, because from what I'm able to sense, the threads of Art tethered to the Shades is different from anything natural in Pantracia. It eats and destroys in a way beyond natural death. I tried to explain it to Kin once, but he wouldn't listen. What Shades do when they soak in the energies from around them is not death. It's something far worse."

When he finished speaking, Amarie's brow drew together, and her shoulders slumped. The toe of her boot dug into the ground as she swallowed. She'd reached her limit, and he felt a wave of guilt for making her find it.

The glisten of wetness at her bottom eyelid dismantled his resolve to keep his distance. He held his breath as his arms dropped from his chest, encircling Amarie instead. He sought to support her with his strength as best he could. His breath blew gently across the top of her hair, blowing back strands of auburn as he closed his eyes.

Her hands touched his vest in front of her, the side of her face against his chest.

"I'm sorry," Talon whispered.

Her breath came slow and even, and her muscles relaxed. "I'm glad you came with me," she admitted, her pledge of honesty appearing to prevail above her pride. Her hand on his chest pressed near her face, and he wondered if she felt his heart beating.

He didn't know what to say without sounding pathetic, so he locked his jaw. She felt fragile in his hands, even if he fought to remind himself that she wasn't. A compulsion within him wanted to hold her delicate form tightly and always protect her.

A few breaths later, her head lifted from his chest, but he didn't quite let go as she tilted her chin to look at him. In an instant, he found himself in a position he hadn't experienced in a long time. With her in his arms, their faces close, he saw the different flecks of blue within her eyes and the rosy edge of her lip. Her expression was impossible to read, but the sadness had vanished.

Her mouth relaxed, her lips parting.

The shrill call of a distant finch shocked him from his trance, and his hands remembered how to listen to logic. He abruptly let go of her, clearing his throat and looking in the direction of his horse.

"We should continue on," he said. "Before it gets too dark." Looking at Amarie would be a bad idea, so he moved towards Lynthenai. He took his horse's bridle to guide her from the sweet grass she munched on.

He urged his shoulders to relax in case Amarie noticed. His highly inappropriate inclinations were the last thing the poor woman needed to deal with. Yet it was difficult to ignore the attraction budding within him. To fully deny it would have been far more hazardous.

They spent the remainder of the day riding in silence, though Talon's mind rambled on with wild thoughts.

Perhaps he imagined the connection between them? A part of him wondered if he over analyzed a simple embrace between friends. The unusual emotional turmoil hindered his attempts to focus on anything except Amarie.

When the forest flooded with sunset colors, they passed by a trade caravan stopped to make camp. Their wagons circled a firepit, swelling with the aroma of their dinner already underway.

Fortunately, they seemed uninterested in Amarie and Talon, who continued past until the sun dipped too low for them to continue. They made camp under a low-slung canopy of branches belonging to a younger oak.

Conversation failed to resume; tense uncertainty hanging in the air. Luckily, their routine for nightly camping was well established, and she removed the edible contents from their packs while he went about setting up a fire.

If Talon listened intently enough, he heard the distant chatter of voices carry over the wind. The lull of their voices kept him distracted.

He caught Amarie's gaze on him in the corner of his vision and stiffened.

She settled herself on the far edge of Talon's bedroll and placed a parchment of dried meats and bread between them. Holding out her hand, she offered an apple which he accepted with a grateful smile. Biting into hers, she looked towards the small blaze of their camp fire, nursed by his Art.

He tangled the weaves of the invisible fabric against his fingertips in a comforting buzz.

The glimmer of orange light played on her face.

Looking from her to the apple in his hand, he debated what to say. She seemed content with silence, but he couldn't be. But what *had* he intended by his actions?

"Amarie, I—"

She cut him off with a raised hand and a sharp shushing sound.

Irritation bubbled in his throat, and he narrowed his eyes. His mouth opened to protest, until he realized her head was tilted, her ear lifted to listen. He obeyed and changed his focus to his hearing.

An eerie lull filled the trees, devoid of birds and wildlife. The murmur of voices had faded, but it was doubtful the caravan camping nearby was already turning in for sleep.

A sharp ring of steel cut through the forest, followed by a shriek of terror. A distant roar he'd never heard before replied. It sounded like the scream of a wildcat gnarled with the inflections of a man's tongue. Rasped and battle worn.

Amarie's gaze flicked back to him, her eyes wide. "Grygurr," she murmured, recognizing the sound. "The caravan."

Talon clenched his fist tight and used a whisper of his will to snuff out their campfire. His power tickled within him, vibrating like a contained whirlwind of potential, but he didn't draw on it beyond dousing the flame and pushing the smoke into the ground.

He refused to pretend he had a hero complex that urged him into action. What happened to the caravan was no concern of his. His focus belonged instead on himself and Amarie and remaining unknown to the grygurr.

With the space between him and Amarie abruptly dark, his eyes took a moment to adjust. When he found Amarie's gaze, she glared at him in confusion.

"Are you just going to sit there?" she asked, voice suspended in disbelief.

He shrugged. "I don't think it would be wise to—"

Before he could conclude the otherwise obvious statement, she rose and jogged to her nearby mount. He watched as her fingers unlatched her crossbow from Viento's saddle, but she didn't lift herself to mount him as he half expected.

What is she thinking?

He stood to follow her. "What—"

She interrupted him again, "Suit yourself and stand idly by," she spat. "But I'm not going to cower while innocent people fall to those beasts." The fire in her eyes warned him not to argue. She slung the quiver of bolts over her back and held the crossbow in front of her.

Why does she insist on arming herself with so many weapons? It seemed unnecessary considering her skill in the Art.

Talon struggled to understand why she foolishly wanted to help strangers. Surprising himself, he whistled low for Lynthenai. He could have sworn he saw a vague hint of approval cross Amarie's face before she turned and bolted off through the forest towards the caravan on foot.

Puzzlement could not sufficiently express the feeling overwhelming Talon as Lynthenai's head pushed underneath his hand, urging him to notice she'd come like he'd called. He'd been distracted watching Amarie maneuver around trees and through the underbrush with agility. The mystery of her continued to escalate.

Letting out a huff of frustration, Talon pulled himself on to Lynthenai's saddle. He didn't completely settle or grab the reins before a click of his tongue and tap of his heel urged his mare into a gallop. She didn't hesitate, even as they turned onto the worn road which echoed with nearby battle.

The air thundered with poised power, manipulated by one or more practitioners of the Art. He suspected Amarie, in the careful way it ebbed against the energies surrounding the battle.

Swords clashed against wood and stone, ripping through the night air.

The firepit at the center of the encampment still raged with life, illuminating all around it. The caravaners scattered, running and shouting, while five grygurr rampaged through their camp. Horses whinnied while children cried. Men and women struggled with swords to fend off the attacking beasts.

The grygurr stood taller than the humans by about a foot, even with a deformed, hunched back. Adapted to camouflage in the forest, their dark skin was dappled with wildcat spots along their backs and sides. Tufts of midnight fur tipped their long, pointed ears, elbows, and knees. Their elongated faces appeared somewhere between that of a man and jungle cat, with an upturned nose and long fangs.

In his futile search for Amarie, Talon's eyes landed on a slower grygurr. He carried a sturdy quarterstaff, adorned with beads and carvings that matched his plethora of necklaces.

Talon recognized him as the source of the hum in the air. The fur along his jaw was flecked with thick strands of white, tinted orange by the firelight. He radiated power, suckling on the energies all around them, funneling it to his companions.

Talon resisted the urge to reach for the same powers; he'd draw the attention of the creature. Instead, he dismounted Lynthenai in a massive shadow at the edge of the camp, ushering her away from the chaos.

A man cried out as grygurr claws slashed his sword out of his hands, and he fell to the ground. Scrambling to get to his blade with his back dangerously exposed, he was most certainly about to meet his end, and Talon could never reach him in time even if he'd wanted to. A blurred streak split through the brush on the left side of the camp and sank deep into the attacking grygurr's skull. The creature's body slumped to the ground in a heap. A roar of rage erupted from his companions.

With the cacophony of sounds, a sixth grygurr emerged from behind one of the wagons. His large yellow eyes narrowed on the origin of the crossbow bolt.

The grygurr wore hardly any clothing, only rugged strips of linen fashioned to conceal the parts any human would. A few were decorated with belts or sashes, draped over concave waists, or awkwardly across their chests.

When a second bolt flew and impaled the newly emerged grygurr, a third turned on its cat-like hind legs and charged into the brush with a maniacal snarl.

Talon remembered his words to Amarie, stating he would ignore her if a circumstance such as this were to arise, but his heart leapt into his throat as he realized she wouldn't have time to load another bolt.

He conceded the weapons must be a temporary tactic, because her use of the Art would draw the same attention he also avoided. He didn't have much time to think this through before a daring set of green eyes, rimmed with gold and amber, met his.

The low growling breath of the largest of the raiding party heaved, gaze locked with Talon's for what felt like an eternity. The creature remained still for a mind-numbing amount of time, as if debating whether he wanted to fight an auer. The rumors seemed more plausible as the large warrior, fur streaked purposefully with mud, hesitated. His chuff drew the attention of another, head swiveling towards Talon and away from where Amarie was certainly dying.

A colorful Aueric curse found his lips as he realized he could no longer avoid conflict.

The two beasts, twenty feet in front of him, turned away momentarily, distracted by a rustle of leaves and feminine yelp. Amarie flew from the brush, thrown by the grygurr who'd gone in after her, and she tumbled over the dirt.

She found her feet in a swift movement, drawing her sword. Her attacker lunged after her, bringing a stolen axe down to meet her blade in a fierce attempt to overpower her.

Talon couldn't watch; his concern for her would negate the opportunity he now had. With the two grygurrs' attention diverted, Talon dropped a breath into his core. It fueled the connection deep within him. He didn't need to draw from around him, but the tender comfort the energies of the forest gave made the link to his own energy easier to forge.

The flow of the Art rippled through his limbs as he twisted the fabric around him to obey his will. The air heated as his hands drew together, the power of his veins pooling in the palms of his hands, creating a purple and amber flame which curled around his weaving fingers. It barely took any effort, the motion easy despite the destruction dancing within it.

Taking a step forward, he braced himself before he drew his hand back. Snapping power sizzled in his ears before the weave ripped itself from his outstretched hand, arcing forward like lightning towards the larger grygurr's throat. Talon's other hand spun in lazy circles parallel with the ground, his power searching for its next weapon.

Unexpected, the lance of fire struck its intended target squarely at his jugular.

The beast tumbled back, slamming to the ground. The flame danced on his flesh, burning. Clawed hands flew up, trying to smother it, but it didn't cease. Choked growls came from the massive writhing form, his legs bucking to fight an untouchable foe holding him down.

The tawnier-coated grygurr eyed his fallen companion and took an unwilling step away from the Art at work. Long talons withdrew a two-handed sword from an awkwardly slung belt. The massive claymore spun easily in one of the grygurr's hands. The warrior flew forward, no longer hesitating in going for the auer who attacked first.

The grygurr's first step came to a rattling stop, his ankle seized by a root which hadn't been there before. It wrapped around his lower leg, squeezing tighter.

Talon steadied his breath as he pressed the energies from his own body to tear the grygurr to the ground. He focused on drawing the Art in slowly to maintain control before daring a glance at Amarie.

Chapter 5

Amarie planted one foot behind her, her blade holding back the grygurr's axe. Pulling from her internal well of power, she strengthened her muscles beyond their natural limits. Otherwise the grygurr's attack would have split her skull.

So close to his cat face, with his ragged stench of breath beating down on her, she saw the confusion in his large round eyes when she didn't buckle beneath him.

Shifting his weight to the side, the blade grazed her upper arm.

Sharp pain radiated, but Amarie refused to let it distract her. She twisted her weapon, catching the edge of his axe to deflect it. The jarring impact forced her fingers from the hilt of her sword, and it fell with a dull clatter to the ground.

The loss of support in front of him caused the grygurr to stumble forward.

Amarie's left hand thrust to her side, finding her dagger. In a swift, practiced motion, she buried the blade into the soft flesh under the grygurr's jaw.

Death came to him with little noise, but a sticky hot ooze coated her wrist. He collapsed at her feet as she found herself facing two more who came to assist in the failing attack.

A wielder of the Art stood twenty yards behind her at the other side of the encampment, but his abilities didn't concern her. The blades held by the two new grygurr posed a greater threat.

She dared to look away from their slow approach, spying two grygurr who had fallen by Talon's hand. A smile twitched at her lip. A part of her doubted he'd participate, but his change of heart pleased her. She couldn't tell how Talon downed the first, a monstrous beast easily twice her size. His claws tore at his own throat, flecks of blood coupled with gargled screams and the smell of burning hair.

The second had a steadily growing root snaking up its leg. The lighter furred grygurr shifted to his back, trying to crawl backwards away from the vines as they clung to him.

Talon stood, his eyes clear in their focus as he walked towards the struggling pair. His hand, shrouded with a strange dark cloud of power, reached for a glint of steel. His right hand pulled a manifested ebon hilt from his sleeve.

Talon's eyes flicked towards her as he stalked closer to the grygurr still fighting against his Art. He didn't return any semblance of a smile, focused on her with wide eyes. His empty hand motioned wildly in the direction behind her, his gaze darting from her and towards the staff wielding grygurr.

She spun around to see the old shaman lifting his weapon, beating its end rhythmically against the ground. Dancing against the decorated wood, the carvings sparked and glowed with an incandescent blue-white light. A swirl of power rushed across the ground into the base of his staff, through the curves of his chipped claws; the beads rattled with electricity.

The metallic taste of an electrical storm formed in the air.

In the corner of her vision, Talon turned from his trapped victims to face the thrumming power instead. He surged towards the shaman with his wicked serrated blade at his side.

Her heart jumped into her throat. A crashing wave of adrenaline flooded her veins, fueling her sprint towards the caster. She ignored Talon and lunged ahead without hesitation. She needed to get to him before the auer did.

He might have been able to do something, but there was no doubt in her mind that she was better equipped to handle the threat.

Neither of them made it to the shaman before his Art unleashed.

Only halfway across the camp, the enveloping flash from his staff blinded Amarie. The bolt of lightning danced towards her with deadly design. She sucked in a hot breath, trying to mentally prepare herself for the impact.

The white-hot crackle collided with her body in searing rage. A boom accompanied it, and her ears rang defiantly. Amongst the shudder, she heard a distant, ragged scream, but it wasn't her own.

Amarie's heart pounded in rhythm with the throbbing electricity, racing faster, her stride unfaltering. A crash of energies erupted within her. At first it felt abrupt, but then her pulsing power, her curse, devoured the new source without so much as a moment of pause.

The unfurling power merged with her own, her body momentarily ablaze as it coped with the unexpected gift. The blue flames she fought to hide before licked her skin in a blaze, before they extinguished as if never there at all. The blinding white flash ebbed from her vision, eyes adjusting through the haze of purple and pink.

A fresh wave of strength pulsed through her limbs as she ran. With the lightning coursing through her, she breathed hard but felt no pain. The Berylian Keystone had been a conductor for the great ley lines when it existed in its original form, and its new form acted in a similar manner.

Everything progressed in slow motion.

In her final stride towards the cat-beast, her hand shot out. Her empty palm impacted his chest. With all her might, she surged every ounce of the Art burning within her soul into him. A short cry of effort left her throat. In their contact, Amarie became hyper aware of the shaman's spider-webbed connection to the surrounding nature.

She pushed the energy from herself, and it swelled within him like an overflowing cup. It bubbled over, streaming from his being where it couldn't be contained. A pop preceded a whoosh as it raged through the grygurr's soul. Like the ember of a wick struggling for life after being blown out.

The glow from the lightning on her skin faded as the power reduced to dull sparks and the old shaman fell limp. His body crumpled with a clatter of stone and clay beads; the haze of his connection to the fabric snuffed out.

Amarie stood in place, gasping for breath as the familiar lust within her begged to use more power. The intoxicating rush of the moment threatened addiction, and she fought to steady herself. Whirling around, her gaze found Talon.

He skidded to a stop five yards away, eyes wide and mouth slightly agape as he stared at her. The blade in his hand hung limply at his side, all intent behind it lost.

The grygurr tangled in the roots howled in rage as he tore the last of the wood free of him. He bounded to all fours and gazed with dark eyes towards the auer, but then past him to the fallen shaman.

Talon was too distracted to notice the threat, but it quickly became irrelevant because the creature fled into the trees, followed by the two previously threatening Amarie.

"Amarie?" Talon questioned, his voice unsure.

She ran a hand over her hair, unflinching as she still attempted to catch her breath, regaining her grasp on the power flooding her. Her breathing slowed as she watched Talon, looking for any sign he might flee from her, as most logical people would.

Talon's chest hardly moved as if he wasn't breathing. He just stared at her, looking at her eyes, her hands, and back up again. He broke the gaze to examine his own hand which closed around the blade as it dissipated into bruise-colored smoke. His fingers brushed away the clouds as he stepped towards her.

"Are you all right?" Talon asked as he walked. His clean hands reached to grasp her blood covered fingers. It felt profound as his fingers closed around hers. He didn't run from her, and she felt a weight lift from her chest.

She nodded. "Yes," she confirmed as her fingers tightened around his. "But we should go."

Curious eyes of caravaners peeked out of hiding places, though they seemed reluctant to emerge. It encouraged Amarie's haste to leave before someone got the idea to start thanking them. She slipped from Talon's grip to retrieve her weapons.

Talon whistled, summoning Lynthenai, who offered a protesting snort before she obeyed. Her hooves avoided the fallen grygurr as Talon urged her closer to Amarie. He mounted and offered his hand to her.

Amarie accepted and drew herself up onto the white mare behind Talon. She didn't hesitate in gripping her arms around his waist. Leaning on his strong back, she let herself relax against him. While harnessing the energy against the shaman caused no exhaustion, fighting it's demand to be set free left her feeling particularly drained.

Talon pulled Lynthenai's reins to spin her back in the direction of the main road to return to their camp. The night was quiet again, except for the pounding hooves. He tilted his head, turning towards Amarie. "Do you think the grygurr will leave the caravan alone for the rest of the night?" he asked, raising his voice just enough for her to be able to hear over the gallop.

She heaved a sigh. "Either that, or they'll send an army seeking vengeance," she said, her tone laced with dry humor.

"Should we move our camp closer to them, then?" he asked, at least pretending to be concerned. "Or should we hope for the best? The grygurr didn't like seeing me there either, so maybe word will spread, and the raiding parties will stay away."

"Grygurr don't like auer," she commented idly, but suspected he already knew it. "They likely won't return, and I doubt there's another shaman close enough to support another attack anyway."

Talon's response came as a single short nod before he turned his head forward again and guided his mare off the main road onto the narrow game trail which led to their camp. He waited for her to dismount first before he followed, boots crunching on the ground. He turned from her, his hand urging the embers of the campfire to instantly reignite. The beginning of the fire appeared darker, more purple than blue. The same she'd seen around the throat of the grygurr Talon killed.

"For an auer, you use a curious amount of destructive Art."

Talon squatted near the edge of the fire, pushing the sleeves of his linen shirt up. The firelight glinted on the tanned skin of his defined forearms. "And you use far less than I expected," he said with a shrug.

Amarie whistled for Viento, who ventured from the shadows. Moving to his side, she rummaged around in a saddle bag before retrieving supplies to clean her injury, plus a new dark-blue tunic. If Talon was going to deflect the conversation, she wouldn't continue it. He didn't need to elaborate any more than she did, and she would respect his privacy.

Taking the supplies to her bedroll, she placed them down without sitting. She gingerly removed her leather vest and her shirt, leaving herself in a sleeveless tunic. She eyed the gash on her shoulder.

"Need help?" Talon asked. His voice was gentle but held a distinct lack of concern.

Kin would have overreacted to the injury.

"Can you stitch?" she asked, meeting his gaze. Doing it herself would be difficult, but possible.

Standing away from her bedroll, she doused her arm in water from the skin, wiping away the blood and dirt with a cloth. She expected him to offer to heal her instead, like most auer were capable of doing, but he didn't.

45

"I'm not particularly practiced," Talon admitted. "But I understand the premise." He stood and rounded the campfire towards her.

Sitting, Amarie took up the small pouch and withdrew a curved needle. She threaded it for him before offering it with a weak smile. "Just a few stitches will close it." She lowered her arm when he accepted the needle, watching him.

He studied the needle, holding it to the fire light, then settled onto his knees at her side. His attention shifted to the laceration.

"Thank you," she added, quieter. She saw the hint of a smile come to his lips with another slow nod.

His eyes traced the her shoulder, followed by a tender touch of his fingertips on her old scars. "From the looks of it, you're used to this kind of injury," Talon said.

She had more on her body, all faded to thin light lines. But the injury she sustained fighting Feyorian soldiers to defend Kin was still new. The memory elicited a small frown.

Talon gingerly squeezed the wound together as he inserted the needle without hesitation.

Amarie sucked in a breath through tightly closed teeth and turned her head back to the fire to distract herself.

Talon's hands were steady, continuing despite her obvious reaction.

"Could've been worse," she muttered.

"I doubt many people can boast your ability to survive such a situation." Talon's voice turned grim as he continued. "If you continue to pick fights with creatures like grygurr, it might be worth your time to practice using the Art to heal yourself." His movements were unpracticed but focused.

His comment made her stomach curl. He hadn't really asked a question but leaving the statement alone didn't feel right. She wouldn't lie. She'd promised not to.

"I can't heal or be healed by the Art," she said, leaving no room for debate.

She felt the first sign of hesitation in Talon's hands. She glanced towards his fingers, half expecting him to recoil.

He didn't. Instead, he took a breath before inserting the needle again. He pulled the thread through her skin, which brought another wince to her face.

"I suppose your inability to be healed is due to the nature of your connection," Talon commented. His eyes finally met hers. "If you're able to shrug off an attack manifested by the Art, then I suspect your body would do the same even if the intention was to aid you. Am I correct?"

His understanding took her off guard, and she couldn't help raising her eyebrows. "You are," she confirmed, wondering if he realized the significance of his understanding. Her mind flashed back to the image of him running towards the shaman who meant to cast the lightning spell on her. "You tried to beat me to the shaman," she said. "What would you have done if you had?"

"Killed him, or tried to at least," Talon said nonchalantly. "Distract him from striking out at you either way."

"He would have killed you first," Amarie whispered.

He gave a half-smile. "Are you certain of that? I've hardly shared much about my ability in the Art with you."

"You're telling me you would've survived that lightning strike?"

"Certainly not as unscathed as you," Talon admitted. "I would've only been able to partially deflect it, likely. I would've sustained substantial injury, and our roles would surely be reversed right now." He paused for a moment, watching her instead of stitching her arm. "Why do you ask what I would've done? Wasn't it obvious?"

"You were supposed to ignore me, remember?" Amarie tilted her head. "For a man less than eager to help people, you sure forgot your promise and rushed to my defense."

"I've grown rather accustomed to your company," Talon said. He turned his gaze down, completing another stitch. "I would've disliked losing it."

Amarie smiled, chewing on her bottom lip for a moment as she appreciated his words. "Then I'll be grateful it played out how it did, because I can say the same thing."

As he worked, she appreciated the fineness of his features and the perfection so many auer were known for. Handsome, in a different way than Kin.

Kin's face was broadly featured, with small imperfections over his chin and cheeks in the form of soft freckles or scars. His beard grew in faster than he could shave it, leaving a constant shadow.

Talon's perfectly smooth skin showed no beard growth, always meticulously shaved off each morning before they resumed their journey.

"Why do you only fight with physical weapons?" Talon asked, disrupting her appreciative gaze. "You don't deny your power in the Art, so why don't you use it?"

Amarie drew a breath at his unexpected bluntness, having grown accustomed to his patience. She paused as he tied off the thread. While he'd claimed to be unpracticed, she'd needed to give no instruction.

"I'd rather use a sword," she said. She looked at the fire in her honestly, not wanting to see his expression as she continued. "I don't know how to use the Art much beyond what you saw. I can hide it; transfer energy. I can destroy any practitioner with a touch of my hand. But I never learned more, not successfully." The words poured from her mouth. "It's dangerous if I try to use it, so I don't." Unable to resist the urge to see his response, she tilted her head up.

Talon's lips pursed together, and his brows furrowed, the look strangely attractive. Finding an auer alluring at all was something she never considered would happen again after the months she spent in Eralas.

An auer had gained her attention the way they typically did, with a beautiful face and charming demeanor. She'd thought she genuinely cared for him, but he'd proven far from deserving of the affection. Since then, the features of the auer had lost their natural appeal. Yet, she couldn't deny her attraction to Talon, auer or not, despite her heart feeling weak.

His chest swelled with a breath as he sat back on his heels. He bit at his top lip as his gaze moved from the ground to Amarie's. "I can infer then, that you've attempted before?" he asked. "I suppose I could imagine it not going well. Power like yours, contained and pooled in a single place, is unheard of, at least in our time. I don't care to guess its origin or how you came to hold it." He shook his head, his face relaxing. "If you lost control... I know it's rare in humans, but I've heard stories of it happening to auer. Those tales are meant to stop us from drawing too deeply... I don't want to imagine." His fingers closed around her hand, squeezing in a way she wasn't sure how to interpret. It was as if he was checking to make sure she was real as much as comfort her.

Amarie squeezed his hand back. "No one gets hurt if I just keep it hidden," she said. "But what I did tonight, to the shaman, I chose to do. I can't do that by accident if I don't try to use it regularly."

"There *is* someone being hurt by denying your power. *You*," Talon said. "You likely haven't had the right teacher. But that's not important right now." His voice grew serious, his grip tightening. "Kin knows, doesn't he?"

She took a deep breath, cringing at the intensity of his question, but she shook her head. "Kin doesn't know the details, what I just told you, or what you saw me do to the shaman... But he can hurt me with his power. I don't understand why, but I'm not immune to the Art the Shades use."

Talon's brow furrowed. "Does Kin know that specifically? That you're vulnerable to Shades?"

Amarie nodded. "He does, but he doesn't know that I'm invulnerable to others."

"How did he find out? Did Kin attack you with his Art?" Talon's tone grew angry.

She shook her head. "It was another Shade. He tried to assault me. Kin saved me and I killed the other Shade."

"But that still means Kin is aware of his potential power over you. His master's power. But if Kin doesn't know the details of your power, what does he know?" Talon asked.

"He knows *what* I am," she said. Her heart pounded in her ears.

He held his breath again, but his reassuring grip held strong. Like a quizzical puppy, his head tilted to the side.

She paused, debating, but concluded that the rest of her secret would come to Talon's knowledge anyway if he was secretly working with Kin. She wanted to believe collusion posed the only possible threat to her.

"How much do you know about the Berylian Key?" she asked, her voice a mere whisper on the night air as she watched his green eyes.

"The Berylian Key?" Talon asked with confusion in his tone. "The thing Kin sought a piece of? Isn't it an ancient Aueric legend? Something from before the sundering of the world?" His face softened, looking as if he would laugh at himself. "I didn't pay much attention to my history lessons as a child."

Amarie couldn't help the vague smile crossing her lips. "I have a book about it you can read," she offered, biting her bottom lip in a habit she still fought to break.

"Are you saying the power of the Berylian Key is real then?" Talon asked. "Not mere legend?"

She sat silent.

His eyes widened, and she swore she heard his heart stop as understanding sank in.

"I'd like to read that book," Talon said. "If you don't mind."

She nodded with her lip still pinned beneath her teeth, offering her other hand as she faced him fully. "Would you like me to show you?" she whispered.

He hesitated, a shallow breath rattling in his chest. He studied her, eyes untelling of his thoughts. If Talon was telling the truth about wanting to help protect her from Kin and the one he served, it was in her best interest for him to know.

"Only if you truly wish to share it with me," Talon replied, accepting her hand within his own. "I can't imagine the burden of keeping such a secret. Or the danger of sharing it."

Her pulse pounded, and she steeled herself not to lose her nerve. The last time she shared this with someone, albeit accidentally, he'd recoiled from her.

"Don't be afraid." With a breath, she released the hold on the tangle of her concealing aura, and it eagerly took Talon into its embrace.

Chapter 6

Wind ruffled the feathers of his wings as Kin glided around massive pines. He'd lost sight of Trist.

The Aidensar forest was thick with a strange buzz of natural energies, laced through the ancient trees like an invisible fog.

She didn't notice me following, did she?

He'd made the decision to pursue Trist after leaving Uriel and Alana, his arm still burning from his demotion.

The grey morning light made the shadows long and easy to hide in. If it were simple for him, Trist's smaller crow form would blend in more effectively than his raven shape.

With a spread of his wings, Kin caught the air to slow his descent towards a branch. His claws scrabbled at the bark, catching his shifting weight. It took an extra flap and a quick grasp at a twig with his beak to right himself. The corvid eyes were less efficient than his human ones, fuzzy at the edges. He couldn't make out the ground clearly, but his perch was as high as the towers in the Great Library of Capul, and he grew dizzy looking down.

Scrambling towards a thicker portion of the branch, closer to the trunk, Kin listened.

At first, he could only hear the angry squirrel, nesting in the branches near him and quite displeased with his appearance. With a flick of his will, a miniature tendril of shadow encouraged the creature away, the needles of nearby pine curling into dust.

He heard the call of a bird in the distance, but it wasn't a crow.

Trist had soared above the Aidensar canopy for days, taking short breaks only in the darkest parts of the night. She'd passed this section of trees already but circled back. It made Kin wonder if she knew something he didn't.

She'd dove suddenly into the tree line, and he feared he'd been spotted. Gliding back and forth from the low-hanging clouds and the cover the pines offered, he'd thought he was hidden.

Trist had to be after Amarie. There was no doubt in Kin's mind now. Amarie could have easily made it this far in her efforts to get away from him. The thought of her running made his claws bite into the bark, splinters digging between his toes.

He selfishly hoped she was alone, but when considering the dangers of the forest, he had to admit she needed an ally. The possibility of Talon being that companion brought a jumble of twists to Kin's stomach. He didn't doubt the auer's ability in battle, familiar with his power. But Talon was also an auer and an insatiable lover of human women. It hadn't made sense to him at the time of their boyish outings, but Talon expressed a fascination in humans. Traditionally slow in everything they did, including love and courting, Talon dismissed his auer customs. He preferred the human haste of mortality when it came to affection.

Could he have changed in the ten years Kin and he had drifted apart? Kin certainly hoped so. He didn't like imagining Talon's charm working on Amarie.

Kin brooded over Talon and Amarie so deeply, he forgot his purpose for a moment. He longed to see her again, feel her. He wanted so desperately to know she was safe and apologize. Explain. She didn't understand the danger she was in with Trist pursuing her.

He'd been afraid to expose her to his darkness, believing she'd be safer not knowing about Uriel. He'd naively thought he could deny his power and keep his will his own. But he didn't know what Alana whispered in Uriel's ear, whilst tangled with him in lust somewhere. The image of Alana in *his* arms, body arching to his touch, made Kin sick.

He debated banging his head against the tree trunk to push the images from his mind, feathers ruffling with the chill coursing through him. A caw gurgled in his throat, following the instinct to retch, which was a human reaction rather than a bird one. The sound nearly covered another, distant and difficult to fully decipher.

The whinny of a horse.

Pine needles rustled as Kin dropped off his perch, wind catching beneath him. He swooped towards the sound, weaving through the trunks near the ground to try to spot the horse. He hoped it wasn't just another caravan.

His clawed feet closed around a branch after he spotted the black and white beasts, close to each other near a fallen tree's cave of roots. Kin could smell a campfire and witnessed Lynthenai trying to force affection on an annoyed Viento. He'd been the one to make the sound, pushing Talon's mare away with his bulky neck.

Hopping down the branch towards its end, the wood gently sagged, and Kin's claws bit in. He wriggled his head through the pine needles to get a better look, and then he saw them.

Talon knelt beside Amarie, her shirt and vest removed, leaving her in a thin sleeveless tunic.

An instantaneous wave of jealousy boiled into Kin's throat before he noticed the white gauze in Talon's hands.

"It's healing well." Talon's voice came strong through the trees, and he sat on his bedroll.

Everything in Kin wanted to soar down and embrace Amarie, but he hesitated. Instead, his eyes ventured to the auer. Talon and he had been through far worse things together and still come out the other side as friends. Kin needed to speak to Talon first. He needed his friend to understand what Alana had done, to help convince Amarie to believe him. Talon knew the truth of his sister's power.

"How does it feel?" Talon asked, his eyes looking from Amarie's stitched wound to her face.

"Better. Think you can pull the stitches out yet?" Hope echoed in her voice.

"Not yet," Talon said with a shake of his head. "They need a few more days. That impatient?" He teased. "It only just happened. And you're lucky the grygurr didn't get you worse, all things considered."

"It's itchy," she complained, but smiled at him. "Though I suppose you're right."

"Don't scratch it," Talon lectured, waving a finger. "Maybe cleaning up a bit will help. That spring is only a short distance back the way we came. We could backtrack this morning if you'd like?"

He's offering to bathe with her now? Kin's chest rumbled.

"I can manage by myself this time, while you pack up the camp," Amarie suggested as she stood.

This time? Jealousy seethed like an encroaching storm.

Talon hesitated. "You sure?" he asked, motionless.

His purpose in confirming was unclear, and Kin urged himself to consider the various logical possibilities. As much as Kin wanted Talon not to tag along, he also didn't like the idea of Amarie alone. Especially when he considered Trist could be nearby. But he couldn't pass up the opportunity to get to Talon.

"I'll be fine," she insisted and lifted her cloak from her bedroll to pull around her bare shoulders. "Perhaps you could attempt tacking Viento again?" she suggested with humor, and Talon gave a wry smile.

He conceded a breath later and put away the supplies spread around the smoldering campfire.

Amarie picked up her sword, securing it around her waist.

"Be safe," Talon said.

She nodded, her lips curving in a reassuring smile, and turned from their camp.

Kin wondered what exactly they'd been through. It took every ounce of willpower not to follow Amarie, but his biggest obstacle was the auer who seemed adamant in protecting her.

Tension lingered in his chest, and Kin acknowledged the jealousy with resentment. The dangerous emotion threatened to make him forget the more important reasons why he needed to talk to Amarie. She needed to know about Trist. About Uriel. About his part in all of it.

His wings rasped against the pine needles as he dropped from the branch and landed on the moss laden ground behind the tree he'd spied from.

No longer able to see Amarie, he looked at Talon's back before reaching for his power. The familiar embrace of shadow rolled over his shoulders, consuming the raven body before swelling upwards like a great monster rising from a tar pit. Flecks of black dripped and flaked from the cloak resting on his broad shoulders, ferns of the forest curling in death around him.

Talon spun around, and Kin drew his empty hand from the depths of cascading shadow in a hasty attempt portray innocence. He'd sensed Kin's power and readied his will. Flickers of deep colored smoke touched his fingertips.

"Hold, Talon," Kin said quickly. He locked his eyes with those of the auer he still wanted to consider a friend.

Talon's pupils contracted, too small for Kin to even be certain they were there amongst the forest green irises. Now on his feet, the pull on his Art didn't stop. His fingers wriggled against the fabric he manipulated, the haze thickening. "Don't presume to order me, Kinronsilis," he hissed dangerously.

Kin had seen Talon angry before, but this was different. A disappointment lingered in his friend's eyes, which flicked in the direction Amarie had gone.

"Forgive me." Kin drew his other hand out from his cloak,

pushing the material back over his shoulders exposing his simple grey tunic, tight at his chest. He wanted to make sure Talon could see the hilt of his short sword and that his hands were far from it. "I didn't come to fight. Merely to talk."

"Talk?" Talon asked, his tone incredulous. "I don't believe I'm the one you owe an explanation to and I doubt your intentions are honorable."

"Please, Talon. You're as close to a brother as I've ever had. Believe me when I say whatever Amarie saw, what you saw... It wasn't real." Kin recalled the horrible sensation of Alana pressing her lips to his, taking away his control. "We don't have time for this. Amarie is in danger."

"Indeed," Talon said, "from you." He stepped forward and circled his wrist as if to stretch it. With the action, the energy he'd gathered dissipated into the dirt at his feet. A tingle of the power remained at the edge of Kin's senses, which Talon certainly maintained on purpose. He wanted Kin to know he was still ready.

Kin had no intention of attack and was certain to keep his hands exposed. "I'm not the danger," he said. "There's another coming for her. Another Shade."

"Then you told your Master about her," Talon growled, his hand moving to withdraw power again, twitching in anticipation as Kin took a step back and rose his hands higher.

Talon knows?

"No!" Kin breathed. "I didn't speak a word of her. It's for another reason. We killed a Shade a month ago, together. Amarie shot him through the neck, and somehow it was traced back to her."

"A Shade you undoubtedly led to her." Talon grew increasingly more frustrating.

Kin shook his head. "I didn't. He traced the shards. If you know the truth, then you know how essential it is that my master not learn it also."

"You should leave," Talon demanded.

"Do you really believe you can protect her better than I can?" Kin asked, finally lowering his hands. He heaved a breath. "You need my knowledge of the Shades. To protect her, you need me. She needs me."

"You ruined all need she might have had for you the moment you kissed my sister. How long has that been going on? I didn't think you'd go back to her after she abandoned you when you needed her most," Talon growled.

Talon's words forced Kin to confront the memory of what had led him to hate Alana. When Kin first received Uriel's access to the Art, it had been a confusing time when his body and mind were subjected to a bombardment of new challenges. He never had the slightest inkling of potential in the Art before. It was like not knowing how to swim and being thrown into the deepest part of a pond, head first.

The moment he needed Alana the most came after he was given his first task. A straightforward retrieval of an object requiring minimal planning. It still required him to use the Art, though, and with no instruction.

Trying to use the power, which in the first rank only allowed him to blend into shadow rather than actively control it, led him to accidentally entrap himself half engulfed. Alana grew frustrated with his apparent lack of understanding and walked away.

Talon stepped in to help the scared teenager begin to understand the depth of what he'd gotten himself into. Talon never liked it and told Kin fervently he needed to abandon his quest and his access, pretend it wasn't there and go back to the estate.

Kin argued and learned all he could from his friend to complete his task. It was when he was given his second quest, requiring him to kill for the first time, that Kin had tried to listen to Talon. He stopped, refusing to use the power or even acknowledge the blight on his soul.

It proved more difficult than he ever imagined. The moment he stopped tapping into the threads of the fabric, his body revolted against him. First with general tiredness, then an uncontrollable shaking. Accompanied with unexpected mood swings, uncontrollable rage, and a constant thirst no drink could quench.

Kin quickly fell back into using it again. If he took too long to complete a task, the Master would start to throttle back on what he had access to, making the symptoms worse. Forced to watch another Shade receive discipline for their failure, Kin realized there was no way out. Instead of death, he chose to embrace his new power and all it required. The killing grew easier to stomach.

"Have I lost so much of your respect and trust?" Kin asked, his voice turning soft. "You know what Alana did to me ten years ago. I could never love or want her."

"Then what did we see?" Talon asked. "It looked like you were enjoying her company."

"You *know* Alana. Better than me. You know what she's capable of. She caught me off guard and I didn't have the power to fight her."

Talon's spine straightened, his eyes darkening.

Kin hoped Talon's commitment to family would not blind him to the truth.

"She took hold of your will?" Talon asked, tone raspy. The concept of forcefully taking control of another was forbidden by all those who practice the Art.

"We both know Alana serves the Master by her own choice and for her own reasons," Kin pointed out. "Is it so impossible to believe she has developed such a skill?"

A crow cawed somewhere, and his body tensed at the memory of Trist.

"Believe me," Kin hurried to continue. "You know all my reasons for hating and distrusting your sister. I don't owe any allegiance to her. I love Amarie." The words came pouring out, and his voice took on a begging tone.

Talon frowned. "Your ties to the creature you serve, make everything you say subject to disbelief."

Another caw and a scrabble of wings.

"Please, we're running out of time. We need to warn Amarie about the Shade who's coming for her. Trist won't be easily dissuaded, and she's more powerful than me. We must work together to keep Amarie safe," Kin begged again.

The auer's power recoiled. "If you're lying, there's no power in Pantracia that'll keep you safe from me," Talon threatened before he shoved his way past Kin in the direction Amarie had gone. "Keep up."

Chapter 7

The itch drove Amarie mad. She wanted to claw the stitched thread from her flesh. She hoped Talon was right, and a simple clean would diminish the discomfort.

Arriving at the spring, she removed her cloak and stepped to the water's edge. Kneeling next to the naturally warm waters, she scooped some onto her stitches. The itch calmed gradually, and she admired Talon's handiwork on her shoulder.

She regretted judging him on his heritage when they'd first met. He was nothing like any auer she'd encountered before. Their growing rapport dulled how sorely she missed Kin's arms. Like the itch, the pain of his betrayal slowly numbed to something more manageable. Her insides ached when she thought of him, and those memories still came too frequently.

A twig snapped behind her and tore Amarie from her somber contemplation.

Assuming it was Talon, Amarie opened her mouth to greet him as she turned her head in the direction of the noise. Her legs straightened when she saw an unfamiliar face and reached instinctively for her sword. As her fingers curled around the leather wrapped hilt, she studied the hunch of the old woman's back, draped with a thick cloak.

Every hair on the back of Amarie's neck stood straight.

This woman looked old enough to be her mother. Despite her

posture, her body seemed surprisingly adaptable to the terrain. A long braid draped over her shoulder showed hints of blonde mingled with streaks of silver shimmering in the low morning light. The darkness in the woman's hazel eyes elicited a stomach-churning memory of Ormon, the Shade who'd attempted to assault her months prior.

A Shade. Amarie felt certain the old woman was one. Kin had told his master of her, and now another Shade had come. Though, sending just one almost felt like an insult. And where was Kin?

"Oh, I'm sorry child. Did I startle you?" The woman's youthful voice sounded deceptively nurturing.

Amarie gripped the hilt of her sword and withdrew it a few inches as she stepped from the edge of the spring. She refused to hesitate, knowing full well what a Shade's Art could do to her. She would strike first and readied her power within her.

The woman's eyes fluttered down to the sword with a frown. She heaved an exaggerated sigh against the heavy air as she stepped from the undergrowth. Pushing her black cloak back, she revealed a plain, amber-colored dress beneath it.

Every nerve in Amarie's body screamed warnings, regardless of the woman's innocent appearance.

"Not going to play along?" the woman said, a pout on her lips. Her stance straightened, and the hunch vanished. "Pity."

Amarie fully withdrew her sword from its sheath with a satisfying rasp of steel. The woman didn't react, lazily focused on Amarie's face.

"You're the girl with the shards," the stranger said.

Amarie's brows knit together.

Why does she still care about my shards?

The woman didn't look physically threatening. She carried no weapons, just a black sash knotted on her hips with nothing strapped to it.

Amarie knew better. "And you're a Shade," she bluffed, hoping for confirmation as she stepped in a wide arc.

The woman walked to mirror Amarie's movement, her hands buried in the ruffles of her cloak at her sides. "Now, how would you know how to identify a Shade so readily, child? Unless you've encountered my kind before?" the Shade asked, her voice sinister.

"Encountered would be a gentle term to use," Amarie said, remembering the sound her bolt made when it skewered Ormon through the throat. "Do you care to *join* your companion?"

Amarie's mind whirled with how to defend herself against an Art practitioner who could do her harm. Her ability to surge her power into the Shade would be useless if she managed to keep Amarie far enough away. Calling for Talon crossed her mind, but he wouldn't hear her.

The Shade gave a wicked grin. "Ormon was an infant in his power compared to me. It'd be best to hand the shards over without incident. I won't be as easily dispatched as the last who discovered your secret."

Another knot tied itself in Amarie's insides. Her mind went to Kin. Was she referring to Kin or Ormon's death? Her stomach lurched. Horrible images of Kin in pain collided with her mind. She gulped for air, forcing herself to breathe.

Amarie brought her sword parallel with the ground and pointed the razor tip towards the Shade. Her left hand touched the small dagger at her thigh, but she didn't get the chance to draw it.

The shadows at her feet shifted. A tendril of pure midnight struck from the ground and closed around her left wrist. It yanked down before she had a moment to react.

Amarie collapsed, her hip slamming into the ground. The vine seared her flesh; it felt like she'd thrust her arm into a dense frozen rose bush. A cry escaped her lips. Agony radiated from where the tug had almost pulled her arm clean from its socket. Trying to block out the pain, Amarie pushed her power into her legs, rising from the ground. She steadied herself, boots catching against the edge of a rock. Resisting the pull of the tendril, Amarie yanked her wrist away, causing the shadows to crackle as they fought to keep hold.

The woman approached in her peripheral vision, eyes narrowed.

Amarie swung her sword in a wide arc, despite the awkward stance. She felt resistance as her blade connected with her target, and a moment of triumph trumpeted through her body as she twisted free of the shadow. Her eyes took a moment to register what they saw.

A wall of darkness, gliding forward from the trees and rippling like low waves at the woman's ankles. Her cloak was no longer simple cloth, it twisted into curved thorns and spines of armor which covered her skin. It ran down her arm in thin chitinous plates, curving perfectly where it needed to fit together to allow her movement.

Horns of onyx ran like a mane down the outside of her arms, ending with a large reptilian claw protruding from her wrist bone. She rotated her joints, flexing her elbow with the deflection of Amarie's blade, which hadn't even left a dent.

Amarie watched in horror as the plating spread, like a rapid growth, over the entirety of the woman's body.

Spines grew from her shoulders and knees, her appearance resembling tales of the Corrupted, housed in the deepest hells. Her fingernails turned to claws, which rivaled even the dexterous fingers of the grygurr.

A wicked clang reverberated as the Shade's hand closed on Amarie's sharpened blade. Wrenching it sideways with a twist, she tore it from Amarie's grip while her other hand reached for her throat. Ebony claws bit into the tender flesh beneath Amarie's jaw, and she gasped for breath as her airway closed.

"I'll ask once more, child." The woman's head was the only thing unchanged by the shadow armor. Her blond hair fell over her collarbone, fading to grey then into the black of the rest of her body. "Where are the shards?" Her tone sounded sickly sweet.

Blood oozed from Amarie's left arm, her skin shredded by the thorny shadow vines. It dripped off her fingertips to the ground at a jarringly fast pace.

"I'm no expert on Shades," Amarie gasped, "But aren't you a little old?" Her voice choked and fear threatened to overtake her.

Fury filled the face of the Shade, washing over slowly and giving Amarie plenty of time to flood herself with energy, drawing from the source deep within herself. It rolled towards her target, pulsing through her veins. The hand on her throat was all the contact she needed.

The familiar purpose filled her, and she surged every ounce of energy she could muster into the Shade.

Expecting the Shade to collapse, just as the grygurr shaman, Amarie braced her legs to catch herself.

Instead, the look of rage on the Shade's face altered to one of enjoyment. A low rumble purred from her throat, but it wasn't one of pain. A sigh of pleasure escaped her lungs as her head rolled back. Her mouth parted, tongue flicking at her lips. Her grip stayed strong throughout, her fingers clenching tighter in a moment of ecstasy.

As the Shade came back to herself, Amarie's stomach filled with dread.

Nothing remained of her hazel irises when she opened her eyes. Amarie saw herself in the reflection of the gold-flecked obsidian surface.

A masculine purr passed from the Shade's lips. "What did you just do, my dear?" It wasn't entirely her voice anymore. A strange tone mixed within it as if another spoke in unison.

Amarie's eyes widened, and she struggled for breath as the grip tightened even more. She gulped a wheeze of air. "Talon!" she managed as loud as she could.

A flicker of amusement passed through the woman's eyes as they faded back to their original hazel. "No one is coming, child," she cooed, rolling her neck.

Amarie needed to stay in control of her aura and contain the azure flames. The Shade didn't know what she held, and it needed to stay that way. Before she could think any further, the world went black.

Chapter 8

Pushing aside the underbrush, Talon strode in the direction of the spring.

Kin's less graceful body thundered behind him, struggling to keep up as Talon weaved over the tangled forest floor.

Talon grinned to himself in amusement of his friend's inability to grasp the concept of stealth when moving through the woods. The irritating noise served as a constant reminder he was being followed. It made his back tingle. The memory of Kin's influence on Amarie's emotional state caused the brief smile to turn into a frown. Could he believe what Kin was trying to tell him? Talon certainly believed his sister capable of manipulating a situation, but to use her power to affect someone else's will?

Has Alana fallen so far?

The old set-in stain of her corruption began when they were banished from their homelands. Their punishment to become *rejanai* hadn't been entirely her doing, though. Talon had to admit his own crimes and their role in the miserable state of his life.

He missed his homeland, and the dim reminder of Eralas that Aidensar provided reopened the wounds. It'd been nearly fifty years since Talon left. Cynically, he noted he'd been in the human lands for a larger portion of his life than he'd been in Eralas. He was still considered a child when they were forced to sail away from the rocky beaches and misty cliffs.

With the only family he had left at his side as Eralas faded on the horizon, he'd sworn to always keep his sisters safe. They were all he had. He owed his life to Kalstacia, his oldest sister. The sacrifice of her station in the revered Mender's Guild and her own freedom to remain on the island saved he and Alana from a worse fate. She chose to become a rejanai like her siblings to keep them alive.

Despite Alana's sins, Talon stuck by her. They had a connection he and Kalstacia would never have because of the way they developed their Art together. They were closer in age and both more interested in traveling than settling down. Their youth drove them to try to find the advantages of being away from the suffocating island, while Kalstacia settled into a secluded area away from prying human eyes. Talon had grown more accustomed to the curious looks and found a new family in Kin's instead.

Kin didn't know his own fortune, Talon concluded as they clambered forward through the brush of Aidensar. His family loved and adored him, no matter what wretched mistakes he made. And Kin had plenty misgivings. He had sacrificed everything Talon wished for in his own life.

On top of it, Kin somehow managed to gain the affection of Amarie and had sacrificed that too. For what? Power? How short sighted it all was. Impatient. How foolishly human.

"Tell me. How is your Master?" Talon asked darkly, his memories leading to a renewed distrust of the man following him.

Kin sucked in a breath, and Talon swore he felt the glare of Kin's steel-blue eyes on the back of his head.

"Where in Nymaera's name did that come from?" Kin grumbled. "I don't care and neither do you."

"You cared once," Talon pointed out. "What's changed?" He stopped abruptly and turned. His occasional tendency towards the hasty actions of humans was getting the better of him with his desire to trust Kin. He needed to logically consider all the angles first.

Kin nearly ran into Talon with his broad chest, fists tightened in frustration.

Talon watched the pulse of muscle at the corner of Kin's jaw. "What's changed?" he asked again.

"This can wait. We need to find Amarie." Kin's voice quavered.

Actual concern? Or was it simply the thirst for the power he might gain by finding Amarie and giving her to his master?

Talon stood strong.

"Dammit, Talon," Kin cursed. "It changed when I met her. I'm not an idiot, I know there's no escaping the choice I made, but it doesn't matter! You of all people should know what that feels like. I'll always need to pay for my mistake, but don't make Amarie pay for it too." He ground his teeth. "I don't give a shit about the Master, and all we're doing is wasting time talking about it. I want to keep her safe, even if she wants nothing to do with me."

Talon studied Kin, trying to evaluate the tone of his voice and the honesty of his expression. He'd once believed he could read Kin like a book. He heaved a breath. "You swear to me," he commanded, gripping Kin's shoulder. "You swear everything you've done is to protect her. And if necessary, you'll walk out of her life to make sure she remains safe. Alana might have done you a favor by starting the process for you."

Amarie would never truly be safe but having Kin around could only make it worse. His connection to the beast he called master would always put Amarie in danger.

Kin's eyes hardened, his lips pressing together into a frown as he shoved Talon's arm away. "What gives you the right to demand that of me? Why in the names of all the Gods do you care so damned much?"

"I can demand whatever I damn well please of you," Talon shot back. "I've earned the right."

Kin's frown deepened, and he took a step forward, bringing his face inches from Talon's. They both stubbornly held the position, waiting for the other to back down.

"You have no right," Kin whispered. "I may owe you for what you did for me ten years ago, but this has nothing to do with that. This is about Amarie. And we're wasting time standing here."

"Wasting more if you refuse," Talon countered. "You're poison, and I won't let you infect her life any more than you already have. She's better off without you."

"And better off with *you*, then?" Kin spat. "Why are you even still here? Is she another human toy? Surely she doesn't need you hovering over her shoulder."

Talon sucked in a steadying breath. He didn't dignify Kin with an answer. Something in the shadows of Kin's gaze and the ones around them on the forest floor made him uneasy. He fought the instinct to step away, refusing to let Kin affect him. In Kin's anger, the air felt colder.

"Does it really matter?" Talon snapped. "Swear it, you bastard. Swear you'll walk away."

"Gods, Talon. Yes! I swear it," Kin glowered, taking the first step back. "I'll do what's necessary."

Talon didn't offer another word, instead turning and continuing towards the spring. Certain now of the danger Amarie faced, he hoped he wouldn't come to regret the pause he'd forced to confront Kin. His motivations for telling Kin to stay away from Amarie weren't selfish and truly for her. A part of him wondered if she'd agree but somehow doubted she would.

She'd forgive Kin despite the threat.

It terrified Talon. She deserved someone who didn't put her at risk every moment. He avoided delving too far into his feelings for Amarie. He was merely acting as her friend. The moment he held her in his arms, even if only once, still lingered in his mind like a haunting dream. It meant nothing, only innocent comfort, and it certainly didn't bias his judgment regarding Kin or his master.

The flora grew denser before it finally thinned. He couldn't hear the gurgle of the spring, but a sickening familiar sensation collided with his chest.

Talon felt blinded, despite his eyes still seeing the trees ahead. Instead it was within his being where he felt a flicker of static within his own power. He may have dismissed it if he hadn't felt it before. His heart leapt into his throat as he recalled watching the grygurr shaman crumple to the ground with Amarie's hand against his skin.

She coalesced her power to overwhelm someone; she was already in danger.

He didn't bother to explain to Kin before he rushed forward. He urged his senses to focus, aided by the gentle thrum of his power within him as he ran. He listened, catching the stuttering breath of some poor forest creature dying and the babble of the water.

"Talon!" Amarie's voice sounded broken but unmistakable in the distant edge of his hearing. He was still too far away, and desperation spurred his run faster.

Kin grunted behind him, racing to keep up through the brambles.

Talon's heart raced, aching within his chest. He burst through the final swell of foliage too late. Time had passed too quickly.

A new stench, mixed with the sulphur of the hot spring, hung in the air. Talon's boot crunched as he stepped onto the dry death surrounding the water. Before he could catch his breath, he was forced to catch his balance as Kin shoved him aside.

Kin's chest heaved as he stepped onto the shriveled grass. It still slowly disintegrated, disappearing into the dirt. Shreds of leaves and other plants barely clung to life, withering away. The disrupted terrain suggested a struggle.

Kin's pale fingers emerged from his cloak as he crouched, touching the ground. "We're too late," he said, his eyes looking at the water and then the trees beyond.

Talon's stomach dropped out, and the decay rose in his nostrils as he hastily looked around. He spotted a glimmer of metal, untouched by the death, and stooped to wrap his fingers around the hilt of Amarie's sword.

"Did you recognize that surge of power?" Kin's voice broke the eerie silence. The air was devoid of morning bird song. They were likely dead too.

Talon ignored him, twisting the blade in the palm of his hand, and let his senses reach out for Amarie. They had to be close.

"Talon?" Kin urged with distinct impatience. "I know it must have been Amarie. You started running as soon as that sensation passed through—"

"It was her; that's all you need to know," Talon said, cutting Kin off. His eyes caught a dark splatter of crimson on the death riddled ground. A primal fury rose within his chest as his gaze moved from the blood and back to Kin.

"This is your doing." Talon said. "You led your master's dogs right to her."

Kin rose to his feet, eyes locked on the patch of blood. He threw the corner of his cloak over his shoulder, freeing his arm from its shadows. He rolled up his sleeves, exposing the geometric tattoo that granted him power. It marred his skin like a twisted scar. A brand.

Without even acknowledging Talon, Kin lowered his hand to hover parallel to the ground above the darkening stain. A whisper of power brushed against Talon's senses as Kin worked the Art, pulling in shadows from the edge of the spring's clearing towards the destruction.

The blackness flicked over the decay before it came to the blood, then gobbled it up into the lightless flames.

It caused the anger in Talon to seethe. How dare Kin use his Art now? The very power guilty of spilling her blood. His shadows consumed what was left of her, and it made Talon's insides tremble.

Talon's power moved differently than Kin's, coming from the pit within his being. In the anger it came easier; the waters of his energy already turbulent. It flicked into his palm, swirling in a dense cloud. The haze grew deeper, black and purple like a bruise, before Talon lashed it forward.

He didn't aim directly at Kin, but at the shadows at his feet lapping at the blood. They hissed and recoiled, as if the shadows themselves felt pain, and Kin's eyes shot up.

Talon readied himself for another blast before Kin could question him.

"Back away," Talon said darkly, passing a second ball of entangled energy to his left hand before his dominant right wove another.

Kin looked towards the power and frowned. "You idiot. What are you doing?" he snapped. The shadows moved to the sides of his feet like obedient hounds awaiting instruction.

"Don't play innocent. You led a Shade straight to her," Talon shouted, his voice growing taut with the power at his fingertips seeking an outlet. "You killed her."

Kin's face contorted with a look of shock, his eyes widening.

Talon's eyes fluttered to the shadows, where he could smell more death occurring behind Kin. The bush they'd emerged from wilted.

"For how intelligent you auer are supposed to be, you have to be the dumbest I've met." Kin returned the heated tone but kept it at a lower volume. "I came to warn you. I told you Amarie was in danger. If I hadn't come to you, you wouldn't have even known to come looking for her until it was far too late. The blood is fresh. We have to hurry." Kin turned away, exposing his back to the power Talon held at his fingertips.

"This could all be a ploy. A game to catch both Amarie and I unaware. To take us both," Talon accused.

Kin laughed. A deep and throaty sound which irked Talon enough that he almost hurtled the Art straight at Kin's head.

Turning back, Kin shook his head. "You give yourself too much credit. Uriel doesn't give a single iron mark about you." His face turned serious again. "She may still be alive. So, stop being dramatic, or I might start to think you belong in the Xaxos street festivals."

His frustration with Kin almost made Talon miss it.

Uriel.

He'd never heard the name before, and it distracted him from Kin's insult. Suddenly unable to form words, Talon lowered his arms.

Kin didn't seem to realize right away what he'd said aloud. When he did, he averted his gaze and sucked in a breath, looking at the ground to summon the energy he'd been using before.

Silence hovered as Talon watched his friend's shadows consume the rest of Amarie's blood. He let him finish, dismissing the power swirling at his fingertips. The heat of it returned into his body, leaving his head buzzing.

"So, it has a name?" Talon's voice rose through the quiet. "Your master?"

Kin didn't answer right away, his eyes darkening as the shadows slithered towards his heels and vanished. Nothing remained of the scarlet splatter of blood other than a vague stain.

Talon waited, and Kin shuffled his feet, causing a thin cloud of dust to rise from the dead ground.

"I shouldn't have said it," Kin admitted, looking with desperation at Talon.

For a moment, the steel-blue of Kin's eyes belonged to a thirteen-year-old boy pleading with him to keep a secret from his father.

"Can you find her?" Talon asked, surprising himself as he acquiesced to Kin's unspoken request. Looking at the rot of the ground, Talon had no way to track where Amarie might be. The displaced dirt and uprooted grass, signs of struggle, were focused only at the center of the decay. There were no tracks beyond its diameter where she might have been drug away.

The toxic aura surrounding the unnatural use of the Art drifted at its border. Talon couldn't trace it either. As much as he didn't want to admit it, he needed to rely on Kin.

Kin nodded, his attention shifting to the far side of the clearing. "I can," he said as he stepped out of the dead circle, headed east. "Are you coming, then?" He stalked into the dense trees instead of waiting for an answer.

"Just remember what you've sworn to," Talon muttered as he followed. "And I'll keep your secret."

Chapter 9

The stagnant air felt wet in her lungs as Amarie gasped for breath. Damp darkness surrounded her. A distant orange glow on her closed eyelids suggested a nearby light source. Her left arm trembled with pain, her body aching at the very idea of moving.

Listening, Amarie tried to decipher her new surroundings without revealing to her captor she was awake.

None of the sounds she'd grown used to in the Aidensar forest filled her ears. No water, wildlife, or breeze amongst the trees. Just the crackle of a small flame she assumed was the light source and a distant drip echoing against stone.

Amarie's head swam, overcome by a disconnected feeling. Hot trails of blood ran down her left arm, but the sensation faded the farther they fell. The hand felt cold, and her fingers refused to respond.

Bound together behind her back, her right hand was awkwardly forced against her left one. Amarie pinched her left wrist but felt nothing. She tried to pull her legs forward, finding them secured at the ankle.

Where am I?

Amarie detected no human sounds around her and dared to open her eyes.

Wall sconces, curved with once elaborate details, provided the hazy light she'd guessed at. An iron beam of some kind, with sharp rusted edges, held her spine painfully straight. It was secured within a crumbled stairwell.

Her head throbbed near her temple.

Dark lumps of shattered stone lay scattered about the dimly lit chamber, but the Shade wasn't in sight. The stone ground was dusted with a layer of dirt, but no sky loomed above her. No canopy of trees. Just blackness, broken by the flicker of the sconces, their bent cages creating thick lines of shadow.

How long have I been out?

What buildings stood in the middle of the Aidensar forest? They were at least a day's travel from any village or city. The dense rock surrounding her didn't belong to a forest hamlet nestled in the treetops.

The crumbling stone walls surrounded five pillars, still fully intact, and stubs of what may have been several more. The bases and clinging capitals, stalactite-like, were intricately carved but chipped and rimmed with lichen.

The ruins were ancient, their origin impossible to discern. A dark bundle of fabric shoved against the wall under one of the sconces looked like her cloak. If the Shade had gone through her pockets, she would've found her coin purse where Amarie kept the smaller Berylian Key shards. She would never find the larger ones, stitched within Viento's saddle.

"Alive after all?" The wicked voice echoed over the stones and made her jump. "I'd begun to wonder."

Amarie turned as much as she could to see the matronly looking Shade enter the room from the broken arch of a doorway. The orange glow made the age lines of her face more pronounced, withering her face like the shriveled ivy clinging to the ruin walls.

Why haven't you killed me?

Meeting the Shade's dim gaze, Amarie said nothing.

"Ten... tiny... shards," the Shade said with disappointment. "None big enough to be the one Ormon tracked to you." She eyed the small burgundy pieces of the ancient Berylian Key within her open palm.

Perhaps Kin had nothing to do with this. Would he have known if another Shade hunted her?

Amarie offered no explanation, her lips pressed together in effort to control the pain and bite back fiery retorts. She closed her eyes, leaning her head back against cold iron to find reprieve.

Her stubborn lack of interest earned her a boot slamming into her ribs followed by another wave of pain. The metal beam rung as her head snapped to the side and collided with it. Her cheek burned where the back of the Shade's hand impacted, and she gasped for breath. The room spun again, and Amarie squeezed her eyes closed tighter.

"Don't ignore me, you arrogant girl!" the Shade barked. "Where's the other shard?"

"Shard?" Amarie managed. Her voice sounded gruffer than she remembered. Her mouth, as dry as cotton, filled with the coppery taste of blood. She spat the red ooze onto the dirt beside her but kept her eyes shut to the dizzying sensation. "I collected those because I like the color. They go well with my hair," Amarie murmured.

Instead of another blow, something squeezed around Amarie's legs, and her eyes shot open.

Black tendrils stretched from the warped shadows cast by the sconces. The thorny vines seared through the leather of her boots and breeches, scalding the flesh beneath up to her knees. Unlike purely physical pain, the agony coursed deeper and raged through her blood as if infecting her with poison.

A cry erupted from Amarie's throat. She kicked her legs out in a failing attempt to rid them of the shadow. The Art-laden vines wrenched at her shoulder, her wrists burning as her bindings cut into her flesh, suspending her weight temporarily. Blood curled in thick streams from her lower legs and feet, staining the stones red.

Screams echoed from the distant abandoned halls of the ruins, all belonging to her. They bore deep into her eardrums, her mind blaring. No matter how she fought, the shadows persisted, their grip tightening and lapping at the crimson pools growing beneath her.

It took every ounce of her focus to maintain control over her hiding aura.

Her wrists collided against each other and the railing they were secured to, shocking pain up through her left shoulder where it most surely had been separated from its socket. Her boots fell to shreds from her feet, her breeches torn midway down her thighs and no longer providing her even the slightest protection against the tendrils lashing at her without mercy. They dug and tore into her flesh, ripping jagged lines bubbling with blood.

Amarie grew dizzy, feeling the pain start to blur throughout her cold body. Her cries reverberated at the agony, desperate but weakening as her strength waned. She held her breath to contain the azure flames fighting for release. She wanted to die with her secret intact.

A moment of respite came when her body devolved beyond the ability to kick, and Amarie's breath rushed, still heaving with sobs of agony she couldn't contain.

"If you don't answer me, death will be the only reward for your insolence." The Shade lowered herself to Amarie, whispering in her ear—the only reason she could hear it above the deafening ringing.

Whatever the woman had armored herself with before had vanished. She knelt in a simple burnt-orange dress, fiery in the sconce light. The sleeves were tight around her wrists and wrinkled hands gripped at the hem to keep it from the blood on the ground. She might have been a common villager, with her plain appearance. The coldness of her eyes confirmed the darkness she was capable of. Her irises expanded as Amarie clenched her jaw, blood pooling in her mouth.

She spat her mouthful of blood at the Shade's face.

The woman lifted an idle hand to wipe the red splatter away as she straightened.

"As if you'd let me live otherwise. Just kill me and be done with it. I don't fear you," Amarie snarled. "Or death," she lied.

The uncertainty and finality of it thrummed against her mind. Unspoken words haunted her, unaccomplished desires. As much as Kin had hurt her, she dreaded never seeing his face again. She never dreamt everything would end quite like this. Not with death so soon. As much pain as there was in her heart, she wanted the opportunity to say final words to Kin. And Talon. Would either of them ever know what happened to her? Would anyone? Or would her body rot down here, and her bones become as ancient as the walls surrounding her?

The Shade tossed her braid behind her shoulder in an irritated motion, stepping backwards through the dust while avoiding the pools of blood. With each step, a different darkness gathered at her feet. Shadow chased after her every movement, swallowing the firelight on the floor with greedy gulps. Tentacles like a great sea beast wriggled at the edges, dancing to a low hum in their master's throat.

"You shall have death," the Shade sneered, tracing her fingernail through the remaining blood on her jaw. "But only when I am satisfied in my amusement with you, child. Fear of death is irrelevant. Rather, I'll help you find your fear of living."

Chapter 10

Amarie had lost blood at an alarming rate and it made following the fresh trail within the shadows regretfully easy for Kin.

The blame he placed on himself went far beyond Talon's accusations. The auer's anger for endangering Amarie couldn't compare to the guilt he already felt. His mere presence had exposed her to Uriel.

Trained to be capable of unfathomable cruelty, like all Shades, Trist would use despicable tactics to force secrets out of Amarie. The knowledge of the inevitable process made Kin want to retch.

His stomach flipped with each step through the underbrush. Amarie's life was in greater jeopardy than Talon could realize. She might already be dead, but he pushed the thoughts away; they would destroy him before he could find her if he permitted it.

The demotion of his power only put him further behind Trist, and he questioned what he might be able to do if they arrived in time. Kin would die for Amarie, but if she was already dead, he hoped Trist would aid him in joining her in the Afterlife. If Trist wouldn't, Talon certainly would.

Several times Kin forgot Talon's presence behind him with how silent the auer's footsteps were. As they followed the trail of blood, it grew stale. The amount didn't diminish but each patch grew drier than the last. Kin watched the ground as he stepped carefully through the brush. The shine of metal, partially buried in a withering fern, caught his eye. He knelt to touch the dagger he'd seen countless times before. His thumb traced the pommel, and he remembered when Amarie used it to smash the glass in the east tower of the Great Library of Capul the first day they met. The leather wrapped hilt felt tacky, stained with her blood. It must have fallen and re-emerged from the shadow, since there was no sign of another struggle. He absently rubbed the sticky liquid between the pads of his fingers, hoping somehow the contact with it would help him find her.

Kin jumped as Talon reached towards the dagger. Pulling the blade flat against his chest, he recoiled.

"I'll carry it," Talon offered, his tone remarkably soft. He could easily craft a makeshift casing with the Art, as he had for her sword already at his side.

It made no difference to Kin, unwilling to give up the one piece of her he'd recovered. He'd rather risk the injury, and Talon seemed to understand. He only hesitated momentarily before withdrawing his hand without argument.

"Let's keep going." Talon's voice sounded raspy, and he wondered briefly if the auer shared in the depth of the worry Kin felt.

Kin tucked the blade into an inner pocket of his cloak, careful in its placement. Its weight brought minor comfort, but urgency fueled his step forward. Nodding, Kin took a breath and pushed on.

They walked for hours, the trail within the shadows filled with dry blood. With the prevalence of Kin's tortured thoughts, it felt more like days. And time kept bleeding on far faster than he wished.

The woods thinned as jagged mountains erupted out of the forest floor. Aidensar's mountains reached to the sky, the rockface cut as if man made. The steep cliffs would be impossible to climb without extreme care.

As they grew closer, Kin feared the trail would venture vertically, and he would have to abandon Talon to pursue alone. The auer wouldn't like that.

The blood became sparse, which either signaled Amarie's bleeding had slowed, or her supply was dwindling.

He needed to find her soon. To his relief, the trail met the mouth a small crevice hidden against the rock side. It was just taller than he and barely wide enough for a man to fit through. He paused, examining the entrance from a short distance away as he debated his options. It was impossible to tell if Trist still lurked inside.

During his moment of thought, the auer behind him brazenly walked past, eyeing the opening before turning briefly back to Kin. "Is she in there?" Talon asked, pushing aside the foliage covering the entrance.

Kin shook away his uncertainty and nodded as he crept to the entrance. He pressed past Talon, eager to enter first both to be the one to protect Amarie, but also to protect his friend. Talon didn't fully understand the nature of Uriel's Art, or that of his servants. It would be better if Kin intercepted first.

Something deep within the entrance shimmered, and Kin narrowed his eyes. He resisted the initial inclination to pull at his energies, manifest them into something tangible to defend them. Trist would sense it. It would be better if he could maintain his stature amongst the Shades, assuming Amarie was still alive.

With Talon directly behind him, Kin made his way into the wide crack, his shoulders scraping the sides. The brightness from the sun faded as they walked deeper, and it grew difficult to see. Pausing, Kin glanced back, and the auer seemed to read his mind.

Talon extended a hand out in front of him and conjured a ball of flame. It danced into the air above them, circling lazily. Their shadows extended out as the crevice opened to a wider area. Talon stepped forward, coming to Kin's side.

With a whisper of his power, the flicker of flame lurched ahead of them. It stopped as it encountered a pair of large doors, easily twice the height of the crevice. Only one attached to a column with an intricately adorned capital and wide base. The other lay crooked, its massive form braced against stone and the other door. It left an opening wide enough for a horse, even though getting a horse to these doors would be impossible. Crafted from bronze, they appeared aged and mossy with time long passed. The detailed inscriptions and imagery on their surfaces faded beyond easy recognition.

Kin didn't have the desire to waste time studying the inscriptions, but he saw a sun depicted, and several tall structures which reminded him of Capul. Great towers reaching towards the clouds.

This was no cave, but an entrance to ancient ruins of a lost world. Ruins weren't unheard of in Pantracia; many littered the flatlands where the winds exposed them. This was something entirely different.

Desperation to find Amarie encouraged Kin to charge through. Unable to detect more of a blood trail through his power, he turned his eyes towards the ground where the lichen was disturbed.

Trist had left the realm of shadow here, resorting to transporting Amarie physically.

Talon's flame zoomed ahead, revealing footprints and drag marks rimmed with dark smears of blood. The tracks traveled deeper into the ruins, but there was no evidence of anyone having left.

Amarie had been here for some time already, and the knot in Kin's stomach grew tighter. Swallowing back the fear of what he might find, he continued on through crumbling hallways adorned with columns and intricate patterns on the stone walls. Some were carved and some painted, peeling in great swaths from the walls. The sense of ancient secrets hung undeniably thick, and Kin wondered how few had seen these sights in so many years. Dark vines of night ivy grew abundant, the air heavy with dampness.

Kin weaved through the wide arches and halls, praying to the gods he barely believed in that Trist was gone. The feeling in his stomach soured with each step, the moist air weighing on his shoulders. Pressure on his chest caused his heart to struggle to beat. As he rounded another corner, the iron smell of blood overwhelmed him, and he paused as Talon's firelight flickered on a crumbling archway.

The viscous smell stung his nostrils. It took all his strength to swallow and prevent his stomach from revolting. Inconceivable dread filled him, but he forced his feet towards the silence as Talon walked behind. Their steps slowed more than he anticipated, and the auer seemed to have no desire to pass him.

Rounding the column of the archway together, the light of Talon's fire allowed them the vision of the gruesome evidence at the forefront of the room.

So much blood. Great pools of it, like oil in the orange flames of Talon's small orb of light. A sulphurous scent drifted in the air. Slow curls of smoke rose from the ghastly glow of embers within extinguished torches on the wall.

Splattering covered one of the low walls, but it was unclear if it was a staining of lichen or something more sinister. The thick liquid on the ground continued beyond the light in Talon's hand and they were forced to take another step forward together.

Talon lifted his hand, the flame growing with an usherance of his energy to reveal where the gore originated.

A form lay crumpled on the dirty floor, dark auburn hair splayed over the ground around her head. Empty dark-blue eyes stared, unfocused and dull. Dry blood caked her face, seeping onto the stone beneath her. While her body had fallen to the side, her bound arms remained entrapped against an iron bar in impossible angles.

Breath ceased in Kin's chest, his insides quaking. His body protested the movement, but he jerked him forward. Feet nearly forgetting how to move, he stumbled towards her.

The echo of his boots sounded distant as he stepped to Amarie. He collapsed to his knees at her side. Unable to control the impulse to touch her, he pulled her broken body against him. He needed her in his arms, but her skin felt frigid.

A ragged cry reverberated through the air from his lips. His hand caressed her hair, pushing it from her face, hoping for the smallest movement.

No breath passed through her mouth, her eyes unblinking, fixated somewhere distant he couldn't see.

Something behind him moved, and Talon cut the ties binding Amarie's wrists to the iron beam. Her body fell heavily against him, and he wrapped his arms about her despite the wet blood. Everything within him numbed. His body shuddered as he tried to force his eyes to see what Trist had done to her once-perfect body.

Her limbs were shredded, flesh torn over her exposed legs and feet. The way she'd fallen into his arms looked unnatural, a leg twisted with the remnants of her boots and leather of her breeches scattered over the stone. What might have been a lace still tried to wrap around her ankle, but it bit into open flesh instead.

Kin, without pause, brushed it away and urged her leg into a more natural looking position.

She couldn't be gone.

He waited for her to breathe, to look at him like she had before. Hells, even if it was filled with hate. All he wanted was for her to slap him, tell him how much she hated him for what he'd done.

"Amarie." His swollen tongue fought to form her name, whispering it into the darkness as he clung to her. "Amarie, please..." he could hardly manage words.

None of what he wished for came. Breath choked in his throat. His body involuntarily quavered and wet heat threatened his eyes. They burned like nothing he'd felt before and his heart heaved. It was as if he couldn't take in enough air. All he tasted was her blood; there was nothing left of the beautiful scent of her hair.

A firm hand grasped his shoulder. It felt as if it tugged him away and his instant reaction was to recoil, take Amarie with him. Pull her closer.

"Kin."

Kin realized the voice had said his name numerous times already.

"Kinronsilis," Talon said again. His tone, hoarse with emotion, tried to cut through Kin's ragged sobs reverberating through the ruins.

"She's gone." Kin's voice caught. "She's gone."

"Is the Shade still here?" Talon asked.

How can he ask such a thing? It doesn't matter.

He didn't care if Trist came and slit his throat. How could Talon care? Talon had delayed Kin. It'd been a mistake to go to him first. Too much distraction in pursuing Trist, in saving Amarie. He wouldn't get to tell her how much he loved her.

Kin ripped his shoulder from Talon's grasp, sliding along the ground, trying to keep Amarie in his arms and in a position comfortable for her.

Talon blanched, taking a step back with a rasp against the stones.

Kin's hand ran through Amarie's hair, fingers trying to part the mats and wipe the blood from her face.

"Kin." Talon's voice came again, sounding stronger this time. "Amarie wouldn't want us getting killed too."

Unexpected anger swelled within the grief rippling through Kin. He growled, his mind jumping to places he wouldn't have normally allowed it to. The emotions found his Art, the tumor of his soul tearing his inhibitions.

The power urged him to let out his anger on the closest living thing he could.

Chapter 11

Until the moment Talon saw Amarie's cold barren stare, he'd denied the possibility of her death. He'd known loss before, the tightness in his chest familiar. The surprise came in how intensely the feeling coalesced within him. His stomach twisted.

His body lurched towards Amarie, but Kin was faster. The forlorn cry from his friend's lips startled Talon, evoking goosebumps on his skin. He swallowed the instinct to tear Amarie from Kin's arms. Kin had no right to hold her after what he'd done to her.

Talon tasted the copper of Amarie's blood in the air as he severed the bonds holding her upright, and his stomach sank as he watched her weight collapse into Kin.

He hurriedly moved away again, pressing the back of his hand to his lips to still the instinct to be sick. The way his boots peeled off the sticky ground made his heart quicken in his steps backwards and from her blood.

As he cleared the dark pools on the ground, he sank to the dirt. He sagged, cradling his head within his hands. His heels scraped across the ground as he drew his knees into his chest, the chill of the stone seeping through his breeches on his backside. He tried to focus on the cold feeling to fight the numbness spreading through his limbs.

Amarie.

Her eyes burrowed into his soul as Kin cradled her head against his chest, weeping. Great smears of blood covered his cheeks. The salt water of his tears bore through the stains, disfiguring Kin's face into a tormented visage of his mourning.

The emotions raking at Talon's chest were far more intense than what he'd felt when he lost his parents. The news had come not horribly long after his banishment, and the grief was tainted by a childish grudge against his father for his role in his children becoming rejanai.

Talon's eyes burned at the sight of Amarie. In such a short time, she'd become a fixture in his life. More than someone he'd merely grown accustomed to.

His life had been anything but predictable after becoming a rejanai and Alana was the only stability he'd ever found. It explained his continued forgiveness for her wrongful deeds. Amarie proved to Talon there were other options. She was strong and resilient despite the human nature of fragility. He saw the tenderness in her, the vulnerability, which led him to respect her attempt to hide it even more. What started as a fascination resolved into an infatuation and desire to know her.

Talon gulped in a breath, forcing his hands to his knees.

Kin had devolved to sobs, and he whispered her name as if she'd hear it.

Watching Kin hold Amarie's body brought a bitterness Talon dared contain. If Kin hadn't been so careless, she'd still be alive. If Kin hadn't met her and forced her into his dark life, Amarie wouldn't be dead. It was Kin's connection to the Master, to Uriel, that damned Amarie to the fate she suffered. Kin was responsible for the actions of any of Uriel's Shades against her.

A sickening thought brought a new wave of nausea to Talon as he forced his head up and peered into the dark shadows at the edges of the firelight.

Were they alone?

The idea of killing the Shade responsible for Amarie's death invigorated him enough to stand, even though his knees shook. Yet, when his gaze fell again on Amarie's still form, he swallowed the knot in his throat and desired nothing above putting her broken body to rest. To clean her skin and bury her so she could be at peace. He thought of her and what she'd want.

Talon tried to pull Kin from his grief crazed mindset, but he only succeeded in angering him further. The man behaved irrationally, entirely enveloped in the wretched loss. Talon saw the truth of it now. Kin's love.

The more Talon spoke, the more irate Kin became. Air stirred around Kin and energy drained from the growths in the chamber. The sudden loss of life brought a tingling on Talon's skin. He understood what Kin did and moved to offer physical comfort again to try to still Kin's reach for the Art.

Before his fingers closed on Kin's shoulder, shadow propelled from the flickering edge of the torches' circle of illumination. A hot pain stung Talon, his hand recoiling as Kin's power drew a line of blood across his wrist.

"Nymaera's breath," Talon cursed in a huff. He shook the wrist where the pain echoed up his arm. The vine drew back like a serpent's head, and Talon yanked up his sleeve to see the slash.

Kin's state of mind was far worse than he expected.

Talon didn't hesitate, the power within him easy to find, and he reached with his Art towards the live vines curled around the iron beam Amarie had been tied to. He drew the foliage into the turbulence of shadow.

They moved akin to Kin's Art, striking at the tendrils of darkness, and twisted in battle. The bark and leaves shriveled as they encountered the shadows, creaking in protest but holding against the striking black tentacle.

Amarie's body slipped from Kin's lap as he reverently placed her on the ground, cradling her head until it touched the stone. His fingers lowered her eyelids to hide the lifeless blue as another wave of despair passed through Talon.

He blinked away the burning sensation in his eyes to focus on the darkness in Kin's gaze.

"This is your fault," Kin scowled. "If you hadn't delayed us..."

"Kin," Talon started, hazy with emotion. "Placing blame won't bring her back. You know I intended to protect her. There was nothing we could have done; we found her as fast as we could."

Kin glowered as he rose from the ground, turning his broad shoulders to face Talon. "I would've been faster," he growled, treading forward with an exhale of power rippling into the writhing shadows at his feet. "I could've caught Trist. Killed her." The air around Kin pulsed with the Art, drawn from the dark source his master infected his soul with.

The corruption tasted acidic in the air. Talon's power wavered as he looked on Kin's gory face, his eyes pitch colored. Talon was once Kin's superior when it came to the practice of the Art, but the way the air hummed caused Talon to question if it was still true.

He took a step back, his chest tightening as he wondered if he would now find out.

Chapter 12

The pain ended.

Breath flooded her body with ice as it drew in. Not by her lungs, but by her soul. Perhaps it wasn't breath, but something else entirely.

Blackness surrounded Amarie, yet it held a sleepy kind of peace. No muscles needed to move; she floated on water, though nothing was wet. Nothing felt warm or cold, except the essence of air continually entering and leaving her body.

Images flashed in front of her of shadow vines ripping flesh from her legs. A gasp reverberated on her lips, but it made no sound. Darkness closed in around her, threatening memories of agony and loss.

Abruptly, she fell and wheezed to breathe, but no air came. Only cold. A ripple of chilling sensations danced across her skin, traveling through her body. Her jaw tensed. A whimper rose in her throat, but it couldn't escape.

A hand touched her, and her mind stilled. Whatever pulled her downward halted, and warm fingers closed around hers.

Amarie wished she could see.

"Amarie." A feminine, distantly familiar voice echoed. "Open your eyes."

"I can't breathe," Amarie said, her voice weak.

Though, words required breath. Perhaps breathing here wasn't as it once had been.

Where am I?

She'd watched pools of her own blood grow wider and darker over uneven stony ground.

"Open your eyes, sweetheart. You're safe."

The voice hummed against her memory, words vibrating within her mind.

Amarie's eyes shot open, only to be blinded by the brightest of lights. Her pupils adjusted as she blinked, and a breeze touched her cheek. The air smelled of cherry blossoms, and her palms brushed spring shoots of grass surrounding her. The ground below her was dry, and she pushed against it to sit up.

She met a pair of eyes the same dark blue hue as her own. Amarie sucked in another breath, and it finally dropped deep into her chest, like a stone into a pool of water.

"Mother," she breathed, her voice hardly a whisper as she took in the familiar face.

Amarie's throat squeezed, hot tears welling in her eyes. All the turmoil, the memories of the Shade, stilled to silence in her mother's gaze, and the embrace of peace returned.

A comforting hand touched her cheek, and tears raced down Amarie's face.

Her mother, Mayen, looked exactly as she remembered. Light-auburn hair, cut just above her shoulders, framed her youthful face. With full lips and the same angled brows as her daughter, but a softer jawline, she appeared in her early twenties, just as Amarie remembered her. She wore a simple dress, snug at her slim waist with delicate light blue fabric.

Isn't she cold?

Amarie turned her gaze down on herself, and realized she wore a white dress similar in style. It had straps tied behind her neck and no sleeves. She remembered the chill of winter, but it was absent in this place. The fabric of the dress covered to her knees, leaving her lower legs and feet bare to the spring sun. There were no marks on her flesh, no hint of the torture she'd endured. Even her old scars were gone.

"You're all right." Her mother tenderly tucked Amarie's hair behind her ear.

"Where am I? How are you here?" Amarie asked. *Is this real?*

Her mother stood and extended her hand to her daughter.

Amarie took it, watching the woman she missed so dearly with a persistent feeling of awe.

"You're... Between." Mayen explained. "And I came to make sure you found your way."

Amarie's mind whirled. *My way to where? Between what?*

"Come, my precious girl, I'll explain."

They walked hand in hand through the tall grass dappled with wild flowers. Amarie finally looked around at what surrounded her, and the pang of familiarity echoed in her very bones.

Home.

She remembered the land from her childhood, far from the forest of Aidensar she'd been in last. The meadows outside Tryth in Olsa.

The vast property grew thick with untamed wild grass. To one side stood a tall barn, painted white but aged against the blue sky. A low fence ran the length behind it, dictating the paddock for horses. A smaller building to the side housed chickens.

They walked past a large maple tree, and Amarie paused to admire the rope and wood swing, tied to a low branch, swaying in the breeze. It swept memories of playful days through her. Laughter, from the time spent with her older half-brother, Ryas, when he visited, was a long-forgotten memory, along with the joy of her mother chasing her around the tree.

Using her free hand, Amarie wiped tears from her face. Looking the other way, she dared to check if the house stood where it once did.

The homestead was built with wood and stone, only landscaped around its foundation. The single level structure looked as it always had. Painted blue and white, Amarie's heart swelled, anxiously fluttering at the sight she hadn't been privy to in sixteen years. A wide porch wrapped around the entire structure, adorned with a bench and worn rocking chair.

As they moved, Amarie outstretched her hand, and her fingertips brushed against flowers and grass which felt so real. The sun warmed her skin, and more memories of laughter resounded in her mind as she pictured herself as a child running through these same meadows. Full of happiness and exuberance for life.

The delicate fabric of her dress swayed as they walked, touching her skin with a softness she was no longer accustomed to.

Off to her far right, her gaze settled on a pond she used to play around as a child. The slimy muck on the bottom had kept her from wading in deeper than her ankles back then, but it looked fuller now than she remembered.

A whinny drew her attention back to the barn, and in the distance, she saw horses playing. A new foal scampered around the fields with an umber coat and white blaze down his face. His mother stood nearby, ears swiveling in response to his eagerness. Patience abundant, the mare chewed on some hay.

The excited sounds of the foal snapped out of her senses during a slow blink. The horses vanished during the temporary black of her eyelids.

None of this was possible. Regardless of how desperately she wished it could be, this wasn't her life. It had progressed very differently.

"This isn't real," Amarie concluded. "It can't be." Her gaze moved to her mother.

Her childhood home's existence ended the same day she had last seen her mother. She'd watched it be set ablaze as her mother perished.

"It is, love. Unfortunately. It's real. Though, this isn't your world, but closer to mine," Mayen reassured, squeezing her daughter's hand. "This is the Inbetween. The place meant for mortals to enter before the Afterlife. I came as soon as I learned of your journey here. But I can't stay, and neither can you."

I'm dead?

"You're taking me to the Afterlife?" she asked, surprisingly feeling no fear at the concept. "Is it... peaceful, there?" She hoped her mother had rested all those years.

Mayen nodded and looked over the field as if expecting something to come.

Amarie followed her gaze back to the pond, which overflowed now. Its surface crawled over the dirt.

"It's peaceful, I promise. But you don't belong there yet," she said with regret. "You must go back, to the world of the living."

Dread crept into Amarie again. *Go back?* But surely only more suffering and pain awaited her. Being with her mother sounded like a better option considering all that had happened.

"Why? There's nothing for me there," Amarie pleaded, wincing at the thought of returning to the blood-soaked ground she last occupied. It held nothing but betrayal.

"There are still those who look out for you," Mayen said, her tone deep with knowledge.

Amarie shook her head. "Kin isn't who I thought he was, and Talon..." She paused briefly. "Talon is better off without me."

To her surprise, her mother smiled, a sparkle in her eye Amarie remembered with fondness. "It's not them I speak of, but still... neither of those things are as true as you believe them to be." Mayen let go of Amarie's hand and wrapped her arm around her exposed shoulders to pull her close as they walked.

The touch soothed her, and Amarie felt her heart calm. Her mother's words were a curiosity, but she didn't question them. She needed to wait for answers to questions she'd already voiced.

"I know well the burden you hold, it is the defining legacy of our family," Mayen said gently. "And that's why you must return. What you hold within you cannot die, cannot be destroyed. It's an ever-present force. The manifestation of the Art, our great responsibility, won't allow you to remain here. Although your lungs don't currently breathe air, they'll do so again."

Understanding settled within Amarie.

"There's much still ahead for you, my daughter. Though it pains me to tell you it won't be easy, I know the strength you carry. And I don't speak of your power. I know the fortitude of your spirit. The struggles you've overcome. The agony you've endured. And I know without any doubt that you'll persevere. You have an important role to play in this life, and while one day you'll be able to join me in the Afterlife, today isn't that day." Mayen stopped walking and turned to face her daughter.

"Amarie, you need to embrace your instinct to stop running and remain strong. I know the power you hold is terrifying, but the loss you've suffered because of it isn't your fault. Your uncle's death wasn't your fault."

Amarie's throat tightened, and her eyes burned again.

"Rennik doesn't blame you," Mayen assured her. "He wanted me to tell you that, but also not to fear it anymore. We may not walk among the world of the living any longer, but that doesn't mean we aren't with you. You need to master it. Unlike me. Refusing it was my undoing and I don't wish the same for you. There's someone to teach you, and you'll know him."

"Who?" Amarie asked. "Who will teach me?" She knit her brows closer together, studying her mother's face.

"You'll know by the way he encourages you. Supports you. It will become his purpose once he finds it."

Kin? She dismissed the notion quickly. Kin had never encouraged her to use the power. He'd never even asked her much about it.

She attempted a smile, and her mother returned it with warmth.

"Don't be afraid," Mayen said. She pulled Amarie into an embrace which threatened to dissolve every ounce of self-control Amarie had. Standing an inch taller than Amarie, Mayen held her close, and she wrapped her arms around her mother in response.

The affection Amarie had almost forgotten filled her soul in a way she could not have previously imagined.

They stayed for a time, content in the moment and reluctant to bring it to an end as the sun dipped lower in the horizon.

Finally, Amarie pulled from her mother to look towards it. "How long until I must go?" she asked, receiving a sigh from her mother, who glanced towards the flooding pond.

The water crept steadily towards them through the long grass.

"Not long, I'm afraid," her mother said sadly, but then a smile danced to her lips which Amarie couldn't help but quizzically return. "Now, daughter of mine, tell me about Kin and Talon."

Amarie shook her head and laughed. "Oh, Mom. You can't possibly want to know about them, of all things?" she asked with raised eyebrows.

"Of course I do!" Mayen exclaimed, squeezing Amarie's shoulder. "You say Kin isn't who you thought, and Talon would somehow be better off without you. I can't fathom either being true, so enlighten me. Let your mother in on your love life. I was never able to give you advice on matters of the heart." Her eyes glittered with delight, but something in her tone begged for forgiveness.

Amarie's heart softened, and she nodded. "If you insist," she conceded. The two of them continued walking towards the homestead as they talked.

Amarie told her about Kin and how they'd met. It felt strange to be honest. She told her mother everything, from the robbery and escape in Capul, to the Delphi estate, as well as her desperate journey to Lungaz.

Mayen listened without interrupting, other than the occasional gasp or squeal of delight as if she was hearing it for the first time.

Amarie told her of Kin's parents, and then, inevitably, about Talon's sister. Her mother's frown mirrored her own emotions.

"Talon came with me, and I still don't really understand why," Amarie continued, remembering his insistence that she needed a friend. At the time, she didn't consider him as such, but now...

"Perhaps he's merely empathetic," Mayen suggested. "Rare for an auer, but not impossible. I wish I could offer you better insight into his intentions. Despite what the priests in those stuffy temples suggest, the Beyond is not a place I can easily watch from. Only glimpses..."

Amarie stepped over a tuft of grass. "So, you can't see my life as it unfolds, then?"

"No." She sounded regretful and reached for her daughter's wrist, giving it a squeeze. "I am only granted a general sense of your emotions, but not much more than that. So, I do understand that recent events in your life have been tumultuous. But I'd hoped you were finally finding happiness with Kin."

Amarie shrugged. "I'd hoped for the same. But I appear to have been the only one. I doubt I'll see him again."

Mayen squeezed her wrist again. "Well, Talon seems like quite the gentleman based on what you've told me," she offered, studying her daughter's face as she spoke. "Perhaps you can find new happiness with him instead. He treats you well, doesn't he?"

"He does," Amarie agreed, but her mother narrowed her eyes at the undertone of reluctance in her voice. "He's just not Kin." She sighed. "I can see how good Talon is to me, and how patient, but when I close my eyes and imagine arms around me, they aren't his. It's always Kin. I can't help it, even if he betrayed me, the memory haunts me. I question sometimes what I saw, and if it was as it appeared," she admitted, and her mother tutted her tongue, shaking her head again.

"Darling, it hasn't been that long. Healing takes time. Talon will just have to wait if he desires more from you. Kin may have misled you, but not all men will. Trust me, I know. And if he didn't betray you, the truth will reveal itself."

Amarie exhaled a deep breath, trying to find comfort in the advice her mother was giving. Her feelings for Talon were rooted in friendship. But the way he looked at her the day he embraced her still buzzed in her memory.

"You don't *think* you'll see Kin, but do you *want* to see him again?" her mother asked, carefully prodding.

They both walked onto her childhood porch and took a seat on the bench.

"I don't know," Amarie breathed, "I feel like it would be easier if I didn't. I'm afraid of what he might say. If he'd confirm it was real, and how my memories of him will suffer." Amarie put her face in her hands, with her elbows on her knees as her mother tenderly rubbed her back. "But I miss him; I dream of him every night." Amarie looked at her mother. "Every night, I see his face, and every morning, there's this renewed pain that he's not there. Holding me."

Mayen pulled Amarie into a sideways hug and sighed. "Time will heal all, sweetheart. I promise. You just need more time." Mayen stroked her hair.

Memories of the times her mother's comfort came when she was a child echoed through her soul. Flashes of images and emotions rustled through her. The gentle embrace from her mother, comforting her through a childhood nightmare. She remembered the warm tanned skin of another set of arms that encircled both her and her mother. The dark, sharp lines of a circular tattoo on his bicep housed a strange cut-out in the middle, like a key's bit. The summer smell of the man belonged to her father, but it was the most she could remember of him.

A few breaths of time passed before Amarie sat straight again to look at her mother. "Did you love my father?" she asked.

"I did," Mayen confirmed with a nod and smile. "More than anything. And he loved us, but being a family wasn't an option." Her mother's dark-blue eyes drifted to the sky, where the sun was setting, and then dropped to the grass.

The water had risen quickly, now lapping at the top of the porch steps. Only the house remained, all around covered by a vast stillness of water.

Mayen frowned, and returned her gaze to her daughter. "Our time is nearly spent, Ree. You need to return."

When Amarie opened her mouth to protest, her mother kept speaking.

"It's all right, we'll see each other again. Just not too soon. You have much to do."

"I'll do my best," Amarie promised, nodding as her mother touched her cheek. She didn't need to force the smile she gave Mayen. Despite the looming end of their time together, Amarie felt grateful for it.

"I know you will. I love you, my precious daughter," Mayen said.

Amarie's eyes burned with salty tears. "I love you too, Mom," she whispered.

She blinked slowly, as the water crested onto the porch and swelled over her feet. The edges of her vision brightened to a blinding white. An invisible force encircled her, drawing her upwards.

Chapter 13

Kin turned his focus from Talon to the wrestling tendrils of vine and shadow, his power seeking to reabsorb that being expelled. The shadow slurped into the ground, taking the dying vine with it.

"Don't!" Talon shouted as his power faltered.

A replacement black tendril Kin conjured from the shadows between them lashed out, striking at Talon's midsection. It nearly hit its mark before the ground quaked, making way for a new root to block the attack just in time, tackling Kin's power.

"Kin, damn it," Talon growled. "Think about what you're doing."

Kin couldn't think. His mind only allowed him the image of Amarie's blank eyes. The streaks of blood on her cheeks. Thick mats of it in her hair. The smell overwhelmed everything. His boots squelched in the ooze as it mingled with soil.

He slid his boot through it, bracing himself. His anger surged into chaotic control and more shadow erupted around him, striking like a nest of vipers at Talon's ankles.

The air around Talon pulsed as he conjured a whisper of wind. Pushing against the fabrics at his feet, Talon sent a raging line of purple fire along the ground. It leapt up, focused by his will to form a wall Kin's power couldn't penetrate. The shadows sizzled like water striking a hot stone as they recoiled.

The wave of heat struck Kin in the face, and he squinted through the burst of violet light. He brought up his arm to protect his eyes, the roar of rapidly heated air reverberating past him.

A rasping gasp echoed through the air behind Kin as the crackle faded. His shoulders tensed as he spun, expecting Trist's return. He forced his eyes to focus on the decayed archway. But nothing was there.

Battle paused mid breath, and Kin didn't dare hope the source of the inhale as he turned his head back the other way. The wall of fire faded, flickering down to a dim line.

Talon stood frozen, his gaze pinned on the ground behind Kin. The auer's eyes widened, and Kin heard another sharp inhale, but from Talon. It mirrored the shock crossing his face. The focus of his eyes remained behind Kin, encouraging him to look.

Another wheeze of a breath came as Kin's eyes centered on Amarie's chest, which had been still moments before. But it rose in the amber light of the sconces. He examined her from head to foot as his brain struggled to comprehend the sight.

The horrendous wounds, which Trist inflicted on her body, should have still been there. Instead, he found her skin intact, and her bones realigned. Blood still marred her skin, but the torn muscle and flesh had mended as if the injuries never happened.

His heart stopped, and the rage ebbed away. Exhaustion from delving into the Art slowed any instinct to approach.

She couldn't be real. His mind was playing tricks on him in the dark, or Talon had fallen further than Kin ever imagined and used nefarious tricks like his sister to distract him.

Talon shifted abruptly, his boot scraping against the stone and drawing Kin back.

Kin couldn't tear his eyes away as Amarie's lips parted for another breath.

Her hands gripped on their own accord, nails clawing at the ground. Her eyes shot open, and she sat up in a swift motion, as if waking from a nightmare, her bloody hair tumbling over her shoulders. Amarie's bare feet kicked out in front of her, slipping in the muddy ground. She didn't stop until her back collided with the wall of the room, a short exhalation shocking through her body. Her eyes lifted and found Kin first. The panic on her face deepened, breath coming fast as she scrambled to try to push herself upright against the wall. Her bare feet couldn't find traction, sliding in the muck. Sparks flickered at her fingertips, evolving into an azure flame which crept up her arms as she shook her hands.

Kin sucked in a surprised breath as his eyes moved to the pulse of power emanating from her hands. Instinctively, he wanted to take a step back, but nothing in his body worked.

Her ocean-blue eyes focused behind Kin, on Talon, and a new wave of confusion passed over her face.

Neither of the men moved.

How is this possible? She was dead, only moments before. She was *dead.*

Kin had held her in his arms, felt the stillness of her chest. No blood coursed through her veins. Kin knew death far better than he wished and there'd been no mistaking it in her.

Yet now, she was staring at him again, with a look of living horror on her face.

Kin surely did look the part of an enemy, mid battle with Talon. Regardless, a new sensation surged through him, bringing fresh emotion to wet his eyes and tighten his throat. Of all the mysterious things he'd witnessed in Pantracia, never had Kin seen someone return from the dead. Some things weren't possible, for good reason, and he couldn't help but question if this was truly her. Especially with this strange appearance of flames on her skin, which he'd never witnessed before.

With a shaky breath, Kin forced a step forward, and her eyes widened, her hands reaching for a dagger no longer at her side. The blue fire spread from her feet across the ground, radiating outwards for several feet, like an oil fire.

He raised his hands to expose his stained bare palms to her while still struggling to find his voice.

Talon was faster, dropping any connection to his Art so abruptly, Kin felt the void left behind. The auer cautiously crossed the room. "Amarie?" he said gently.

She didn't recoil from him as she did from Kin.

Talon stepped into the blue flame, confidently striding through. Nothing happened to him as he knelt within it beside her. He positioned himself between Amarie and Kin, blocking her line of sight to him, and there was no doubt in Kin's mind it was intentional.

Amarie surely saw him as a threat, and he tried to tell himself her reaction was expected but not permanent.

Please don't let it be permanent.

He desperately wanted to touch her and vanquish those stinging memories of her cold skin and dead eyes. Looking at her, he thought he could still see it.

Her breath heaved hard, echoing through the chamber as if she had just run a long distance.

Kin collapsed, his knees unable to support him any longer. All strength he clung to with every sinew of his being failed, the energy seeping into the darkness of the ruins. He rubbed his hands, still caked with her blood, on the tops of his thighs. Everything felt distant, as if they weren't really his hands touching the leather of his breeches.

"It's all right. You're safe. The Shade who did this to you is gone," Talon said calmly to Amarie. "Kin won't hurt you. I don't believe we've been witness to the truth of his actions, and he poses no threat right now."

Kin appreciated the vote of confidence, even if unexpected. It was better than having the auer against him. Even with the inferred temporary state of safety.

Talon couldn't expect Kin to leave her after such an ordeal, regardless of Kin's promise, could he? She was traumatized and would need support. Comfort. She would need him. Kin felt incapable of following through on his word to exit her life now. If he'd reached her in time, he could have protected her. He didn't want to let her out of his sight again.

His eyes stayed on Talon's back as he spoke to Amarie.

Her arms slipped over Talon's shoulders to wrap around his neck. The dim glow of blue flames ebbed away, extinguishing into the ground.

Kin closed his eyes as quickly as he could and tilted his head away. A crashing mix of wild relief tainted with the agony of jealousy filled him. He channeled his focus to swallow the deep boil.

It's just a comforting embrace, he assured himself silently.

Talon let her go gradually and glanced back at Kin. To his surprise, the auer's eyes were wet with emotion and glistened in the flickering firelight. In the heat of the moment, he'd accused Talon of feeling nothing for her.

As bravely as he could, Kin gazed at the woman he'd lost in many ways, to find her watching him. Less fear clouded her expression, but uncertainty remained.

She looked once more at Talon, who offered his hand to help her rise to her bare feet.

His mind and body protested the movement, but Kin urged his feet beneath him. Once he managed to stand, he resisted the desire to propel himself towards her and pull her into his arms. Tears left wet trails down his cheeks, but his feet remained where they were.

Talon's green eyes stared hard at him, but Kin barely noticed while he struggled to look away from Amarie.

Despite the blood, her skin looked perfect, her eyes bright.

"We should get her out of here," Talon said firmly.

The words failed to register, and Kin remained frozen.

Talon glared, clearing his throat to rock Kin from his trance.

Kin nodded vehemently, still unable to find his voice. His eyes hurried to take her in again. Her breeches ended mid-thigh, and her grime-covered feet stepped gingerly along the wall of the room as she avoided her own blood.

Talon hovered close to her shoulder but didn't support her. She wouldn't have wanted it.

Her wide eyes watched Kin, and he wished he could know her thoughts. She lifted a dark bundle and pulled her cloak around her shoulders without looking away.

His apologies had to wait, he tried to tell himself. Now wasn't the time. The metal scent of her blood hung thick in the air. Death hovered both from the use of Kin's Art and the horrible reminder of Amarie's last moments.

Leaving such a place couldn't happen quickly enough. He wanted to see Amarie in the sun, amongst the trees where she belonged. Not in this dank ruin he never wanted to set foot in again.

"I'm so sorry," Kin whispered. His voice sounded haggard. A ragged cough choked past the tightness of grief in his throat.

Amarie's eyes narrowed, and she sidestepped to dry ground without looking away from him. Her lips parted, and for a blissful moment, he thought she might speak. No words came, and she set her jaw.

Her expression haunted him, overpowering the logic suggesting they should leave and demanding him to explain. "Amarie..." He sucked in a breath, but there was too much decay in the air, and he stopped. "I had nothing to do with Trist finding you. She somehow knew about Ormon."

Talon stepped forward, placing himself in between them, encouraging Kin's vision to him instead. He held up a hand towards

Kin. "Now isn't the time, and this isn't the place," he said. "We need to get away from here in case Trist returns." Talon turned sideways between them, facing Amarie as he continued. "We'll explain it all. There's much to discuss." His hand grasped her upper arm. "And I'm relieved we'll have the opportunity to do so. But we need to leave this place."

Her eyes left Kin and moved to Talon, a twitch at the corner of her mouth. Another splintering fear rushed through Kin. She needed comfort, and it destroyed his insides to know he was unable to provide it.

Kin turned away. It was the only thing he could do. He tugged at his cloak, his body insisting he felt cold despite the muggy air. He stepped away from the light of the sconces. The walls seemed too close, the ceilings too short, and he needed the sky.

They all moved through the hallways without speaking, with Kin leading the way. The scent of blood eventually faded from the air but clung to his clothing.

He didn't look back, hearing Talon and Amarie behind him, their footsteps together in rhythm. Kin stepped through the crevice, eager for the freshness finally filling his lungs.

The sun hovered at a mid-afternoon angle. It'd been morning when he approached Talon.

Amarie stepped into the sunlight first, and Kin examined the fierce tightness of her jaw as she peered up at the sky. She must have known she would die in there, and her upturned brow above her glistening eyes nearly brought him to his knees again. Stepping over the grass, she closed her eyes and breathed slowly as her bare feet brushed against the needles of the forest floor. Her chin quivered as she came to a stop, blood smeared over every inch of her.

Kin wanted to wash it all away, help her forget.

Appearing to steady herself, she drew in a gradual deep breath before opening her eyes again. They were glassy, but no tears fell.

"Amarie." Kin said her name again as he dared a step closer to her.

Talon shifted his feet, but Kin refused to look at him. He didn't need Talon's permission to speak to her.

Her features softened, and she turned to watch Kin, her expression impossible to read.

He wanted her to speak, to hear her voice.

Amarie stood her ground, eyes focused yet distant at the same time.

The words weren't enough, but she needed to know.

"This shouldn't have happened." He felt his resolve to stay in control of his emotions weaken. His body insisted that if he didn't express his feelings through the Art, then they would manifest in other ways. Kin's eyes grew blurry with tears again and he sucked in a breath to try to steel the outward show of anguish.

He had to be strong. How many experienced death and lived to remember it? This was harder on her than on him.

Amarie hadn't spoken one word since awakening. She showed recognition in both he and Talon, but how much did she remember beyond that? Did she remember dying? He didn't want her to have those kinds of memories to burden her on top of everything else she already carried.

She opened her mouth again as if about to speak but closed it. Her eyes left his, moving to her blood caked hands. She swallowed, trying to process what was happening as much as he and Talon were. Her eyes flicked to Talon, a pleading within them.

"There's a stream," Kin managed, hoping she would understand he wanted to help.

Her eyes darted back to him.

"It isn't far and will be safe." He gestured towards the thicket. He looked to her bare feet, though knew better than to offer assistance.

Stepping forward, she nodded barely enough to be recognizable as a response. She walked in the direction he pointed, and he didn't reach to stop her. Instead he eyed Talon, who moved to follow.

Talon's mouth opened as if to say something, his gaze on her feet like Kin's had been. Talon was about to protest, offer Amarie help, or insist they go a different way. Or ask if she was all right.

Kin stopped him, his hand closing firmly over Talon's shoulder, and he shook his head. "Time," he managed, his voice catching. "She needs time. Don't ask. She'll speak when she's ready."

Talon's face contorted to a frown, and he brushed Kin's hand away. Talon's clothes and skin were untainted with Amarie's blood, which Kin was covered in.

Kin's cloak weighed heavily, and his hands stuck together in the creases. He needed the stream as much as Amarie did.

"Fine," Talon said, moving away from Kin to catch up to Amarie.

Kin looked back.

The crevice gaped like an open sore, a wound in the mountain side. It radiated with the smell of decay. How had his life turned to such a violent path? He wished it would end, but it was too late for such peace.

The truth needed to be hidden from Uriel. He could never find out Amarie lived.

It took Kin longer to focus than he wished, his mind lethargic and hesitant to pull on the power. But shadows swelled, grasping rock, dirt, and trees. They clawed at the stone bordering the crevice, sealing it into a jagged scar. No one had seen the ruins within for centuries, and now it would be more before anyone found them again.

The vibration made Kin light headed. He'd closed his eyes to remain standing. As the hum of power faded from his veins, he managed to lift his feet to follow in the direction Amarie and Talon had gone.

Kin didn't bother trying to catch up. It was better to give Amarie space from him for the time being despite his own desires. But he needed to understand more about what happened, and he needed to be near her. He wanted to make sure nothing like this could ever happen again. He had so many questions.

His knees ached, his steps unsteady as he followed the trail Amarie and Talon left behind. He could have easily replenished himself, but Uriel's power felt more vile than ever. He'd sensed the depth of Trist's energies in the ruined room where Amarie had lain dead. It clung like a fungus on the air, still feeding on the life within.

When Kin stepped through the thick underbrush, Amarie had already waded partway into the stream. She sat cross-legged with her knees still above the surface of the water. She'd cleaned her face of most of the blood, and shook her head at Talon, but Kin didn't hear what the auer had asked her.

Rolling hills with sparsely placed pine giants curved lazily towards the water's edge. Ferns thinned to become luscious grass until they gave way to eroded rocks and sands of the stream's beach. One part of the shore on the opposite side was broken up by the weaving roots of a massive willow tree, its long cascades of leaves reaching to gently kiss the surface of the water. The scent of mint and rosemary was a wild contrast from the acrid stench coming from his clothes. Sunlight failed to fully penetrate the thick canopy except above the stream. Beams traced through the air, fracturing into small reflections of light cast by the babbling waters.

Amarie rubbed her arms, the current drawing away the sullied brown and red she washed off. Stilling her hands, Amarie remained in the stream facing Talon, who stood on the shore like a protective watchdog. Reaching, her fingertips touched its flowing surface, and Kin could only imagine the thoughts her mind held.

Painfully ignorant of her suffering, birds chirped, adding to the cheerful symphony of the woods.

Talon seemed intent on speaking, and he crouched at the edge of the water near her. "Do you remember anything?" he asked in a gentle tone.

Kin crossed his arms, a flare of frustration boiling through him. The auer just wouldn't take his advice.

Amarie closed her eyes and cringed. She let water pool in her palm before lifting and watching as she poured it out.

If Kin had the energy, he would have reached into the Art and used his shadows to slap Talon. He wanted to tell her she didn't need to talk. Didn't need to tell them. But perhaps they all needed to know.

"Yes." Her voice came finally, but it was rough. "Everything." Lifting her chin, she eyed Talon.

Kin took a deep inhale at her voice, the sound of it tightening his chest.

Talon glanced at Kin, hesitating. Perhaps he didn't know where to start. Something in Talon's motion told Kin he wanted him to ask instead. Kin shook his head.

Talon rolled his eyes, turning back to Amarie. "What happened?" he questioned, but it sounded harsh. "Can you tell me?"

Kin tightened his arms across his chest. He remained near the edge of the forest line, granting space between them, but he wished he didn't need to. The stream gurgled, tempting him to join Amarie in cleaning, but he couldn't yet.

Amarie took a breath, her eyes calmly meeting Kin's during the silence. "Trist... I suppose her name is... wanted my shards," she started, and her gaze fell to the water in front of her as she let it flow between her fingers. "When I refused, she knocked me out. I tried, but... It didn't work, my..." Her voice trailed off as she looked at Talon with a shake of her head. "It didn't work; it didn't work on her," she tried to explain.

Kin didn't understand what she was talking about. He gritted his teeth and shifted his posture. He suspected she spoke of something regarding her Art.

Talon nodded solemnly and waited for her to continue.

With her eyes back on the water, she spoke again. "I woke up in that chamber. She found my smaller shards, but she wanted more. She wanted information." She sucked in a weary breath. "Where were my other shards; how did I manage to kill Ormon... by myself..." Her voice grew hoarse at the recount, and she paused to swallow.

Kin's heart pounded. Did Trist now know of his involvement?

"Once she realized I wouldn't play along, things got worse. I knew I would die, but she took her time." Her jaw clenched again.

The glassiness in her eyes ate at Kin's soul. His stomach twisted into nauseating knots.

Talon's questions forced her to relive it.

Amarie shook her head. "What happened leading to my death makes little difference," she whispered. "In the end, I wanted to die. When it finally came... it was a relief. Like falling asleep." Falling silent, her eyes glazed over at the memory Kin wished she would've been spared. Her chin quivered again, and tears raced down her face. Her bright eyes moved to Kin, delving deep into him. "I saw my mother," she choked out with a sob.

It was too much for him, and his arms fell loose when she squeezed her eyes shut. He walked to the shore, taking the step necessary into the water to get close to her. His joints protested kneeling, but he ignored the discomfort. The cold of the stream helped ease the ache. He lifted her hand from the water, closing it in his. His grip remained light so she might pull away if she wanted to. He couldn't stand to be away and watch her like this. He had to be at her side trying whatever he could.

Amarie's eyes opened again, as if she wanted to see which of them touched her, and they bore into Kin. Her hand didn't move away, and he dared a squeeze.

She rolled her shoulders back, flexing her jaw as her gaze diverted to Talon. Her hand felt limp in Kin's, ambivalent to his touch. "Is sharing sensitive information a bad idea right now?" she asked Talon.

Kin's grip on her hand loosened, but he steadied himself to

remain calm in the silence Talon let hang for what felt like an eternity. Kin kept his eyes on Amarie, and hers flickered back to him.

"I think he needs to know," Talon said. "If he was going to tell his Master anything, he would've already. Perhaps knowing will help him understand the gravity of his promises."

Kin gritted his jaw, recalling the oath Talon forced out of him. How could he ask such a thing after what they'd both seen? When Amarie's gaze hardened on his, it brought his attention back to her.

"Promises," Amarie repeated, briefly biting her bottom lip as if the word irked her.

Kin resolved his grip on her hand again, giving it a squeeze to usher his own reassurance. "I swear I've kept your secrets. I will never share them," he whispered. "No matter the cost."

Her brow twitched, and she squeezed his hand so tight he felt her pulse. "My mother was the Berylian Key before me," she said, watching Kin as she recounted. "That's how it's passed. From mother to daughter, when the mother dies. I don't have a daughter, so the power had nowhere to go. My mother and I talked, for what felt like an entire day, and she explained it to me. I can die, but not until the Key has a new vessel to go to."

Kin couldn't help but feel grateful for her willingness to share such pertinent information, even with Talon's encouragement. Ever since he first accidentally discovered her secret, she'd been incredibly silent about details. He couldn't blame her. He'd been the same with his secrets about his Art and the truth of his service. He didn't want to be like that anymore.

"Then I woke up," she concluded, and looked at Talon. "To you two trying to kill each other..." The dryness of her tone bordered on humor as she raised an eyebrow at them both. "Why was that, if you mean me no harm?" she asked.

Kin bit at his lip but resisted the urge to defend himself. He looked instead at Talon whose eyes widened.

The auer's surprise resolved into a faint smile, and Talon shrugged. "Emotions," he said. "Grief. Anger. It can bring out the worst, and Kin is clearly not immune."

Kin pursed his lips but had to appreciate how Talon worded it. It was Kin's fault, and he wouldn't pretend it went any other way. But Talon didn't seem angry about it.

"I wasn't in any danger," Talon added, a vein of arrogance in his tone. "And Kin is the only reason we even found you. I wouldn't have been able to follow the trail he did. It wasn't visible to me."

Amarie listened, and then shifted her gaze to Kin, as if debating something. Her jaw worked, and he swallowed under the weight of her gaze. Smudges of blood remained under her chin, and he wanted so desperately to wipe them away.

"My *hero*," she finally said, voice thick with sarcasm.

Kin grimaced and averted his eyes.

Her hand pulled from his.

"This probably wouldn't have happened if you'd never met me. It all started there. And with Ormon," Kin whispered. "For that I'm deeply sorry."

Had Ormon's death been the catalyst for Trist and Uriel discovering Amarie had more of the shards? It was possible. Kin should have claimed the final blow in Ormon's death. Then Trist may not have had the task to find and kill Amarie. Kin would have been the only one punished.

"I don't even deserve the opportunity to beg for your forgiveness," Kin admitted, forcing himself to stare at her chin. At the streak of blood, to remind him of the danger he caused. "I don't deserve the chance to tell you the truth." He sucked in a breath, his gaze flickering back at Talon. There still had to be hope for forgiveness. "I'd like to speak to you alone, if I might," Kin said to Amarie. "Talon, perhaps you could give us some time?" He tried to be as gentle as he could in the request, but his voice sounded hoarse.

"Not a chance." Talon shook his head. "I'm not daft enough to leave you alone with her. Not after what one of your kind did."

Kin glowered. "I've already proven I'm no threat. I came to protect Amarie. I love her." The words came tumbling out.

Talon narrowed his eyes. "You have an interesting way of showing it. With lies." He opened his mouth to continue, but Amarie cut him off.

"It's fine, Talon," she said. "I want to hear whatever twisted explanation he has."

A wave of relief crashed through Kin.

Talon froze, his shoulders rising in tension. "It's dangerous."

Amarie didn't waver in her resolve. "If he tries anything, I'll kill him myself," she said halfheartedly.

Kin eyed her carefully, but he'd gladly face death just to have another moment with her. If she did kill him, he surely deserved it.

Talon grumbled a protest and shook his head again as if about to argue with her, but she turned her gaze hard on him. A silent conversation took place that Kin could only guess at before Talon finally gave in. "I'll fetch the horses, then. And meet you where the main road crosses this stream when you're ready," he conceded, rising from where he knelt. "Don't be too long or I may come looking."

Kin studied the dark ruby stains on his fingers as Talon stalked away. They made his stomach ache, as much as Amarie's threat. He bit his tongue as he placed them under the water at his knees, rubbing the stains.

Talon didn't bother to say farewell before he disappeared into the thicket, his auer grace keeping him as silent as a deer. Walking back to their camp to retrieve the horses would be slow going, even for Talon, and Kin would cherish the time.

The stream felt warm, thanks to the more temperate climate of the forest and because it likely came from a hot spring farther upstream before mixing with the cool melting snows of the mountains. Springs were nestled everywhere within these mountains; it made for the perfect temperature in the air.

With only a little scouring of his nails, Kin managed to rid his hands of Amarie's blood. From his squatted position, he unfastened the large button on his shoulder which kept his cloak in place. The weight of it shifted, his hand catching the hard edge of Amarie's dagger buried within it. He dug into the folds and slowly withdrew it. With a gentle toss, the cloak fell onto the shore.

A quick scrub of water removed the blood stain. He took the blade in his palm. "Found this," he said. "I figured you'd like it back."

She eyed the dagger with a certain darkness in her gaze. An undercurrent of pain lingered on her face. Was she still recounting her last moments of life and seeing her mother again? Perhaps focusing on her anger towards him was a good distraction from the torment. He deserved it, regardless.

She stood, taking the dagger from his hand. Stepping to the shore, she turned the blade over in her hand as she eyed it.

He turned as he stood to watch her from behind, wondering if she already thought about using the weapon on him.

Flipping it in the air, she caught the tip of the blade before propelling it through the air. The dagger sank into the dirt next to her cloak.

He took it as a gesture of trust.

Amarie unlaced her torn and bloodied vest, along with her equally ruined shirt, and let them fall to the ground. Wearing her sleeveless tunic and what was left of her leather pants, she folded her arms in front of herself and faced Kin, silent.

"I owe you so many answers," Kin said as he met her eyes. He ran a wet hand through his hair as he tried to collect his thoughts. Every time he looked at Amarie, he felt her dead body in his arms again, making him shiver. The combination of relief and grief was certain to be a bad one.

Her movement and the glimmer of a stray sunbeam on her shoulders fractured his determination to be strong. "I thought I'd lost you forever," Kin managed, his voice cracking. "I held you in my arms, but you weren't there anymore. I'd lost you."

Amarie paused, body frozen for a strained moment. Her brows knitted. "You lost me when I saw you with Alana," she whispered. "I don't understand why my death would cause so much grief for you."

A pang of residual anger towards Alana coursed through him. "That wasn't real," Kin said. "I would *never* kiss her willingly. I love you, *only* you." He took a tentative step towards the shore and her.

She looked at his feet, hers mimicking his with a step in the same direction, keeping the distance between them. "I'm assuming you convinced Talon of this?" she asked, her tone softer.

"He knows Alana," Kin said. "He didn't want to believe she would use the Art in such a perverted way, but he knows she's capable of it."

Amarie didn't respond right away. Instead she walked past him into the stream again. She waded deeper than before, until she stood near the center of it. The water flowed around her waist. More browns and reds trailed downstream, leaving her clothing and skin. She sank into the water and gradually submerged herself completely.

Kin stood ramrod straight, watching her. What had he hoped she would do if she learned the truth? Did he really expect her to jump back into his arms? Disappointment lingered. His eyes fell, examining the splotches of blood on his brown breeches and tunic. He sighed, steadying himself and trying to find the next words to say.

Amarie emerged from the water and stood, her head tilted back with her hands smoothing over her hair. Little waterfalls cascaded from her skin. Wiping the drips from her face, she took a sharp inhale. Her sleeveless tunic clung to her curves while her hair gleamed its natural auburn, now free of blood.

She was beautiful. More than beautiful. Kin's chest thudded. The accentuated rise of her chest and tangle of her fingers amongst her hair was like a drug he didn't know he'd missed. Something more intense than the addiction to Uriel's power. Swallowing barely helped as his mouth dried.

"Amarie?" Kin called softly.

Her gaze turned to him from where she stood in the water. "I want to believe you," she said, letting her fingers drag in the current. A droplet caressed over her lip, her eyelashes flecked with water, framing her crystalline blue eyes with feathered darkness.

"What can I do to convince you?" Kin asked, taking a step back to the water.

I'll do anything, he thought.

She blinked. A new drop of clean water rolled down her cheek to her flexing jaw. "Come here," she said, her voice barely audible over the gurgle of the stream.

His heart leapt into his throat. It spurred the banishment of his tiredness, and he bent quickly to remove his boots before wading into the stream. He urged his body to relax, slowing his steps across the slick stone. His breeches resisted the water until it touched his hips. The bottom of his tunic and the shirt under it grew heavy as they soaked through.

Amarie stood motionless as he walked towards her. "You have blood on your face," she whispered with a twinge in her voice.

"And you missed a spot," Kin offered as he moved closer with a reassuring smile, hoping to soften the surely grisly appearance of his face. The smear he'd wanted to clean away before still clung to her neck. He stepped closer to her, lifting his hand. He paused, logic taking hold. Fingers recoiled back towards his chest, and he looked from the stain to the warmth of her face.

"May I?" he asked, his voice barely a whisper. "Please?"

Her hands rose from trailing in the current and touched both sides of his face, hot against his skin.

He hastily buried the memories of her cold flesh within the ruins.

Her fingers caressed over him with agonizing slowness, leaving a tingling trail behind where they cleaned. She studied his face with each tender movement, searching, as if looking for the truth inside him.

Kin's fingertips brushed against the stain on her neck, bringing the cleansing water to her. He noted the perfection of her skin. No scars marred her, no blemishes. Even the ones he remembered bandaging himself were no longer there. His eyes slid gradually across her shoulders, following her collar. He'd once lovingly memorized all her scars and now found them all gone. Taken away in her reincarnation.

The startling reminder of her death rippled through him, tearing open the internal wounds he'd tried to stitch shut. The feeling of her hands on his face couldn't push away the images of her limp body. Looking into the living swirl of her irises couldn't overcome the memories. A swell of emotion stung his eyes again. He'd shed more tears today than in the past ten years and more escaped as Amarie watched.

Her fingertips delicately brushed them from his cheeks.

"I was so afraid," he whispered. "That it was my fault." A sob racked his chest, even as he fought to control it. "I should've been with you. Should've told you it all so you could protect yourself. So, I could..."

Her hands slid from his face, but instead of recoiling, they wrapped around his neck, and she pulled herself into him. An embrace he'd yearned for.

Finally able smell her hair, sweet and without the metallic taint of death, he enveloped her in his arms as another choking sob shook him. Lips pressed against her wet hair, his body trembling.

Amarie held him tightly, her breath coming in shaky exhales against his neck. "This wasn't your fault," she whispered against his skin, her voice raw. "I collected the shards long before I met you, and

Ormon would've eventually found me. Without you, my encounter with him could've been much worse than the one today."

Kin's stomach twisted at the thought of Ormon's intentions with Amarie. It pushed the grief towards anger just enough for him to start to regain his composure.

Pulling from her, he kept his arms encircling her waist. He took a breath as their eyes met again. "I need to tell you the truth," Kin said, and the nervousness of what it meant brought goosebumps to his skin. His hand found her face again, tracing her jaw. "I've missed you." The words came before he could stop them.

Amarie hesitated, but her jaw loosened, and eyes softened. "And I, you," she admitted. Kin's heart swelled, but then deflated as she continued. "Talon told me what he knows. He told me that day at your family's estate. I wanted you to tell me he was a liar and you'd never do such things, but... when I saw you with her, I..." Her arms remained around his neck, fingers touching the base of his hairline.

He frowned, running his hand over her hair. "I wish I could," he said. "But Talon knows the truth, and I suspected he might tell you. You shouldn't have heard it from him; it should've been me." His free hand rose to her other cheek. "I meant everything I told you about Alana. She destroyed my life. She's the reason I can't call Talon a liar. The reason my existence has been orchestrated by the man I call master. But there's one thing I know for certain now..." He hesitated for only a moment to trace a line towards her lips, his thumb curving with the bottom edge. "I won't idly accept his manipulation any longer. I need you. And nothing can change that. If you'll still have me?" His chest tightened in the silence that followed, stomach writhing. Her expression was painfully unreadable.

Amarie's lips parted in a way that implied her desire to say something but inability to find the words. Her chin tilted upwards, but she bit her bottom lip instead of speaking.

A rush of heat pulled raging desire from the most buried depths to surge through his veins in unexpected fervor. He inhaled sharply, finding consistent thought necessary to keep his knees straight.

Why must she do that?

The familiar curve of her lower lip gently pressed against the pearl edge of her front teeth made him hungry for her mouth. He couldn't act on it, though, for she'd given him no answer to his question. As much as he wanted to hold her in his arms again, love her and protect her, he couldn't without her wanting it as much as he did. That would be worse than not having her. He didn't want to imagine her regretting being with him.

Chapter 14

Kin found himself entranced with the smallest details that had changed on Amarie's face. A tiny round scar once marked her left cheekbone, and a narrow half-inch white one had been located on her chin. Both were gone, and somehow even her eyes were brighter; her lips pinker.

His gaze lingered on Amarie's mouth, before he finally met her eyes again. A slow smile spread across his face, and she returned the hint of one on hers. Old habits fought to return, as if they'd never been apart. Rising his hand to her cheek, he traced the line where the scar on her chin had resided, leaving a wet trail across her skin.

Kin whispered, "Tell me what thoughts are racing in your head." His hand brushed her forehead gently, index finger tracing another disappeared line.

Amarie's brow twitched beneath his touch, and she inhaled a deep breath. "I didn't think we'd be here again," she replied. "Like this, or otherwise."

"What do you mean?" Kin asked.

"It feels like only breaths ago when I knew my life would end. I knew I'd never see you again and have the chance to tell you how much I hated you for what you did." Amarie shook her head. "I would never have guessed I'd not only get that chance, but then change my mind about how I feel."

Kin steeled himself from reacting to what she said. He'd imagined how angry she'd been after leaving his parents' estate, but it still hurt to hear her say the word hate. How had things become so complicated? He cupped her cheek, encouraging her head up to meet his gaze more evenly.

"*Have* you changed your mind?" Kin asked. "I couldn't blame you for hating me after the danger I've put you in. After all the secrets I've kept."

"We all have secrets," she whispered. "I don't hate you, so I suppose I have changed my mind. But what's it all lead to? Are you saying you're here, with me, for good?"

"I'm here," Kin said, tightening his hold on her. Their bodies touched beneath the water's surface. "I want this. I want us. I love you more than I ever believed possible. Seeing you..." Dead. He couldn't say it. His throat squeezed, and his head drooped as he fought to control the emotion rising in his chest.

Amarie pulled him towards her and met his mouth with hers, banishing the cold from his heart. It pounded in surprise, body stiffening as he questioned if he merely dreamed. But the current of the stream gurgling around them reminded him of the truth. When Amarie showed a moment of hesitation in response to his own, his lips parted to welcome hers. He'd sorely missed the taste of her, and the fear he'd never experience it again demanded more.

The hand around her waist tightened, beckoning her closer as the heat between them rose with unprecedented speed. Feeling her pulse and breath against him vanquished the dark images from the ruins. The grief fueled a desire for passion deeper than he'd known before. A need to feel her skin and body. A need for all of her.

The swell of heat ignited a popping sensation in the air as Kin became aware of Amarie's power. In many ways, the engulfing feeling was the same as before, but there was an edge of cold that hadn't been there before. The parts of him sensitive to the Art vibrated in response to mingling with hers, causing an intoxicating dance within him.

Her fingers traced his chest, following the curve of his muscles. He vaguely recalled her fingers tangling with the hem, and then his shirt was gone. Their breaths came in tandem, sharp inhales through their noses as lips parted only to rejoin again. Each time they moved away to explore other areas of skin, it only lasted so long before they craved the feeling of each other's mouth.

Kin's hands gripped just below the curve of her backside at her upper thighs, and he lifted her from the water. Her legs wrapped around him as he waded to the side of the stream opposite where they'd started.

The warmth of the afternoon stretched over the grass, and he carried her beneath the massive weeping willow, treading carefully between its roots. Its long, soft limbs of leaves touched the grass.

The kisses she laid on his neck and shoulders proved distracting while he walked through the curtain of willow vines. She nipped at his skin, making his soul vibrate. He managed only a few more steps before he sat, lowering her onto his lap. Her knees straddled his hips, and he was finally free to tug off her tunic.

Her palms pressed on his shoulders as her lips moved against his. His body burned, screaming for her affection as his bare back met the ground.

Lowering with him, her breasts felt hot against his chest. She filled his hand as he pinched, a moan echoing from her lips. His hips arched up from the ground. Amarie's wet hair cooled the side of his neck as it cascaded down. Her hands wandered down his sides. She leaned back. His kisses attempted to follow before his head fell back to the grass. Her fingers unlatched his belt buckle as he admired her.

Water glistened on her skin, dripping languidly from her hair. Her auburn locks glowed in the dim forest afternoon, curling along the roundness of her breast to the hardened tip.

Kin watched his hand trace the muscles of her abdomen, tickling along her skin to embrace her perfect chest. His mouth felt dry.

It didn't take much effort to rid themselves of the rest of their clothing, and her body was quickly against his again. All logic lost, his mind held only his love for her.

Her mouth echoed soft whimpers of desire matching his own, and her hips rocked, drawing a moan of anticipation from him. Her dark eyes watched him as he gasped for breath. The next shift of her hips proceeded with no warning, and her body sank down to completely envelop him within her warmth.

The kiss suspended with a gasp of air from them both. His entire body hummed with a fury to feel more of her, hear more. His hand tangled in her hair, grasping at the roots near her neck, holding her close as they moved together towards faster breath and beating hearts.

Her knees pressed against his hips, and he felt the entirety of her energy merging with his. With it came intimacy beyond the physical. He felt her muscles tense, pulling tight, and her moans rising as the buildup of ecstasy grew within him.

She gripped hard at his sides, nails biting his ribs. Her lips parted from his in need of air, and she breathed fast against his neck.

His lips found her shoulder, his teeth leaving little indents on her skin, but his focus waned as they pushed each other closer to the brink of bliss. He felt it pulse through her as she gasped into his mouth. The cry of pleasure tore through her and dissolved his willpower to hold out any longer. It washed through him like a steamy wave, and he moaned against her lips, meeting the end of hers. His Art danced with hers, intensifying at the zenith before fading as their bodies slowed.

Breath came in great heaves before Kin guided Amarie's lips back to his. He ran his fingers through her drying hair. Slowly, they parted so Kin could gaze at her beauty.

He admired the gentle flush of her cheeks as he took her hand, and brought her hand to his lips. Kissing the tips of her fingers, he found his mind betraying him to think of what could have happened with Trist.

"I'll always protect you," Kin whispered, touching her jaw. "We'll find a way for us both to be safe. Regardless of what it might take to ensure it." It was a promise he wasn't qualified to make, but so ardently wanted to be true.

Amarie's eyes flashed with doubt, and she moved beside him. Propping her head up with her hand, her elbow on the grass, she had a somber look about her. "No more secrets," she ventured with a cautious tone.

Kin rolled onto his side to face her. He hesitated with an inhale of breath, his eyes averting to watch his fingers trace the curve of her hip.

"It's the only way," she insisted.

"I know," he replied. He pressed a strand of her hair back behind her ear. "I just worry. Sometimes it's safer not knowing everything."

Amarie sighed, and shook her head, her hand leaving his skin to rest on the grass between them. "And sometimes not knowing gets you killed," she stated firmly.

A swirl of guilt rippled through Kin.

"If I'd known my ability wouldn't work on Trist, I could've resorted to other means of protecting myself." She slumped her shoulders. "Or perhaps cooperated."

He recalled the questions Amarie had hinted at, old fears boiling to the surface. "Did you tell her anything about me?" he asked, quelling the shame for asking about himself, even if to protect her.

Amarie tilted her head and raised a brow. "Are you asking if I told Trist how you helped me kill Ormon?"

He couldn't look at her, forcing his eyes to the grass, his hand between them. "Yes."

She sighed again, and he could tell she was less than impressed. "No," she said. "I didn't say anything about you."

Kin hid his relief by gritting his teeth. He reached his hand back to her, tracing her jawline as he looked at her face. "Tell me what happened?" he asked. "Maybe there's things I can explain."

Amarie studied his face, and he wasn't sure if she was hesitating with offering the information or if she was simply reluctant to relive it yet again.

"The power I have," she started, "I'm able to... force it into another practitioner of the Art to kill them."

Kin's brow furrowed.

"I killed a grygurr shaman a week ago that way, and I tried to do the same to *Trist*." As Amarie said the Shade's name, her tone sounded distinctly bitter. "It didn't work. She almost appeared to... enjoy it."

Kin sucked in a breath and held it to keep himself from interrupting. A pit of snakes coiled in his stomach.

Amarie's gaze shifted to watch her fingertips play with blades of grass, but at her next words, her eyes returned to his. "Then it felt like someone else was there. With her. Or *in* her. I'm not sure." She shook her head. "Her voice sounded like a man spoke at the same time. And her eyes turned to this... blackness, with strange gold flecks."

Kin's eyes widened, but she closed hers. A shuddering breath dropped into him as he imagined the eyes she explained; he'd most certainly seen them himself. His muscles tightened and his hand fell away from her.

Uriel had spoken through Trist, overtaken her. If Uriel could do such a thing with her, he could perceivably do the same to any of his Shades.

The corruption in Kin's soul suddenly felt impossibly heavy. He withdrew, averting his gaze from Amarie, and pushing himself up to sit. His Master couldn't learn she was still alive, and if Uriel peeked through Kin's eyes, he would. He might also learn the truth if he could somehow tap into Kin's senses. Perhaps he was already aware and playing every emotion Kin felt towards Amarie to his own advantage.

Amarie's hand brushed against his back, and he leaned forward, standing. He tugged at the roots of his hair to remind himself he was still in control. Not Uriel. Everything felt frigid inside his being.

"Kin?" Amarie's voice resounded clearly as he heard her pulling her clothes on.

His mind whirled too intensely to dare look back at her. He kept his eyes low as he scanned for his clothes and hastily picked them up. "Amarie," he said her name wistfully as he looked at the ground. "I can't stay with you. I was wrong." He drew up a leg of his cold, wet breeches, getting into them as quickly as he could. He felt suspicious of every sway of the power within him. The gentle pulse now an enemy as he questioned its intentions. He doubted his own mind. How much control did Uriel truly have?

A feeling of icy isolation hit him as Amarie hardened her hiding aura to exclude him. The pain it brought tangled with relief.

"What are you talking about?" she asked, her voice touched with frustration. Her hand closed on his shoulder, trying to force him to turn and face her.

Her touch sent an array of conflicting emotions through him, and he shoved her hand away. He took a step forward as he fastened the buttons at the front of his breeches, forcing his blurring eyes to look at the green grass nestled between willow roots.

"We can't be together," Kin said, forcing his voice to be strong. "It was naive to think it was possible. If my Master can do that to Trist, he must be able to do that to me. If he sees you..." He needed to be as far from Amarie as possible, to keep her safe. Even if it meant breaking her heart, and his, in the process. The memory of his promise to Talon burned in his mind as he squeezed his eyes shut, forbidding the rise of tears. He rubbed his forearm, digging his nails into the shapes of his tattoo.

To his horror, Amarie stood in front of him when his eyes opened. The glassiness of her gaze nearly crippled his resolve, and he ground his jaw tighter.

Her tunic and breeches dripped with water. "You don't know that he can. We can figure it out together." She stepped towards him.

He refused to look at her, shifting his vision so he could only vaguely see her movements in his peripheral vision. "No. We can't. You don't know what he's capable of." Kin turned and stepped away, creating a necessary gap between them. "You can't imagine what he'll do to you if he finds out the truth. I endanger you further every moment we're together. Trist proved that. I love you and can't stand to imagine his hands on you. He can do so much *worse* than death."

It shouldn't have happened this way. He hated himself for the decision. The recent memory of their tangled bodies made it more difficult than Kin ever imagined. He forced himself to imagine the unspeakable things Uriel would do to Amarie if he found her. Kin would see her broken body again if he allowed Uriel to obtain her. He would see her death over and over.

His life was already gone, already over. It ended when he was seventeen and he'd been dead for ten years without knowing it. He only fooled himself into believing he was still alive while with Amarie. He had to accept his fate and let it go. She needed to do the same.

"You can't just walk away," Amarie said, grasping his arm from where she stood behind him. "If you love me... You chased me all this way, and now you want to *give up*?"

"Me loving you is what puts you in the greatest danger. I wish there was another way, but there isn't. Not with *him*," Kin said.

"Don't I get a say in whether we're together? What about what I want?" Amarie asked, pulling on his arm.

Kin turned with her pull, letting himself look at her. Everything in him weakened.

She advanced, wrapping her arms around his neck and met his lips in a heated kiss.

His body reacted before he could deny himself, hands slipping to her waist as his lips moved against hers. His gut twisted as he forced himself away.

"Don't do this," she whispered, pulling his forehead to hers. "I just got you back. Don't give up on us."

For a torturous moment, he wondered if it could work. He met her eyes and imagined the blue of her irises turned to oil black. Bile rose in his throat. He leaned away, hands on her waist pushing her as he twisted from her embrace.

"I shouldn't have allowed myself the delusion that there could be an us. We both shouldn't have. We should be enemies, not lovers," Kin whispered, his voice catching. He cleared his throat before hardening his tone. "I'll do what I can to distract him from learning the truth about the Berylian Key. I'll keep you safe, but the only way to do that is for me to leave."

"He thinks I'm dead. I'm as safe as I've ever been," she said and then growled. "Why did you come back? To make promises and then break my heart in the same day?"

"They were promises I had no right to make." Kin sighed. "I have a different one I need to keep. You're safe if he thinks you're dead, but I threaten that. He could use me at any moment to learn the truth. All he must do is look through my eyes. He already knows about my love for you. Alana saw to that."

"I know the risks. Running doesn't solve anything. I'm no safer without you. It would be smarter to devise a way to *beat* him rather than hide," Amarie insisted. "I'd never betray you."

"This isn't a matter of your strength. It's a matter of mine. *I* could betray *you* unintentionally. And if I'm close, the danger you're in is far worse. He holds sway over me in ways you can't understand. I'm not my own man and haven't been in ten years. I had no right to give you any part of my soul. Uriel already owns it."

"*Uriel*," Amarie hissed, and it drew a thudding from Kin's heart as he gaped at her.

"Please, don't say his name," Kin whispered, pursing his lips. "I shouldn't have—"

"What promise are you trying to keep that's more important than the ones you made me? Your promise to serve *Uriel*?" Amarie's tone darkened with underlying pain.

Kin flinched. "My service is beyond a promise. It is absolute and no longer my choice. But this choice *is* mine. And I've made it." Kin locked eyes with her, risking the danger to force her away. "Forget me. No more pretending we can have a happy ending."

"You coward," Amarie glowered, shaking her head. "You're just going to make this decision without me and not tell me the truth of why?"

"I'm telling you the truth. I said I would protect you, no matter the cost. I'm doing just that. Why can't you see the threat I am to you? I'm a *Shade*. Your enemy. One who would torture and destroy you just like Trist."

"Then get it over with, enemy of mine," Amarie challenged, stepping closer to him. Her eyes flashed with a purple hue and her hand closed to a fist. "Torture me, destroy me. Why don't we summon Uriel to finish this for us? I just came back from the fucking dead, and you're going to run away because of some beast."

Kin stepped back, careful to keep her an arm's distance away. She wouldn't try to force Uriel out of him, would she? The wild look in her eyes dared him not to call her bluff.

"You don't get it," Kin said, his voice rising in frustration to meet hers. "You—"

"No, *you* don't get it," Amarie interrupted. "I was fine. I was even happy without you, but you had to come back and ruin it."

"You'll find it again, then," Kin grumbled. The pain that echoed through his chest threatened to be permanent for him. "Go back to Talon," he said, gesturing down the stream with a wild arm, defeat rolling through him.

Her hand caught his, and she gripped too tight for him to yank it away.

Terror washed through him. "Don't." He gasped. His hand felt hot in hers, and he could tell her power hovered at the surface of her skin.

Her eyes glistened, and her jaw worked.

"Amarie," Kin begged, digging his nails into her hand. "Let me go."

Amarie's eyelashes fluttered, and she sucked in a breath, releasing his hand so suddenly he stumbled backwards. "Then leave," she whispered, voice cracking. Backing up as a cringe crossed her face, Amarie shook her head. "But if you leave, don't come back. What Uriel might do to me is nothing compared to the torture you've already inflicted."

The urge to embrace her shook through him, but he drowned it with the darkness he breathed as he summoned the Art. Continuing the conversation would be futile. There would be no changing his mind.

"I'll always love you," Kin blurted before he could contain it.

Tears sprang from her eyes.

His chest seized as shadow rolled up his body. It consumed him, licking down his limbs, tingling with his raw emotion. The power came easily as his body shrunk into the billowing blackness.

Amarie closed her eyes as his feathers grew.

Chapter 15

Talon didn't enjoy the long walk back to their camp.

Not to mention, he left Amarie with Kin. Alone. But he respected her enough to obey her request, even if he vehemently disagreed. Regardless of Kin's apparent innocence regarding Alana, he remained a danger to Amarie. The entire ordeal exhausted Talon. And he despised the idea of Amarie forgiving Kin, his imagination tormenting him with images of them embracing like they once had.

As he walked amongst the trees, Talon forced his mind to more productive thoughts. He'd finished reading the book Amarie shared with him, which detailed ancient legends, like the Berylian Key, from before the great Sundering. All speculation, of course, and Talon wished he could return to his homeland to question elders who might have been alive when it happened.

Once a crystal of sorts, the Berylian Key emerged from the collision of ancient powers present in the birth of Pantracia. It acted as the keystone connecting five volatile ley lines, shrouded in secrecy and carefully protected. A human family lived nearby, tasked by their auer masters with caring for the nearby lands, as well as the Keystone itself. When the Sundering struck, shattering the continent and the lines of power that fed into the Key, everything changed.

Rumor spread of the Art of the Berylian Key being utilized in the initial human struggles for power after the Sundering. Its energies helped forge the new kingdoms of Helgath, Feyor and Isalica. Then the Key disappeared, resurfacing one hundred years later in the great civil war of the Northern Isle.

Through history, scholars believed the Key an object. Thus, the search for the original Keystone's shards began.

But Talon considered an alternate history with the new information Amarie granted him. A power passed through a bloodline, from mother to daughter, instead of being trapped within a stone. He wondered if Amarie's ancestors might have been one of the founders of Ziona after the war that split Isalica. It seemed appropriate considering Amarie's headstrong and independent nature. She would fit in well with the ranks of female leaders in Ziona.

Talon had refrained from questioning Amarie about her mother further when she mentioned seeing her. He hated the tormented expression she showed, and Kin's hovering presence. He didn't need to know more yet. There was still time to learn from Amarie. If she ever arrived at their meeting point.

If she forgave Kin, would Talon's company become unwelcome? He hadn't been supportive of their destructive relationship before, and he wasn't about to change.

Grumbling to himself, Talon tied Viento's reins to Lynthenai's saddle. Their saddlebags hung heavy after he finished packing them. The only assurance Amarie would meet him again was that she would never leave her horse.

Talon arrived at the bridge over the stream, where he had suggested they meet. While he waited, he leaned against the bridge's railing, twisting threads of the Art in his fingers to pass the time.

When a stocky black raven joined him, landing clumsily on the wooden beams of the bridge opposite him, it was hard not to look surprised. It was easy to tell the creature wasn't a real raven, since its eyes were a glassy unnatural blue.

Talon stepped forward before the shadows fully flecked away, and

Kin rose to his full height. "Where's Amarie?" he demanded. His skin flushed in anger; Kin must have left her somewhere, alone and still in danger. How could even Kin be so careless?

Kin's face emerged from the shadows, and he pushed his hood back. His damp hair clung to his temples, framing swollen, bloodshot eyes.

Panic replaced the anger in a sweeping wave. "Is she all right?" Talon rushed to ask.

His clothing disheveled, Kin's sunken eyes looked down. "She's as well as she can be right now," he said. His voice sounded hollow. "You were right."

Talon's brows knitted together, and he relaxed the Art he'd forgotten he held ready. His eyes widened as he glanced back the way Kin had flown from. "What did you do?" he asked.

Kin flinched. "I ended it," he said. "I only endanger her further if I stick around."

Talon pursed his lips, sensing Kin had more information.

"Something happened with Trist," Kin continued after a breath. "I'm certain it's somehow related to my master's connection to the Art and how he shares it with those who serve."

"Uriel, you mean."

Kin flinched again. "My *Master*, yes," he said. "No matter how much power is granted to one of his Shades, it always traces back to him. The connection is deeper than I thought." Kin heaved a massive breath and swallowed, his jaw twitching. "He somehow... emerged within Trist. Saw through her eyes and spoke through her mouth. To Amarie. If he somehow sensed the power she expelled... he'll want to find her."

Talon's entire body numbed. "He has the power to project himself like that?"

"I haven't witnessed any limits to what he's capable of," Kin admitted, running a hand through his hair. "And if he can enter

Trist, I have to assume he can do the same to me. I can't risk him learning she's alive. Instead, I'll try to divert his attention elsewhere, while you hide her from him." Kin's voice took on a begging tone, unlike any Talon had heard from him before.

"Where can I hide her?" Talon asked. "If he's so powerful, where could I possibly take her that he couldn't simply follow?"

Kin's jaw tightened, and he averted his gaze again.

Talon sucked in a breath and braced himself.

"Eralas." Kin sighed. "It's the only place Shades can't go. The auer are too powerful and distrust any Art outside their own."

Talon nodded, chewing the inside of his lip. "They would track down the aberration and destroy it without hesitation. But Kin..." Talon looked at him. "You know I'm a rejanai."

"I know," Kin said, his tone regretful. "I wish there was another option, but it's the only place. It's been years; perhaps they won't recognize you?"

Talon couldn't help but laugh. "I haven't changed much in fifty years, Kinronsilis. And people who knew me are certainly still alive. But that won't stop me from taking her there."

As much anxiety as the idea of going to Eralas brought him, necessity outweighed it. Especially if such a sacrifice was the only way to keep her safe from Uriel and his Shades. Talon would go despite the personal peril. The opportunity arose as a chance for him to do a little good to help balance the evil in his life. Nymaera might spare him from the deeper hells of the Afterlife if he did this.

Kin looked up and offered a weak smile. He stepped towards Talon and held out a hand.

The auer took it, gripping Kin's forearm as they embraced each other. Kin's hold felt half-hearted, and he understood the man's willingness to sacrifice himself to keep her safe. Talon would be doing the same by taking Amarie to Eralas. But the cost was far steeper for Kin. Death was all Talon risked.

Talon cautiously released his friend. "Is she coming to meet me?" he asked, resting a comforting hand on Kin's shoulder.

Kin shook his head. "I don't know, but I suspect it'd be best for you to go find her."

"This is the right thing, Kin," Talon said reassuringly, trying to catch his friend's eyes.

Kin let out an exhale that might have been a laugh if he had the energy for it and shook his head at the ground. "I know," he said, "or it wouldn't be so fucking painful." Kin took in a deep, steadying breath before he backed away. The air hummed as Kin tugged energies from beneath the bridge to summon his alternative form. Black wings beat down, brushing wood as Kin rose into the air.

Taking up the reins of the horses, Talon turned upstream, leading them into the underbrush. He followed the shore, listening to the sounds of the forest around him for any clues to where Amarie might be. Finding her proved easier than he feared.

Amarie sat cross-legged in the stream's current. Facing downstream, she must have seen him, but she stared at the flowing water with a blank expression.

He stopped where her cloak and ruined clothing rested on the bank, her dagger protruding from the dirt next to it. Where she sat, the water reached her ribs, but her sleeveless tunic was entirely soaked. The water rolled up her back, gently protesting the obstacle her body presented. Her wet, clean hair dripped from the ponytail at the back of her head.

Her expression and the way her shoulders slumped compelled him to go to her immediately and soothe her. He could sense the rawness of her emotions affecting his own, and he wanted to take them from her somehow. To spare her.

Talon stooped to untie the laces of his boots, leaving the horses to wander the shore. His bare feet avoided the sharp rocks between him and the flowing water. Wading towards her through the shallow current, he felt certain she heard him. She didn't react, even as he crouched beside her. He wanted to reach out and touch her but hesitated.

"Amarie?" Talon said, his voice barely audible over the babble of the waters.

The only response he received from her was a slow blink, her eyelids encouraging the remnants of wetness to renew down her cheek. Her bright eyes were bloodshot, and painfully vacant. Carefully, he placed a warm hand on her bicep. A subtle flinch twitched her muscles, but she didn't recoil.

Talon waited for a time before he sat directly in front of her, occupying the space her gaze hovered on. His knees touched hers under the flowing water. His dry hand moved to her cheek, thumb brushing at the tears.

She flinched again, but he hoped it was subconscious after such a tumultuous day. Her dark eyes lifted from where they'd been focused. "He left," she muttered, watching his hand retreat from her face before meeting his eyes again.

He slipped his hand down over her arm to find her hand beneath the water and brought it into both of his. He struggled for the right words. "I know," Talon said, squeezing her hand as her eyes dropped down to the water between them. "I'm sorry. I shouldn't have left you alone with him."

Her eyes returned to his. "Why come back, just to leave again? And of his own free will... I've never felt more disposable."

"Kin is a difficult man to understand," he said. "It may hurt now, but you must know, somewhere, that this is best." He dried his hand on his tunic before lifting it to her cheek to brush away more of her tears. She didn't flinch, so instead of withdrawing his hand as he had before, his fingers trailed down her jaw as she nodded. "But no. You're not disposable. I'll remain at your side as long as you'll have me," Talon whispered. "I have no way to prove it to you but with time."

She held his gaze. "Time works for me." Her voice grew stronger, but her eyes remained closed as her head tilted into his touch.

"You've had a trying day to say the least," Talon said, tucking a loose strand of her hair behind her ear. "And I'm here to listen if you need to talk about any of it."

"I don't think I want to waste any more breath speaking of Kin," Amarie grumbled.

"I'm not talking about Kin," Talon said.

"Oh," she said. A silence settled for a moment before she shook her head. "I didn't want to come back, you know. Once I realized I was dead, I wanted to stay that way. That's messed up, isn't it?"

"I don't think so," Talon assured. "Not after what I'm certain you endured from that Shade. Life must seem like the greatest trial to endure right now. I understand. I wasn't keen on it either after my banishment from Eralas."

Amarie looked at him. "What changed your mind?"

"People," Talon said without hesitation. "And purpose. It's hard to know the purpose we will serve in someone's life when we meet them, and I learned to stop guessing. Like with you. I don't yet know my purpose for you, but have faith there is one. And for that, I choose to keep living."

Amarie's expression turned thoughtful, the hurt vanishing as she focused on his face. Her lips parted, and she paused but then spoke. "Then I will make the same choice," she whispered. "Because you might just be right."

"I'm grateful, because perhaps you are meant to serve a purpose in my life. You have already begun to," Talon said, smiling.

"And what would that be?" she asked, tilting her head.

"Your influence on where we must go. Somewhere Shades can't follow."

Her eyes narrowed. "Where?" She breathed out the word.

"Eralas," Talon said, the name sweet and languorous on his

tongue. He continued before she could question his status as a rejanai. "So, what is the cause of your sudden fascination with water?" he asked, changing the topic. He'd noticed her affinity for it since waking from death, seeking comfort in the flow of it.

A hint of color rose to her cheeks, and she looked down briefly. "It..." she started, cringing just enough for him to notice. "It was there. Water. When I walked with my mother, it overflowed from a pond. It rose and rose, until nothing was left of the land. I don't understand why it did, but now... something about it brings me peace. Love, maybe."

The implications of what Amarie spoke rushed through Talon's mind. The scholar in him wanted to ask many more questions about what her experience in death had been like. So few had come back and could speak coherently about what they had witnessed on their journey to the Afterlife.

He squeezed her hand beneath the current of the stream instead, offering her a reassuring smile. "It reminds you of your mother now?" he asked.

"More than that," she said. Looking him square in the eye, she added, "It reminds me of home."

Raising his hand from the water, Talon touched her chin. It couldn't be easy for her to share such information with him, considering all she had been through. It made him feel profoundly privileged. He couldn't find the words to express his gratitude. Instead, he leaned forward and tenderly kissed her forehead.

Amarie's shoulders relaxed at the touch, and when she met his gaze again, she offered a hesitant smile. "We can't go to Eralas," she said and shook her head. "You're—"

"I'm not who matters in this case," Talon interrupted. "We'll find solutions to those problems. But I do believe Eralas will also be a good place for us to work together on something you can control." He tapped his thumb on her jaw. "You need to learn how to channel your energies effectively in the Art, and I have some skill in what you could call obscure forms of focus. Eralas will be the safest place for you, both to learn and to live for a time."

Her eyes widened, her mouth slightly agape as if momentarily lost. "You... want to teach me?" she asked, and he wondered why she needed further clarification.

"I may be overestimating my qualifications a little," he said. "But I'm willing to be the teacher if you would like to be the student."

Amarie's smile became more genuine. "At the time, I thought she was speaking of Kin," she admitted, "but she meant you."

Talon furrowed his brow, head quizzically tilting to one side.

"My mother," she continued. "She likes you, by the way, and told me I needed to learn, and that the one who would teach me would make himself known." Amarie spoke of her mother with absolute certainty in her tone.

The offer to teach her distracted her from asking questions about the journey to Eralas. He didn't doubt the questions would come later, but he hoped she wouldn't remember them until they'd already booked passage.

"Your mother likes me?" Talon asked with a raised eyebrow. He gave another gentle tap of his thumb on her chin. "I'll take that as a compliment, I suppose."

Her smile lingered for another moment before it faded, and she shook her head. "I may not know your motivations, but I'm grateful to have you with me," she said.

He didn't fully understand his own motivations either but supposed it might be better that way. He cared for Amarie in a way he didn't yet understand. He'd already tried to tell himself his willingness was because of his friendship with Kin, but it was more than that.

"Then I'll continue to strive to be worthy of such gratitude," Talon said as he finally slipped his hand from her cheek. He'd forgotten it was still there. "We should be on our way. It will be a long journey to Eralas, and it's best if we don't waste time." He stood and offered his hand.

She took it and rose with him, using his strength to maintain her balance. Her soaked clothing clung to her, and he forced his eyes to linger only on her shoulder. There had been several scars he'd noted while stitching her wound, but they were all gone. Without thinking, he touched the unblemished skin.

Her gaze never left his face, and she tilted her head. "Is this your idea of haste?" she whispered.

Wondering what all had changed in the rebirth she experienced, he zig-zagged his fingertip slowly over where he'd stitched her arm closed less than a week before. Her complexion was perfectly smooth, causing a knot in his throat.

"Compared to the pace auer typically do things, this is particularly speedy," he said softly. "Does your body feel different to you now?" he asked, unable to contain the question. He cupped his hand over her shoulder, caressing down her arm.

Amarie considered his question briefly. "A little," she said. "It feels lighter. Stronger, maybe."

Talon smiled, his hand retracing its path towards her collar. "Unburdened by your past. Ready for new beginnings?" he asked, lifting his gaze to meet hers.

"Something like that," she whispered.

Her acceptance didn't mean she understood both meanings of Talon's question. His mind whirled at the possibilities if Amarie decided to move on from Kin and accept new love into her life. He caught himself imagining being with her, and the realization rocked him from his daydreams.

Pulling his hand away, Talon swallowed the lump in his throat. "And now we approach the auer definition of an appropriate pace," he teased. He stepped towards the shore and turned back to offer a hand without fully thinking it through. He remembered Amarie's independence too late and wondered if she would mock him. He didn't retract his hand though, willing to make a fool of himself in the name of manners.

Amarie took his hand, and they waded to the shore.

He released her once their feet touched dry ground, water pooling in the sand.

"Makes me curious what slow to an auer looks like," she commented, walking to Viento. She stroked his nose, speaking quietly in Aueric, telling him she was glad to see him again.

Talon crossed to Lynthenai and smiled towards Amarie. "Trust me, you don't want to see it," he said. "It would take years."

His breeches dripped around him as he picked up his boots, knotting the laces together to toss them over the saddle. He wouldn't bother putting them on until his pants had at least partially dried. He brushed all the water he could from his clothes before mounting his white mare.

He looked at Amarie to make sure she was ready. "If we push hard, we could reach Zola in a week. Eralas is another week's journey by ship from there. A Zionan ship would be safe enough for us to employ. And there will be plenty of time for you to try to figure out more about me and my motivations as we go." His own mounting desire for her wouldn't stop him from pursuing a friendship.

She smiled at his offer and nodded. "Perhaps we can spare a moment along the way for me to get new boots," she suggested and pulled herself onto the back of her horse. She didn't bother placing her bare feet in the stirrups. "And probably pants."

He nodded. Looking at her legs, it was strange to consider what they'd looked like when he and Kin found her in the ruins. It sent a shiver down his spine. Urging it from his mind, he whispered to Lynthenai, tapping his bare heel against her flank to encourage her forward.

It was hard to believe they would soon be under the canopies of Eralas. It made his heart ache with joy, but his stomach rumbled with fear.

The scarcity of villages and cities on the island, an annoyance in his youth, would now work in his favor. He would teach Amarie how to harness the Art, while maintaining anonymity. It sounded impossible, but he wasn't about to send Amarie on her own. She needed him. It was a pleasant feeling to have, being *needed*, and he hadn't experienced it in some time.

Chapter 16

Spring, 2611 R.T.

The week-long journey to the port city of Zola went quickly with
the steady pace they maintained through Aidensar. Amarie and Talon
left little time for anything but riding, other than sleep. Amarie
gratefully focused on the tangible plan. It gave her time and space to
process everything that had happened.

Returning from death left her vulnerable to Kin's affection, and
she fell into it wholeheartedly. But he broke her. He chose to leave
under a cowardly pretense of keeping her safe. He'd made the choice
for them both, and anger burned in her stomach.

Kin gave up on her, on them, and now she needed to do the same.

Talon helped her sort through her feelings. He never pressured
her, yet she often found herself spilling each painful emotion without
needing encouragement beyond his gentle tone.

Talon would teach her how to properly practice the Art. As much
as it still terrified her, she understood the necessity. If she could learn,
she could defend herself against Shades. Against Uriel.

Recovering from Kin somehow felt less difficult this time. The
wounds had started the healing process once before and still
remembered how they stitched together. If anything, she now felt
closure; she'd never see him again.

Resuming the routine Talon and she had established came
naturally, but she often found herself curiously watching the auer. He
was nothing like the man Kin initially described to her. She looked

forward to the time on the ship when she would get a chance to talk to him more often, like they had while sitting together in the gentle current of the stream.

Amarie still felt his fingertips on her face, tenderly brushing her tears aside. It didn't seem like usual behavior between friends. The kiss he'd placed on her forehead had felt intimate, but her memory of those moments was unreliable. The ordeal of the day left her questioning much of her interpretations of Talon.

Talon hadn't touched her in such a tender way since that day. Part of her wanted it again, but another part questioned if the comfort he showed her was out of obligation. A burden which fell to him simply because there was no one else.

When they reached Zola, Talon arranged passage for them and their horses. The ship was scheduled to restock on supplies in Rylorn, the home of the Helgathian armada, before sailing the rest of the way to Eralas.

Amarie loathed the idea of docking in Helgath. The militaristic nation had a pension for kidnapping and brainwashing practitioners of the Art, forcing them to become part of their war machine. With the lingering rumor of a building civil war, they were bound to be 'recruiting'. But it was the only transport they could find going in the proper direction. And they would only be in Rylorn a single night. If she could keep her power secret from the auer on their own soil, she could hide it from the Helgath military.

The ship hailed from Delkest rather than Ziona, which was another benefit for them. It meant the trade vessel was less likely to draw the attention of the dock masters and inspection agents of Helgath, well known for its ongoing rivalry with Ziona. It also meant the ship was run mostly by men, rather than women. She felt some comfort in the tedium of being worried about boisterous drunk sailors trying to get too friendly. It was a menial problem, one she would rather focus on than thinking of Shades.

They boarded in the morning, and Amarie tended to the horses while Talon arranged the details of their accommodations. He'd been able to secure a private cabin, assured there were two beds within it.

She remained with the horses through the launch of the ship, listening to the creak of the timbers straining with the sails as they caught the sea winds. The rear hold had been converted into tight stables, the large loading doors to the deck tied open behind Amarie. In the corner, a pile of hay rustled in the wind rushing down the ramp. The chill wind passed over the Dul'Idurr waves, but a temperate breeze came from the jungles of Ziona.

Lynthenai shook, agitated with the sway of the ship, her ears swiveling in distaste. Amarie whispered to her until the waves smoothed as they drifted farther into the azure sea. Once both horses had settled, and Lynthenai munched on some oats, Amarie went to find Talon.

Thick, fluffy clouds hovered on the horizon, promising an easy journey.

Her new leather boots, not yet broken in, echoed on the planks of the massive three-mast galleon's decks. She made her way towards the bow's stairwell, which led below deck to the sleeping quarters. Hands brushing both walls lining the slim hall, Amarie eyed the row of doors and paused at the one ajar, peering in.

Bent over, Talon crammed their bags beneath a bunk bed, narrow and inset on the right wall.

Her eyebrow quirked at the sight. His breeches fit tightly against the curve of his backside. She'd have to be blind to not appreciate the view. Keeping silent so she wouldn't alert to auer to her presence, she leaned on the doorframe.

He struggled with fitting the bag into the tight storage compartment, his muscles flexing within his shirt. The gentle flicker of light from a lantern hanging from the ceiling in the middle of the room glowed on his warm, brown skin.

Stepping silently inside, Amarie slammed the door behind her. She smiled as Talon's body convulsed in surprise.

He might have lost his balance and fallen if he wasn't graceful enough to pop a booted foot out to catch himself. He released his bag, half-sticking out of the compartment, and stood to face her. His hand came up to smooth his black hair, loose around his shoulders, and he gave a smile in an obvious attempt to hide that she'd startled him.

"Are the horses all settled?" he asked. He leaned one hand against the opposite wall, yet his shoulder still nearly touched the wooden frame of the top bunk.

The cabin rocked, listing to the side when the occasional wave struck the side of the ship. The sway was the only indication they were at sea, since the room had no window.

His short-sleeve tunic was an ash grey with silver clasps, accommodating of the warmer climate. The top two were undone, revealing the collar of his bare, smooth chest.

"Yes, settled," she replied. "They'll be fine, I'm sure." Her gaze shifted to the bunk beds. It wasn't exactly what she'd had in mind at the promise of two beds.

"I'll take the top," Talon assured, having noticed her baleful glance. "Wouldn't want you tumbling off. But the seas should be smooth." He used the toe of his foot to finish booting his pack into the small compartment.

She smiled absently. "*Should* be," she murmured, "until they aren't and your delicate auer backside lands on the floor in the middle of the night." Her tone was playful. It felt good.

He gave her a grin with pearly teeth. "I'll try not to wake you as I plummet to my certain death," he teased.

"I appreciate that," she said.

"With such a stealthy approach, I have no way of knowing just how long you stood in that doorway admiring my aforementioned backside. Dare I venture you have a genuine interest in maintaining its condition?" Talon smirked, his eyes glittering mischievously in the lantern light.

His borderline flirtatious response surprised her, but she felt her mouth twitch into a broader smile. "I suppose you'll never know," she admitted. "Delicate as it may be, it's a great ass. Does my admiration offend you? Because I can refrain next time."

"Not at all," Talon quipped. His lips parted as if he was about to speak again but then closed, and he chewed on the inside of his lip like she'd seen him do when thinking.

With her back against the door, and the settling silence, she rapidly became aware of the tightness of their quarters. He was only an arm's reach away and standing in the center of their cabin. They'd never been alone in a room together.

The awkward silence held strong, their previous banter dissolving within her uncertainty. He looked like he didn't notice, his eyes locked fervently with hers.

Amarie inhaled slowly, averting her gaze from the intensity of his.

"Ironic, isn't it?" Talon asked through the humid salty air. "Finally, time to talk and neither of us can think of anything relevant to say." He took a backwards step towards the wall, dodging the hanging lantern as he did so.

Gods, the room is only the length of the beds. She wondered if it qualified as a room at all. Perhaps a closet.

He leaned his broad shoulders against the back wall, slightly to the side to peer around their swaying light source.

A huff of a laugh passed through her lips, watching his torso for a moment before meeting his gaze. Her immediate urge was to offer a teasing response, but she stifled the instinct.

The admiration she felt when she looked at him caused underlying feelings of guilt to plague her, as if she should be stricter with her thoughts. Amarie wanted to forget Kin, to stop loving the memory of their time together. Talon seemed like a worthy distraction after the week she'd been granted to sort her thoughts.

"Talking isn't usually my strong suit." Amarie found her voice, studying the features of his face and the way the lantern light accentuated the strong line of his jaw.

"It hasn't always been mine either," he said with a small shrug. "But we hardly know anything about each other. Don't you wish to remedy that?"

"Well," she started. "You could tell me your motivations. You're taking me to a place you're exiled from, which I can't imagine is a good idea for you."

"I'd hoped you'd forgotten that little detail," Talon said, his expression unreadable. "It's not the wisest decision I've ever made. But it's the safest place for you and I'm willing to take the risk." Little green fires reflected in his eyes.

"But why?" she pressed. "Why are you willing? Do you do this for Kin? Because I can't imagine why you would take such a risk for me." She searched his face for a hint to the answer.

Talon had no semblance of a hero complex, so what made her different? He'd so far proved honest in word, but his thoughts were difficult to decipher. And he hesitated now, averting his gaze, which caused her stomach to tighten. Hesitation was rare for Talon, and it reminded her of how Kin would react to a difficult question.

"I once believed there was nothing that would take me back to Eralas. I miss it, but that is expected of a rejanai. It's been fifty years," Talon said, focusing on the dancing flame within the lantern. "I suppose Kin is how this started, I can't deny that. But if it was for him alone, I wouldn't return. I do this for you. To keep you from whatever the beast is that Kin serves. To keep you, and your burden, safe."

He spoke of her power as a burden. It buzzed within her as if responding to the thought.

"Why?" she whispered. "Why does it matter to you if I'm safe?" It was an emotional question to ask of an auer, who often struggled when answering questions revolving around feelings. But Talon wasn't a typical auer.

Talon hesitated again, and she couldn't help regretting her push for more.

"Forget it," she hurried to say, lowering her gaze to the floor and feeling her face flush. "Forgive me. I should be grateful for your willingness, rather than question it."

He was protecting her, wasn't that enough? He hadn't left her as Kin had and projecting her skepticism onto him was unfair.

Her palm slid to the handle of the door behind her in an absent motion.

Talon gave a half smile and lifted a hand in a gentle wave. "No, I apologize," he said as he closed his eyes. "You deserve to know why, but there are a multitude of reasons. Not all of them are completely clear to me yet, and I'm still deciphering them. I'm not often good with examining my emotions without time to dedicate to them, which I understand to be a trait of my people." He rubbed his clean-shaven jaw before continuing.

"Part of my willingness stems from my concern for you, which, in turn, comes from my friendship with Kin. There's also the fact that you need an ally, and I find myself in the position to fit the role. Who else would if not me? Yet another is a greater concern for the power you contain, and a need to keep it from those who might misuse it. But those reasons feel too shallow, considering you're perfectly capable of traveling to Eralas without me, as well as making your own decisions."

He looked at her again, his eyes gentle. His words confirmed her thoughts, and she struggled for a response. He continued before she could find it. "Another is a vast, overwhelming desire to ensure I have the opportunity to get to know you better. To explore the potential purpose we have in each other's lives," he said, each word spoken with great care.

Nodding, Amarie breathed a deep exhale. "Well, I suppose you have the chance," she invited and hoped he would take advantage of it. "I've managed, surprisingly enough, to keep my pledge of honesty, and I plan to continue. I can't say with any certainty that anyone has ever truly known me," she admitted as his smile broadened.

"Then I take great honor in having the opportunity," he said. "Curiosity drives me to learn as much as I can about you." He pushed himself to stand, maneuvering closer to her again. "Would you like to walk with me? I believe these accommodations are a little too cramped for us to have anything but an awkward conversation. And I'd like to learn more about your mother and your family," he said. "You did say she likes me."

Amarie smiled wider, biting her lower lip for the briefest moment before she released it and nodded. She stepped towards him, her hand still on the doorknob. "She does," she confirmed and rolled her eyes. "Only the gods know why." She pulled the door open.

She felt his warmth on the back of her neck before she left the room and entered the hallway again.

He followed directly behind, not offering a response while tugging the door closed. The hallway wasn't wide enough for them to walk side by side, and Talon gestured towards the stairwell which led to the deck. The only instruction they'd received from the captain was to stay out of the way, and if they did, they could go wherever they pleased while aboard.

Amarie made her way up the stairs. Once on the main deck, the welcoming breeze of ocean air invigorated her. She walked to the rail of the ship and looked down at the water sloshing against the side of the hull before glancing back for Talon.

He arrived beside her, and she hadn't even heard his footfalls on the deck. He leaned casually against the banister, his back to the sea, the wind whipping his hair against his neck. He crossed his arms. Unlike Kin, the stance still felt open, rather than shut down. The sun radiated against him, making his skin gleam.

"Do you really want to know more about my mother?" Amarie asked, leaning sideways against the railing to face him. The sun warmed her skin, hinting at the arrival of spring. Not a bit of her missed the frigid weather in Delkest and Feyor.

"I do," Talon murmured with the sea breeze. "Anything and everything you wish to tell."

Amarie turned her head to look out over the water, forcing her thoughts to sort themselves. With her recent time in the Inbetween, her memories of her mother had never been clearer. "She was always beautiful. So full of life. Most of the time, it was just the two of us. I have an older half-brother who'd visit sometimes. I spent my youngest days in Tryth, in the eastern meadows of Olsa. I was six when my mother died, and my uncle took me north to a village just outside of Arboral. I remember thinking the trees there were so big because I'd hardly seen any before as a child." She paused and looked back at Talon.

"She told me... when I saw her in that place... the Inbetween?" Amarie shook her head. "My mother believes you to be *quite* the man. Her words, not mine," she clarified with a teasing smile before returning her gaze to the ocean. "Of all the things she could have asked about after she finished explaining the hard stuff, she wanted to talk of men." She laughed.

"Sounds rather natural to me." Talon smirked. "Typical thing a mother is supposed to be curious about, isn't it? Concern about who might care for her daughter after she no longer can?"

Amarie shrugged, supposing he was right. "Her name was Mayen," she added. It felt easy to share with Talon, even though she'd never told anyone else. "I never knew my father, but she told me she loved him."

"Do you know his name?" he asked, but she shook her head.

"I know nothing about him..." She paused and then squinted in recollection. "Except his arms... wrapping around my mom and me. He had a tattoo, but it's hard to remember. It looked like a sun, or something. With a symbol in the middle."

Talon stood perfectly still, watching her with a curious glint in his eyes. It made her stomach flutter.

Taking another wonderfully deep inhale of the fresh sea air, she nearly laughed at herself and ran her hands through her wind-tangled hair. "I didn't even think to ask my mom more about my dad when I saw her. By the time he came up at all, we were out of time. But I guess there were more relevant things we needed to talk about."

"In this case, you're probably right." Talon nodded and relaxed his arms. He put them behind him, palms resting on the railing. "What about your half-brother and your uncle?" he asked. "Mayen's brother, I assume?"

Her mother's name sounded strange coming from another person's mouth, yet oddly comforting at the same time. Someone else to remember her.

"Yes, my uncle was her brother. His name was Rennik. My brother, Ryas, didn't visit much after that. I think I only saw him once or twice, and not again after my uncle died eight years later," she explained.

Telling Talon about her family felt entirely normal. His casual stance kept her talking. In the briefest span of time, Talon already knew bounds more than anyone else. Even though time with her family felt short, she had fond memories, and the sting of their deaths had long since faded.

Talon nodded, turning his gaze to the horizon on the opposite side of the ship. "I'm sorry for your loss of family," he whispered against the wind. "It's a testament to your strength, to have seen so much and still have your spirit and determination. To experience such loss, and learn to protect yourself so young, couldn't have been an easy task."

"Why do I feel like I could say the same thing about you?" she asked. "You haven't told me details of your banishment, but you must have lost plenty yourself. How long has it been?"

Talon's gaze dropped, but he didn't hesitate in his response. "Far too long. I've been a rejanai for forty-nine years, which is longer than I lived in my homeland. I was young, only forty-three when my trial determined banishment. To the auer, I was a child, but old enough to be punished as an adult in the eyes of the Sanctum of Law."

Amarie slid her hand across the bannister to cover his. "That couldn't have been easy, either."

"No." Talon's hand turned over, his fingers entwining with hers. "But it gets easier with time," he admitted, giving her a soft smile.

"You're nothing like the man I expected you to be," Amarie whispered.

Talon's head quirked up, his fingers twitching in surprise. "Oh?" he asked curiously. "Now you can't say something like that and not elaborate."

Amarie shrugged. "I was led to believe you were a rather typical auer who believed human women were simple conquests. That you use your charm to get whatever you wanted without a care who it might hurt. Didn't seem like a reach considering my previous experiences with auer. "

"To my shame." Talon slipped his hand from hers, and she lost her smile. "That's not entirely untrue. But that was years ago, encouraged by certain company I kept. It wasn't who I wanted to be."

Amarie hadn't expected the admission but stepped towards him. Her hand closed on his again and squeezed. "I don't judge you for who you were," she said. "Who you *are* is much more important to me. I still stand by what I said. You're nothing like how I expected."

Looking to their hands, Talon's closed around hers once again.

He drew it towards him in a smooth motion, lifting the back of her hand to his mouth. He kissed her knuckles tenderly, provoking a shiver up Amarie's spine.

Her eyes widened, and her breath hitched.

His lips pressed against her skin again, this time at the inside of her wrist.

Amarie could hardly hear the waves over her heart pounding in her ears. Swallowing, she pinned her bottom lip under her tooth for a moment as she watched him. Tearing her gaze back to his closed eyes, she whispered, "Talon."

As if waking from a dream, Talon's eyes opened, and his lips stilled. Clearing his throat, he rose his head and lowered their still-grasped hands. He watched the movement instead of meeting her eyes.

"Apologies," he whispered, letting go of her hand and tucking his behind his back.

Amarie shook her head. "Don't," she said, taking an embarrassed glance around.

Only the bare minimum of sailors traversed the deck, and no one was interested in them. Boisterous laughter echoed up from the bowels of the ship.

"I think you're—" Amarie started.

"I should get back to sorting our things," Talon interrupted. "I'll be just below, should you need anything." He gave her a nod, keeping his hands against the small of his back as he backed away.

"Talon..." Amarie tilted her head, wishing he would stay.

"I'll come find you later," he said, disappearing down the steps.

Amarie sighed, touching her wrist where his lips had been only moments before. Venturing to the bow of the ship, she faced the evening dimness creeping onto the horizon. Leaning on the wood, the wind whipped her hair back and from her face. The gentle swells of the sea encouraged the sleepy sway of the ship.

It felt like far longer than a week since Kin had left. Especially when Talon's presence worked to erase her thoughts of him. Taking a deep breath of the ocean air, she let it out slowly. She needed to stop thinking about Kin.

Her fingertips ran over the smooth, water-worn wood at the bow's railing as her mind wandered back to Talon. While he was handsome, whenever she closed her eyes when she was alone, she imagined Kin's arms enveloping her. Perhaps finding another, being held by another, would be a more effective way to change those inclinations. Talon's kisses to her knuckles had effectively banished Kin from her thoughts.

Being unattached wasn't new. She'd never experienced much of anything else. Not companionship, not friendship, and certainly not love. Kin had spoiled her, making it hard to go without after enjoying the luxury of a partner.

She assured herself that time was all she needed to feel normal again. And she had plenty of it.

The sky on the eastern horizon shifted to darker blues and purples which met the sea, the sun's colorful descent flickering off the waves. She didn't turn to appreciate it, ambivalently facing the encroaching night.

"You're missing quite the view."

A voice behind her made her jump, and she turned around to see its owner. She hadn't heard footsteps approach and silently chastised herself for being so aloof.

A few feet away stood a man she didn't recognize. The distant orange clouds highlighted the tips of his sun-bleached hair, cropped short at the sides and longer on top. He dressed in the usual attire of the crew, with clothes meant for work. Dark-brown breeches and a cream-colored tunic. A dark vest, the color of his pants, draped loosely on his shoulders, hanging open.

Forcing a smile, she reminded herself to be polite.

Before she could speak, however, his rough voice came again, "Though I might argue *this* view makes the sunset behind me seem plain," he said, his eyes sparkling. He offered his hand.

Amarie tightened her jaw and hid an eyeroll behind a slow blink.

"I'm Jael, and I'd be honored to learn the name that goes with such a beautiful face."

She hadn't expected anything quite so polished from the crew of a trade vessel. Or possibly Jael was just well rehearsed. He had the confidence and attractive features to suggest the tactic usually worked.

"Mia," Amarie offered, giving him her new alias. She accepted his offered hand, expecting him to shake it. Instead, he turned it within his and kissed the back. None of the fluttering emotions Talon's kiss had caused came with it. Her eyes narrowed.

He lowered her hand, and she noted how calloused his were. His skin tanned, but not in the natural way Talon's was.

"Mia," he repeated, before he released her. "It suits you. I hear you're with us all the way to Eralas. Have you been there before?"

"No," she lied, "have you?" She wondered why he cared.

"A few times, though only the port towns. Can't say I venture far from the sea." He stepped forward and leaned on the bannister next to her. His subtlety resulted in her turning towards the sunset to watch it with him. He certainly was smooth.

"Shouldn't you, you know, be working?" she said sarcastically.

"My shift doesn't start until after the sun is down. Ends about midway through the night. Perhaps I'll see you out here? Gets a little lonely in the darkness." He smiled at her, and she felt herself smiling back out of the sheer absurdity of the scenario. It was entirely possible a roll in bed with a crew member was exactly what she needed. But it wouldn't happen, regardless of Jael's charm.

A cabin boy ran to light the lantern hanging from the main mast, drawing Amarie to notice Talon emerging above deck. Firelight flickered off his exposed skin.

Talon spotted Jael and tilted his head as he strode towards them. "Good evening," he said. "I was just coming to check in with you about dinner, Mia. But I apologize if I'm interrupting?" He posed the question towards her, but his gaze drifted to Jael.

"Not at all," Amarie said. "This is Jael. Jael, Talon."

Jael offered his hand to the auer as he had to her, though she doubted it would result in the same greeting. "Pleasure," he said as Talon accepted and exchanged grips with him. They maintained silent eye contact for a few breaths, and Jael's jaw flexed.

"I apologize, Mia," Jael said, "you'll have to excuse me. I should grab a bite before my shift starts. Perhaps I'll see you tonight?"

She only smiled, and he returned it. He gave a short nod to Talon before heading below deck.

Talon's eyes followed Jael as he walked away with an interested quirk of his head. He backed up to join Amarie in leaning against the banister. "Am I so intimidating?" Talon asked with an air of amusement. "Didn't think it would be quite that easy to discourage him."

Amarie couldn't help but laugh. "Was that your intention?" she asked, voice low in the night air as she met his eyes. "To discourage him? Whatever would possess you to do such a thing?" Her tone held a mocking timbre of disappointment, which he frowned in response to. At least his previous discomfort appeared to have passed.

"Not my immediate one," he assured her. "But you tell me. What might possess me to do such a thing?"

His playful tone caused an interesting flutter in her chest. "Are auer capable of feeling jealous? Because he could teach you a thing or two about being charming," she teased. Her smile never waned as she watched his face, stray strands of hair dancing in front of her.

Talon frowned again and raised a hand to grasp at his chest. "Teach *me*?" He looked appalled. "You wound me." He feigned stabbing himself in the heart, making her laugh. Leaning his hip against the railing, he continued, "Are you implying I've overlooked opportunities for charm when presented with either environmental cues or societal expectations? It'd be a little pretentious of me to point out the *obvious* superiority of your beauty when compared to refractions of light in the clouds."

Amarie wondered briefly if it was sheer coincidence, or if he had exceptional hearing "Perhaps Jael is teaching you after all. He already used that line. You get points for eloquent wording, but none for originality," she said and turned her body to face him.

He smirked. "My attempts are trite then," he said. He drew his hand from his side, lifting it towards her cheek. His fingers brushed back the loose strands of her hair, tucking them behind her ear.

Her skin tingled at the touch.

"I find even the most eloquent words in the common language hardly adequate to convey my thoughts. They're too shallow for a woman as rare and exquisite as you." Talon's hand lingered near her cheek, tracing her skin. "*Araleinya'thalos* perhaps," he whispered. The intricate Aueric language glided across his tongue.

She recognized the phrase, having heard it used in context to an event which took millennia to occur. It described the wonder around the Art laden budding of a rare flower worshiped by the auer culture. She'd never seen it, only heard stories.

He'd managed to completely stun her, and her smile faded. With seeming effortlessness, he'd taken her breath away yet again. She hadn't expected the playful banter to take the direction it did, and he frowned as her expression shifted.

"I apologize." He dropped his hand to his side in a reluctant gesture. "I overstepped... again..."

"No," she said, finding her voice and taking a small step towards him. "You haven't." Her mouth fell agape as she watched him.

Everything between them seemed to electrify with tension. His smile returned, and she felt like his eyes engulfed her.

"I don't want to be unfair to you," Talon breathed. His hand slid around her waist. "Nor risk what you've already given me."

She swallowed hard, consumed by the rising heat in her chest. Her heart raced, and she tilted her chin up, just enough to brush her lips against his jaw. She felt his back stiffen as his hand caressed to the small of her back.

"Amarie," he started, but she didn't want to hear what he was about to say.

She lifted her hand and pressed her index finger against his lips while her thumb moved over his jaw.

He stopped, eyes closing as his breath caught, his lips parting ever so slightly.

"I'm not as delicate as the flower you compare me to," she whispered against his skin and watched his eyes as they opened to gaze at her. Her pulse pounded furiously fast in her ears.

Talon's lips met hers after an eternal breath. She inhaled at the taste of his lips, warm against her own. It was tender, without an ounce of urgency. A tension lingered beneath as the kiss danced through unfathomable passage of time.

Yet, no time passed as Amarie drew another deep breath, enjoying the newness of his scent and unfamiliar feel of his mouth. She sensed his hesitation as if Talon was unsure of what she wanted. Instead of pulling away, she renewed the action and pressed her mouth against his again.

His lips shifted against hers, parting with the gentle tilt of his head as his hold around her tightened.

After another moment of allowing herself to be lost to the rest of her surroundings, Amarie reluctantly parted her mouth from his. She didn't rush to withdraw, feeling his breath touch the damp surface of her lip. Gradually, she increased the distance, until she opened her eyes to look at his. Part of her could hardly believe the escalation, and her mind wanted to spin with the implications, but she held it at bay.

His eyes were impossible to read as they fluttered open to meet hers. His chest rose with another breath, his eyelids half closed as his hand traced her waist.

"That was," his voice came low, "unexpected." A hint of a smile graced his lips, and she couldn't help but glance at them again.

She felt her mouth twitch in response, but she bit her bottom lip instead of smiling. "Mmhmm," she agreed with a breath as she felt a touch of heat rise to her cheeks. "Perhaps Jael should take pointers from you, after all," she said coyly and slid her hand down from his neck to his chest, her hands resting side by side.

His fingers caressed her hip, encouraging her close. His free hand came to brush more of her hair from her face, tucking it again behind her ear before tracing her lobe.

"I told you I was charming," Talon said with a broader smile. "Perhaps too much for my own good?"

She smiled and shook her head. "I think I'd be all right seeing more of that side of you."

"That..." He lifted his chin and placed a dreamy kiss on her forehead. "I will remember."

Chapter 17

Talon's emotions got the better of him. Twice. He'd be a fool not to admit he craved Amarie, but a shadow within him murmured it was wrong. He tried to reconcile if her willingness for new physical affection was fast for a human or not. It felt as if no more than a breath had passed since Kin's departure, which made it seem even more outrageous. Yet, he kissed her. In the moment, Talon's brain was silenced by his foolishly ardent heart. She'd tasted sweet.

While staring at the dark ceiling above his bunk, he considered his doltishness. Amarie slumbered peacefully below. The inclination to join her surfaced, as was expected, only to be promptly squelched by his analytical mind. They both needed time to evaluate. Time. The thing he kept saying there was plenty of.

Avoidance would be childish and suggest what happened between them was wrong. It was merely a kiss. A lovely, enchanting kiss. Mysterious guilt hung like a thundercloud threatening a downpour.

Even though he'd left, Kin still loved her. But Kin's emotional attachments weren't important anymore. Amarie's feelings mattered. Talon just couldn't believe she'd already forgotten him. Perhaps Talon served as a mere distraction.

He'd come to respect and care for her more than he expected possible. She kept up with him in a way so few could. He lavished in the joy emerging amidst their banter. It fed the affection growing rampant inside him. A glorious infection.

Auer courting routinely took decades, he tried to remind himself. Not weeks. Such haste was a human habit. But human traditions were all he'd known as a rejanai. Wasn't it natural for him to have developed some of their tendencies after almost fifty years?

When the ship made good time and arrived in Rylorn ahead of schedule, Talon felt unexpectedly grateful. A chorus of gulls sounded as they docked; the clouds turning pink with the sunset.

Talon didn't mind the close quarters he and Amarie shared. They smelled of her now and matched what he imagined the araleinya's aroma was like when it bloomed once a millennium. Like honey and jasmine blown in a rainy breeze. Fresh. Difficult to resist.

He watched as the first mate leaned precariously over the railing, shouting back and forth with the port master about cost to dock. The pouch of iron marks jangled boisterously when the port master caught it, and he gestured for the boys at his side to assist in docking the trade vessel. The crewmen worked quickly, dragging the gangplank noisily across the deck before it lowered, and the crew poured off to seek taverns and entertainment for the evening.

Talon watched Jael leave the ship and couldn't help the absent-minded smirk. The crewman had managed to succeed in spending some time with Amarie that day, and Talon had watched Jael laugh wildly while giving Amarie lessons on how to climb and maneuver the rigging of the ship.

Amarie acted less graceful in her lessons than Talon knew her to be. She enjoyed the distraction but always rolled her eyes in Talon's direction when Jael wasn't looking.

Her attention to Jael was simply to appease the man, and Talon found comfort in the knowledge. He was the one who knew Amarie, not Mia. And had kissed her. Jael could not claim the same, and Talon felt a strange bloated pride, even if he was questioning the appropriateness of his affection.

His fingers twitched idly on the smooth, weatherworn edge of the banister, beating a rhythmic pattern as he watched for Amarie to emerge from below deck. The click of boots behind Talon prompted his gaze to turn.

The captain offered a quick respectful tip of his tricorn hat, a smile beneath his dense greying brown beard. "We'll be in Rylorn just for the night," Captain Tykor said. "If the tides are with us, we'll set sail by midday tomorrow. If you want to spend any time in town, best do it tonight."

Less time in Helgath was all the better, limiting the risk of either he or Amarie being taken by the Helgathian military to join their ranks of war magisters. The kidnapping of auer was rare, but not unheard of.

Talon nodded at the captain, who returned it before making his way towards his quarters.

A new set of footsteps echoed, and Talon turned to see Amarie crossing towards him. She wore a light grey tunic with laces at the neckline, and her new leather breeches and boots, but lacked the usual vest she wore. They hadn't been able to find her one that fit right after her last was ruined. Even with the material of her tunic loose around her abdomen, tucked in at the belt, it suited her form. A shape Talon appreciated for the appealing curves, uncommon among auer. Though he saw no short sword at her side, and no cloak to hide it under, he knew better than to assume she was unarmed.

Her eyes roamed the skyline of the city behind him before she met his gaze. He half expected an awkward tension to form between them, but she seemed unaffected. In fact, her mood had improved.

"Waiting for me?" she asked with a smirk as she approached, stopping an arm's length away in the fading daylight.

"No." He grinned. "I was waiting for the other alluring human with a pension for hidden daggers," he teased. "Did you see her?"

Amarie glanced behind her and shrugged. Her ponytail swayed with a shake of her head as she turned back to him.

"Nope, sorry, but good luck," she said, disembarking the ship without him. "Hope she shows up soon," she called back, giving him a wonderful opportunity to enjoy the view as she walked away.

He gave it a moment, unable to control the wander of his eyes no matter how much he debated with himself.

It doesn't hurt to look.

Talon quickened his steps to catch up as she crossed onto the main floating dock of the trade district's port. "I suppose you'll have to do as a replacement," he said with a bump of his shoulder against hers.

She laughed at him. "Gee, thanks," she replied sarcastically with a glimmer in her eye.

The docks stretched out into the bay, presenting them a long walk before they'd make it to the mainland. The port itself was a maze of decking built out over the sea with a mix of floating piers and those built on ancient sunken ruins of stone that disappeared beneath the salty waters. There was no counting the number of ships. Hundreds, at least.

Smoke billowed from thousands of chimneys and drifted out over the docks in a sleepy fog. Through it, Talon observed masts as tall as the trees of Aidensar. Their sails were cinched, the towering tops adorned with vibrant maroon flags tipped with gold.

The Helgathian Armada. The military presence in Rylorn was bound to be suffocating. It made Talon nervous, but more for Amarie than for himself.

She can protect herself, he reminded his overzealous instincts.

Talon summoned the dense cloud of his hiding aura, protecting his power in the Art from headhunters. As auer, he would already be suspect enough. He had no means to hide his contracted pupils, the feature most likely to give away his heritage.

Amarie walked next to him, her hands tucked into her pockets as her low-heeled boots clicked rhythmically on the wooden surface, the murmur of trade and commerce ahead.

The sun warmed his skin despite the season, and the stillness of the air gave reprieve from the constantly blowing breeze on board the ship. The stagnancy led to the odor of salty fish, which Talon hoped didn't linger through the rest of the city. Fortunately, as they grew closer, the smell of cedar wood fires burning in hearths became more prominent.

Entering the packed streets, Talon reached for Amarie's hand to keep from being separated. The feeling of her fingers entangling with his sent a pleasurable shiver up his back which only succeeded in adding to his confusion. He forced himself to think of Kin and seek distraction in eavesdropping on the conversations in the bustling marketplace around them.

He'd never understood how humans could stand living crammed so close together. They all but shoved past each other to get down streets and through narrow walkways between merchant carts and shop awnings.

Amarie made her way towards a tanner's shop, and Talon was satisfied enough to follow her. Splitting up in such a densely crowded place sounded less and less like a good idea. With how many people there were, he had no way of being aware of who might mean them harm.

He squeezed her hand, wriggling through the crowd to keep up with her while his free hand stayed on his money pouch.

The conversations he managed to overhear were mostly, well... human. Concerns over money, trading embargos, war. Rumors about tension between the Helgathian Armada and a privateering vessel with ties to Ziona. Speculation of another Dul'Idurr War around the bend for the proud Helgathian monarchy, which would be the fourth of its kind. Further speculation that the privateering vessel was being taken care of discretely. Yet another that the whole thing had been a ruse to trick Ziona into utilizing their new alliance with Isalica.

Politics. Something Talon had little taste for.

A whispered conversation centered on the academies caught Talon's attention.

"Ya remember my niece Iralynn? Damned soldiers came right up to my sister's house and took the little girl while she cried the entire time. Says she's got the Art. But I's never seen it," a man said.

"Poor thing. Them academies are gettin' greedier. And ain't no chance to sneak her out with all the crackin' down of securities since that deserter and the mess he's caused," a woman replied.

"Damn selfishness making it harder on the rest of us. I hear he got away, too," the man huffed.

"Nah, they killed 'em dead, just like all the others stupid enough ter try. But it ain't stoppin' them rebels from causin' us more problems."

"Nope. They're still looking for the guy. He was leading them rebels. I'd bet ye ten iron marks. My sister's husband's cousin knows, and he'll tell ya it straight," the man concluded.

The conversation lost Talon's interest. He'd hoped for more about the academies than some deserter.

It was when a familiar phrase sank into his ear that Talon froze.

"—said he found it, the Berylian Key, I swear."

His grip on Amarie's hand tightened, and she jerked against him at his abrupt, albeit unintentional, stop. She stared back at him, looking to where he gripped her hand, then to him.

Talon tugged her towards him, against the flow of people streaming past them.

A disgruntled old lady with a shawl gave him a nasty look for having stopped in the middle of the walk way.

He dragged Amarie towards a merchant cart selling thick pelts. Drawing her close, he wrapped a hand around her waist so they might appear as merely an affectionate couple. He refocused his hearing and found the voice who'd uttered the words.

Amarie's hand moved to his chest as he pulled her close. In his

169

peripheral vision, he recognized the quizzical tilting of her head.

His jaw flexed in concentration as he tried to tune his Aueric hearing carefully. Upon finding it, he casted a careful glance their direction.

"What the hells is a Ber-il-inized Key anyways?" a guard holding a tall spear asked. A thick chainmail coif covered his head and neck, topped with a heavy looking, wide-brimmed helmet meant to keep the sun from his eyes. It was a wonder his neck held it all. He spoke to another guard, who'd pushed back his chainmail hood, and held a similar helmet under his arm. They looked to be on a break, leaning against opposite walls in an alley on the far side of the street.

Talon partially turned his back to them, keeping one in the absolute edge of his vision. They were at least twenty feet away, with a sea of people in between. It took all of Talon's focus to make out the next words, uttered by the younger, brown haired man.

"Ber-ril-ee-en," he said the word deliberately for the older man. Something crunched as if he took a bite of an apple, before he continued with his mouth partially full. "Gods only knows, but Handerford says it would totally turn the tide against them rebels. And some guy just showed up with it. Dropped it right in front of old Admiral Jandis' gnarled mustache. On his desk even."

"A key?" the bearded man grunted. "Handerford's tugging your balls again, Sells."

"Not a really a *key*," Sells insisted, kicking at the bottom of the spear the older guard was leaning on, causing another grunt and stumble to catch himself.

"*What is it?*" Amarie hissed, causing Talon to start as she turned his face towards her with a firm grip. She might have asked him the same question a thousand times, and he wouldn't have heard it.

Her gaze narrowed at him, a glint of frustration in the corner of her blue irises. Maybe she *had* asked several times.

"Talk about the Key," Talon said quickly before he tried to hone back in on the conversation. He felt her stiffen under his hands, and her voice came quicker.

"*Who?*" she insisted, eyes scanning the nearby crowds.

His hand moved to touch the bottom of her chin, in a way anyone else might have mistaken for affection. He gently guided her head to point in the appropriate direction.

"In the alley across the way, two guards. Eating apples, I think," he said.

It took a moment before he found the older guard's voice again, urging his senses to tune back into it as he watched Amarie's eyes for recognition.

"Sounds fandangled and made-up to me," the older guard said, stamping the end of his spear on the ground.

"Ain't made-up, Landen" Sells insisted. "And Jandis is struttin' around talking about how he's got it in his office and it's going to be taken to the Academy in the morning."

Amarie shifted suddenly, pulling from his arms too quickly for him to react. He caught her wrist, but she twisted free before being swallowed by the crowds. She'd started in the direction of the guards, but Talon didn't dare turn around to watch her and risk drawing unwanted attention to either of them. Instead, he concentrated on the familiar pattern of her footsteps sidestepping anyone who blocked her path across the cobblestone street.

He sighed in relief when her steps didn't take her into the alley itself, and he turned sideways to examine the goods on the cart beside him. It changed his field of vision just enough that he could see the entire alley and Amarie hovering near its opening. He ran his hands slowly over the pelts at the cart, pretending to inspect them.

"The Academy?" Landen huffed. A well-practiced curse followed. "Shit, what them war mages going to do with the thing? It's a Key."

"Ain't you been listenin', or your hearing getting that bad, you old windbag," Sells grumbled, but there was a hint of a smile in his tone. "Ain't a key like you're thinkin'. At least that's what I'm hearin'. I don't rightly understand it either, but I heard that the Chief Vizier, all the way from Veralian, is comin' here to look at the thing. It's got them all running like a bunch of hounds 'round a bitch in heat."

Landen's frown was accentuated by the greys of his beard, and he itched at his brow beneath his chainmail coif. "And I was hoping for a quiet evening," he grumbled.

Sells chuckled. "Gotta earn them ales now. No nappin' tonight. Why I wanted to warn ya since Jandis already got those beady eyes of his on you for last time."

The conversation devolved to idle chatter about how Landen had fallen asleep during a prisoner shift, and it hadn't ended well for the old guardsman.

Talon looked at where Amarie had been listening, only to find her no longer there. Panic flooded him, and he gulped. He didn't feel confident enough to let his senses seek her out, though the temptation was strong. Using his Art would light him up like a campfire on a dark ridgeline to any other practitioner within several city blocks.

A hand abruptly gripped his arm from behind, and he nearly released his aura in surprise. An exhale of relief relaxed his body when he met Amarie's eyes.

"You startled me," he admitted but couldn't smile. His mind whipped around the implications of the guardsmen's conversation.

"Sorry," she muttered absently, her grip like a vice on his arm. "We need to go to the Academy."

Talon shook his head, grabbing her elbow to emphasize the point. "It's better if we don't get wrapped up in this. This is good news. It means they're distracted and won't notice us passing through town," he said.

Amarie scowled with a tightly set jaw. "I need to have all the information I can get to stay safe. That includes learning of imposters, and the people who might have a motivation to fake its discovery," she said, her words pointed. "They said it was at the Academy, that can't be too difficult to find."

Talon's grip tightened but took care not to hurt her. "Amarie," he hissed. He hardened his gaze, hoping his tone would sway her conviction. But the defiance in her raised chin told him this was a battle he couldn't win. He sighed and gritted his jaw.

"It's not at the Academy," he begrudgingly admitted. At least this way he could be at her side, instead of her sneaking off in the middle of the night. "It's being transported in the morning. They said something about it being in an admiral's office. I suppose that's in a barracks near the docks." He lifted a hand to her caress her cheek. "Are you sure this is wise?" Talon asked, running his fingers over her jaw. Rather than the hope of dissuading her, his proximity to her made it harder for him to tell her no.

Amarie frowned, and her shoulders drooped. "Are you trying to use how I feel about you to manipulate me?" she asked and then sighed. "How very auer of you." Disappointment clouded her features.

The insult stung fiercer than he expected. It might not have been taken negatively by most of his people, but to him... and from her, the intention was unmistakable.

Damn it, he cursed inwardly. He averted his eyes and drew away. "I apologize," he said dryly. "We shouldn't waste time then. It might take awhile to contrive a way to get into the barracks undetected. They'll have wards against the Art."

Her expression remained distant, unconvinced at his less than genuine apology.

He often neglected to consider how much time she'd spent in Eralas and her ability to see through the mannerisms he forgot he still had. Wondering the depth of his error, he stubbornly refused to say more.

Without speaking another word, she walked past him in the direction they were originally heading. He didn't reach for her hand again but was careful to keep an eye on the back of her head as they made their way towards a part of town that smelled of tanned leathers.

Amarie steered into a narrow alley lined with dangling signs of various shopkeepers and seemed to pick one at random before pushing open the wooden door. She let it go after entering, and it would have slammed into Talon's face if he hadn't caught it.

Talon glared at the wood grain on the door before taking a long, steadying breath. He frowned as he stepped off the front step of the tanner's shop, back into the narrow alleyway. Whatever spurred her desire to pursue the rumors of the Key wasn't dire enough to disrupt her wish for material commerce. The minor misunderstanding tasted sour on his tongue as he leaned against a brick wall beside the doorway. He bent a knee to brace his boot on the wall, rubbing at his temples as he considered his instinct to protect her. Did he even have the right to do so?

While understandable, her reaction to his accidental attempt at coercion seemed more immediate than he would have predicted. The way she sneered the word 'auer.' He must have accidentally hit a nerve.

Talon passed the time by reading the array of billings and posters plastered to the stone exterior wall of the tanning shop. One's corners curled over the face of a thief sought 'alive' for their knowledge of a criminal guild called the Ashen Hawks. Another depicted the sketch of the deserter he'd heard rumblings about on the street. Both looked so young yet would now always lead lives of running or death. He imagined his own face in the place of theirs, his poster hung in the streets of Quel'Nian, which had once been his home.

The shop door opened, tearing Talon from his daydream, and Amarie silently padded down from the entryway, a new strapless black corset with laces at the sides fitted on her torso. It held in the previously loose linen of her tunic and covered her chest. Her grey shirt protruded from the bottom, which she adjusted as she spotted Talon.

She walked past him without a word, a haunted look on her face.

Not unexpected, but not entirely what he'd hoped for, either.

Only a tiny window of opportunity existed for whatever it was they were going to do to find out more about the Berylian Key imposter. It meant he'd have to rush to fix things between him and Amarie when he normally would have given it much more time.

He pushed himself from the bricks and stepped after her. "Amarie." He tried to put every ounce of his regret into his tone

Luckily, she stopped and turned to face him. The side alley they stood in was quiet and uncrowded.

"My actions were inappropriate," he admitted as he met her eyes. "I regret them. And I'm sorry."

Amarie looked at the ground. "It's not entirely your fault," she whispered. Her brows knitted upwards.

She's not upset at me, he realized. *It's something else.*

"I still owe you an explanation. I didn't intend my actions the way they seemed. You're hard to think around. I lose track of what part of me wants to be in control. I have no desire to manipulate you. I'm sorry if I've unintentionally reopened a previous wound my people may have caused."

Amarie took a steady inhale of breath, looking at him. Stepping forward, she placed her hands on his chest, fingers playing on the silver clasps of his tunic. "You did," she admitted with a subtle nod. "I'm not easily swayed by handsome features anymore. And I don't think you'd use yours on me in that way. But I hope you understand that I need to pursue this rumor."

He nodded and touched her wrist. "I'll be at your side for this. I'd never leave you to fight alone." Even if he didn't believe in the importance of the rumor, he believed in her.

The wrist he touched turned within his hand, and she entwined her fingers with his.

He wondered at her power to convince him of anything.

"Please. Can we go to the barracks? That'll be easier than an Academy full of war magisters."

He sighed. "All right, but only to gather information. And if things get complicated, we leave immediately."

She nodded in agreement. "I promise."

He resisted her first tug, and she glowered at him, but he offered a half smile. "So, you think I'm handsome?" he teased, and she rolled her eyes.

Reluctantly, he followed her second tug towards the barracks. Coming to walk beside her, they entered the busy street once more. Talon's eyes lingered on a cloaked figure as they moved back into the crowd. He could have sworn he'd seen the person earlier in the day. A nondescript hooded man, he guessed gender by the stance. A common sight, he assured himself. But his instinct was to be suspicious, demanding he pay closer attention for another reappearance.

Talon conjured greater awareness of the footsteps around them. He was glad Amarie guided him, because it allowed him to pay less attention to where they were going, and more to what followed.

Even with the sun below the horizon, business continued. Lanterns dangled from street signs and porches above, casting great shadows in the gaps between merchant carts.

Talon heard clicks of old men's wooden canes on stone, the patter of children dancing at their mother's skirts, and the scrape of worn work boots in a hurry to the next trade. The sea of sound changed constantly, always shifting to a new set and cadence as they moved in varying directions. However, despite several turns and shifts in pace, one rhythm persisted.

The steps remained steady behind them for several more

buildings, and he wondered if it was his paranoid imagination, or someone tailing them.

He tugged Amarie to a stop next to a merchant cart selling various trinkets. "Humor me?" he asked when she tilted her head at him.

The footsteps he paid careful attention to halted, and his eyes darted back the way they had come. There was no hooded figure, but that didn't ease his suspicion that they were being followed. He became more certain of it with each passing moment, especially when the steps he'd heard before didn't resume.

Amarie stood patiently at his side, watching him.

He saw the hint of uncertainty on her face, in the haze of his relaxed vision, but paid little attention to it. He'd have to test the theory again. He could have simply lost track of the footsteps and gestured for Amarie to take the lead again.

"Dare I ask?" she inquired, falling in step beside him.

Talon barely heard her as he concentrated to try to find the beat. He listened as the familiar rhythmic steps resumed and heaved a slow breath.

"I'm fairly certain we're being followed," he whispered.

"Is it a Shade?" she asked. She remained facing forward and kept her voice low with his.

"I don't think so," he concluded quickly. "I wouldn't typically hear boots with a Shade's preferred method of stalking."

The footsteps abruptly ended, and Talon's stomach lurched. The shock interrupted him from contemplating the consequences before he turned to look behind them. Seeing no sign of the cloaked figure, he shook his head. His black hair rustled around his cheeks, forcing him to tuck it behind his ear so he could listen.

After they began to walk again, his chest remained tight. Relaxing just because their pursuer had seemed to vanish would be a mistake. Perhaps their shadow had changed their walking pattern?

They walked another long block before he felt a light tap on top of his shoulder. A pebble clattered to the ground at his heels. Talon turned his gaze in the direction the stone had come from, looking up.

Amarie followed his gaze.

The cloaked figure looked down from his perch, standing on the rooftop of the building next to them. The shadows of his cloak hung thick in the night, his frame a dark hole against the star-riddled sky.

Raw instinct took hold of Talon. "Run."

Amarie didn't need any further encouragement and released his hand to move fluidly through the thinning crowds.

Keeping sight of Amarie was his priority, and he kept close behind her. It was difficult to move through the crowds with a consistent speed, slowing to dodge a family or customer at a cart, then speeding in the brief gaps between.

Shouts of aggravation were thrown in their direction. Merchants quickly palmed their coin purses and goods. They must have looked like fleeing thieves.

So much for not drawing attention.

He wished they could get off the main roadway, and as if aware of his thoughts, Amarie ducked down an alleyway to her left.

It was occupied by merchant carts already closed for the evening and far fewer civilians, allowing their strides to lengthen. As Amarie rounded the corner ahead of him, leaving his sight for a moment, he heard the oof of air leaving her lungs.

His heart leapt, and he rounded the corner in time to see the hooded man pull Amarie through an open doorway, arms encircling her struggling body.

How did he get ahead so quickly?

Talon plowed through the doorway after them. He didn't even give himself the chance to consider the danger of it, his mind screaming afterwards at the foolishness. He instantly delved for the Art, to hold it ready, but hoped he wouldn't have to use it.

Amarie wriggled in the grasp of her captor, who wrestled to keep a hold of her while Talon prepared to draw his weapon.

The door behind him slammed shut before Talon heard the second set of footsteps. He whirled around and saw another figure in the same cloak.

The room they stood trapped within was mostly empty. Four wall sconces alight with fire casted a glow about the room, but there were no windows. Light from the moon came in from an open ceiling hatch with a rope ladder at the side of the chamber. It would be too high for Talon to get up and out before being pulled back down. A second door on the innermost wall remained closed. The stone floor looked well-worn, while two rickety chairs sat off to the side with a small oak table between them.

As Talon accepted his Art might be necessary, his focus of energy was interrupted by both men stepping back.

The one holding Amarie let her go, gently shoving her from him before he raised his hands as if surrendering.

Amarie whipped around, yanking her dagger free from where it had been hidden under her corset at the small of her back. When her captor made no move to retaliate, she hesitated.

"Amarie," the man behind Talon said evenly, his voice reverberating against the stone walls.

She turned to face the speaker, wide eyed.

Had the man overheard them in the alley when Talon said her real name? He silently cursed himself for not being more diligent in sticking with her alias.

"We mean no harm," the other cloaked figure said, drawing Talon's attention back briefly. They were on opposite sides of them, making Talon uneasy. Stepping back, he formed a triangle so he could watch them both. As he did, they removed their hoods.

One man appeared to be in his thirties, while the other was older, in his late fifties. Similarities in their features led Talon to believe the two men were related. They both had the same dark-brown hair, but the older man's was streaked with silver. Both men appeared to be in good physical shape, which had also been proven with the run through the city.

The older man stepped towards the other, keeping his hands visible. His startling blue eyes locked on Amarie but glanced at Talon from time to time.

The door behind him remained unlocked, sealed with only a basic latch Talon could easily release. His brow furrowed as their would-be captors stepped away from the door, leaving an obvious escape point.

Amarie hardly moved, her body angled towards the older man. She lowered her blade.

Talon stood close behind her, looking at the two men. Father and son, he concluded.

"How do you know my name?" Amarie asked, her breathing even but quick.

"I've always known your name," the older man said. "It wasn't a surprise either when your mother gave it to you. It was always Mayen's favorite for a girl."

Chapter 18

Amarie looked at the man who knew not only her name, but her mother's as well. Her chest ached from the run through the city but felt stuck and unable to breathe. She took a step back from the cloaked men, her shoulder brushing past Talon with another step, eyes darting from one unknown face to the other.

How is this possible? They didn't feel like a threat anymore, but why the chase through the streets? It was too much of a coincidence that two men who knew her name were in the same city as a false Berylian Key.

"You don't need to fear us," the younger man said.

She narrowed her eyes as the older man removed his cloak and draped it over the back of one of the chairs. The short-sleeved tunic he wore beneath drew her attention to his exposed arms.

Dark bracers covered most of his forearms, matching the brown tunic. The skin was heavily tattooed. Ink ran all the way up both his arms and disappeared under the sleeves of his tunic.

"Explain," Amarie demanded.

"My name is Deylan, and this is my father Kalpheus," the younger man introduced, and then his gaze turned to Talon. "It's an honor to meet you as well, Talon. I apologize for the theatrics in getting you here, but your safety is our highest priority."

Talon stepped between her and the two men with a single confident stride, clearly unconvinced.

She didn't listen to all Deylan said, distracted by the name of the older man. Kalpheus. The name resounded within her consciousness in a vaguely familiar way.

Kalpheus stepped towards her, into the faint light provided by the open ceiling hatch.

Amarie stared at the tattoos on his arms. On his left arm, a sun, with rays radiating outward from it. Details of circular patterns expanded even farther. In the dim light of the room, it was difficult to determine if she was merely imagining the familiarity of the markings, or if she'd truly seen them before.

He stood completely still, as if patiently waiting for her.

Talon's arm curled behind him to touch Amarie's side.

Amarie's eyes widened as his name and the tattoos settled, finding their place in her memory. But it couldn't be true. She gripped Talon's forearm.

Kalpheus' right arm was tattooed with an abstract symbol, with sharp edges and a bleed of ink outward.

Amarie knew immediately where she'd seen it before, and her gaze met his. With a steadying breath, she released Talon and stepped away. She moved around him, pointing her dagger towards the ground.

Talon's jaw locked, and his eyes followed her.

"Is it really you?" Amarie asked, her voice low as she stepped towards Kalpheus. Her heart thudded in her chest.

When he smiled, she recognized the shape of his cheek to be like her own, even partially disguised by a short, well-kept, brown beard.

"It is, Ree," Kalpheus said.

Amarie's mouth went dry, like the sands of the Gilgas Desert, and her hands slacked. Her dagger fell with a clatter to the stone floor.

Talon touched her arm, but the contact felt far away.

Unable to pry her eyes off the man in front of her, she shook her head. Wetness pooled on her lower lids. "This isn't possible," she whispered. "You can't be..." The words barely carried over the still air of the room. Even as she said it, she wanted to be wrong. She hoped it was possible.

"It's all right," Kalpheus said, striding towards her.

She swallowed hard as Talon's grip tightened on her forearm.

"Dad?" she breathed.

The grip on her arm fell away, and she heard Talon's sharp inhale directly behind her left shoulder.

Kalpheus nodded, and Amarie took a shaky breath as her father pulled her into an embrace she needed so desperately. His arms were warm, and his skin smelled of sun and worn leather.

Amarie wrapped her arms around his middle, listening to his heart beating.

This isn't a dream, she assured herself.

The room stilled, and the hovering tension melted away. She tilted her head, her cheek against his leather tunic.

Kalpheus held her tightly, and Deylan exhaled.

Deylan's boots scraped over the dirty stone as he walked towards Talon and offered a hand in greeting. "We aren't your enemy. And we appreciate the protection you've given my sister over the past several weeks. It truly is an honor to formally meet you," he said.

Talon eyed the offering for a moment before he accepted. "You're Amarie's brother?" he asked but continued before Deylan could answer. "And you make it sound as if you've been watching us for weeks."

"Half-brother, technically," Deylan clarified and released Talon's hand. "Watching... in a way, you could call it that. She's important and not simply because of our familial connection, but you already know that," he said. Deylan appeared to defer to his father as he glanced at Kalpheus.

Amarie released Kalpheus, looking from him to Deylan and then back again. "I feel like there's a lot I should know," she started, and then her gaze settled on Talon. A smile graced her lips, grateful he was with her.

"There is," Kalpheus confirmed. "Come, this storage room is no place for discussions."

Talon didn't seem to relax. A tension prevailed in the way he stood. He watched her, silently conveying his thoughts but her brain, distracted, had difficulty deciphering. Distrust?

She supposed she couldn't blame him. But it was misplaced.

"Come," Kalpheus said again.

Talon eyed her, waiting.

Amarie held her hand out to Talon and waited for him to take it.

He stared at it briefly but came to a decision before long.

Once she felt the comfort of his palm against hers, she stepped towards the door at the back of the room.

Her father moved ahead to open it.

She needed to know, no matter what. If her family knew her, knew who she was, what she was, she needed to understand.

Crossing through the doorway, the warmth of the new room welcomed her. No light from the outside penetrated the dense curtains drawn across the windows. Amarie stepped towards an overstuffed armchair, lit by a glowing lantern atop a side table. Her boots quieted on a lush patterned rug.

Kalpheus walked close behind her, swooping around Talon to encourage her with a gesture to sit wherever she liked. He seemed surprisingly relaxed, considering the circumstances.

She lowered herself into the well-worn chair, releasing Talon's hand as she did so, still watching her father as he took the seat across from her. A wood-burning stove occupied the space next to him, though it remained unlit. Everything felt surreal.

Talon moved to stand behind Amarie, putting his back towards one of the thickly draped windows. He crossed his arms tightly over his chest.

Kalpheus settled at the edge of his chair, leaning forward, grasping his hands in front of him. "To cut to the heart of the matter, Amarie, your brother and I have been watching over you for some time. We are part of a hidden faction tasked with the protection of the Berylian Key."

She immediately tensed at his casual mention of such a secret.

"We've watched over the Key for many generations, using ancient objects crafted prior to the Sundering. We don't have the time to explain the details. What's more important is that you should *not* be here. The diversion we've created by tricking Helgath into believing they've found the Berylian Key was intended to pull pursuers off your trail. We've already captured one and suspect others will come as well."

Amarie sucked in a breath. "Who did you capture?" she asked.

"A Shade," Kalpheus said solemnly, his eyes grave.

Amarie's heart felt as if it dropped out of her chest, clattering to the floor like her dagger. *Kin?*

But Kalpheus continued, "I believe you're already familiar with her, unfortunately, and justice will be dealt."

Her.

She exhaled; they'd captured Trist. Amarie felt a shiver dart up her spine with the knowledge that her murderer was nearby, and she understood why she needed to be far away from these rumors. Talon had been right all along.

"You're planning to use her as a scapegoat?" Talon asked, his voice laced with skepticism. "The Shade. Lay blame on her when the object you're parading as the Key disappears from under the admiral's nose?"

Deylan shifted his feet.

Kalpheus' gaze rose to Talon, his expression unfazed. "It's an option," he confirmed. "One we're debating. I can't pretend to have empathy for the soul responsible for killing my daughter," he said darkly.

Talon uncrossed his arms. "A death you may have prevented, had you watched as carefully as you suggest."

Kalpheus narrowed his eyes at the auer, but he remained sitting. "Spoken by the man who was closest to her during her capture. Just because we watch does *not* mean we're close enough to interfere, even if it weren't forbidden. We knew she would return, and unfortunately, in the eyes of the faction, there was no urgency to attempt rescue."

Talon fell silent again, and Amarie felt his gaze on her for just a moment.

"Is it usual practice for a member of this faction to be related to the Key?" Amarie asked.

Kalpheus shook his head, shoulders relaxing as he looked at her. "No," he admitted. "In fact, it's strictly against the code we follow. Even speaking to you now is forbidden, but these unusual circumstances prompted extraordinary measures." He paused, rubbing his thumb along his other hand. "I fell in love with your mother. It wasn't supposed to happen, but it did, and losing her was, and will forever be, my greatest failure. I can't lose you too; to death or otherwise. You must return to your ship and leave Helgath." His voice hardened, and his gaze shifted to Talon. "You plan to accompany her to Eralas, I understand. What are your plans once you arrive?"

Amarie followed her father's gaze to Talon, who pursed his lips in a defiant gesture.

All were patient as the auer took his time. "Keep to the denser parts of the woods," Talon finally said. "Out of reach of my people, and away from prying eyes."

Amarie wondered how much her father knew of Talon's predicament with returning to Eralas. How much did he know about her, where she'd been, and what she'd done over the years? She didn't know what to feel, considering he'd been watching her all those times she believed herself to be alone.

"Am I to understand you've witnessed each day of my life?" she asked.

Her father looked at her again and shook his head. "No. There are many of us within the faction and watching over you is only part of our duties. We have measures in place that if something happens to endanger you, we're alerted, and you gain our attention. However, for day to day activities and travels, we attempt to respect your privacy as best we can. The goal is always for you to be your first protector."

Amarie nodded, looking at Talon. With a little gesture of her head, she gave him the opportunity to inquire further if he desired.

"Will this faction of yours follow to Eralas?" Talon asked faster than she expected. He leaned forward, resting his hands on the back of her chair. His jaw had relaxed, but she could still feel tension in the air.

"No," Kalpheus admitted. "We'll still be able to watch for threats from the mainland but entering Eralas isn't an option. Physically, or by proxy."

Amarie felt a wave of understanding. This meeting was their way of personally vetting Talon. If he didn't pass their test, she wondered what his fate would be. It made her feel on edge, but her innate trust in her father eased her discomfort.

Idly, her hand ventured over her shoulder, fingers closing over Talon's, trying to convey her trust to him.

His fingers twitched. "I'll take care of her," Talon said confidently. "I'll help her grow in the ways she must to be able to guard herself."

Kalpheus nodded and rose from his seat. "I believe you to be genuine," he said, the hint of a smile at the corners of his mouth. "As much as I selfishly wish to see her again, I urge you to remain there as long as possible. It's the safest place for the Key, and unreachable by many who seek to harm her. But don't be fooled. There are plenty of others, and not all are unable to walk the island. You must be vigilant, both of you." He looked back at Amarie. "It all begins with you leaving Helgath without delay. Now isn't the time for the stubbornness you got from your mother." He gave her a knowing, humorous look.

Amarie nodded with a sheepish smirk. "We'll go," she promised and stood. To Talon, she said, "Unless there's anything else you'd like to know first?" She had to admit the auer had a knack for asking the right questions, while her mind was too busy recovering from emotional shock.

Talon hesitated, but then offered Amarie's dagger back to her, hilt first.

She hadn't realized he'd picked it up. She took it, slipping it back where she'd hidden it at her lower back.

"May I have a moment?" Talon asked, looking past Amarie towards her father. "I know it's not entirely my place, but if you might be amenable, Kalpheus, I'd like to speak with you alone."

Amarie's brows knitted together.

Kalpheus nodded once and walked to the door they'd entered from. He opened it and spoke to Amarie. "It's been the greatest pleasure of my life to finally be able to meet you in person, my dear," he said, and she walked to him. His hand came to rest on her shoulder. "I wish I could've been more of a father to you, and I hope you come to understand."

Amarie wasn't sure how she could understand. He'd left her to be raised by her uncle when he clearly knew of her mother's death. Even after her uncle died, he hadn't stepped in. It stung, knowing he saw but didn't help. It didn't ease the pain of being alone or the guilt of her burden. She wanted to ask him more, talk to him more.

How was this already coming to an end? Why was she already hugging him and saying goodbye?

He happily returned the embrace, but her chest felt hollow. She tried to hide it. The wounds, still fresh from seeing her mother, and

188

now him, were hers alone to bear. Seeing him gave a torturous glimpse at what could have been. She wanted to understand, to forgive.

"I'll try," she whispered and closed her eyes before releasing him. "One day, I hope we meet again."

She forced herself to cross through the doorway and leave her father.

Deylan followed back into the barren space her father had referred to as a place of storage.

Not much to store.

The door behind her latched shut with a rattle, hiding Talon and her father from view.

Deylan smiled. "I remember meeting you when you were little. Barely a year old, I think. Walking around on those wobbly legs," he teased, and she scowled.

"Why did you leave me?" she asked, unable to mask the bitterness in her voice. "All those years ago, you knew me, and yet you let me grow up alone when I needed you."

He bowed his head, and his shoulders slumped. "I had no choice. I wish I did," he pleaded, in a way she hadn't expected. "I wanted to, many times, when I'd learn of what was happening to you, but your location was kept from me. For all I knew, you were on the other side of Pantracia, going through it all alone. Once I was finally old enough to know, and a high-ranking member of the faction, I had to follow the rules. The faction has been around for millennia, since the Berylian Key entered your family line, and its sole purpose has always been to protect the power, not the person. Dad believes that's why relationships are prohibited, because when you think of the Key as a person, it makes choices harder and emotional rather than logical." Deylan exhaled, gently grasping her wrist.

Amarie met his gaze and tried to quell the anger in her chest.

"What we do now... what I'm doing, is to protect my sister, not some hunk of stone or well of power." His tone was soft, which encouraged her not to argue with his logic, as much as it pained her.

"Will I see you again?" she asked cautiously, tilting her head.

He smiled and patted her shoulder. "I'm certain you will," he said. "Especially since the faction is bound to be rather displeased with Dad and me after this is all said and done. Gods only know, maybe we'll come join you in Eralas." He playfully nudged her shoulder.

It felt good, but made her ache. For the relationship with Deylan she'd never had. Her eyes burned, and he pulled her into a hug.

"You're the strongest woman I've ever known, Sis. It'll be all right," he assured, and she took a steadying breath against his chest.

Only a sliver of time to experience what it felt like to be held by her brother. She tried to etch it in her memory before pulling away.

The door behind them opened again with a click.

Talon emerged first, his face grim, followed by Kalpheus.

Amarie felt her world blur, overwhelmed by the new information and stir of emotions. It was all hitting her so close together. She had learned and endured more in the past month than the past ten years; Trist, Kin, her father's abrupt appearance. It was dizzying.

The ache in her heart drove her towards her father again, seeking his arms despite having already said goodbye. She needed them again, something about the feeling being so different than any other embrace. Staying there as long as she could, she memorized the feel of her father's arms.

When the fresh night air outside hit her lungs, she gratefully sucked it in.

Talon walked beside her as they started back to the docks.

The streets had emptied out, merchant carts closed and locked shut. A dim haze of light flickered from street lamps and windows lining the streets. Dodging civilians no longer a concern, Talon didn't reach for her to maintain physical contact. But she found herself missing the feel of his hand in hers.

"What did you wish to speak to him alone about?" she asked, voice distant as she looked ahead. Her feet felt unsteady, her body rejecting reality and moving numbly forward.

"Telling you would defeat the purpose of it being in private, wouldn't it?" Talon asked, but his tone held a teasing lilt.

"Oh," she said. "I thought your aim had been to remove Deylan. I didn't realize..." She shook her head, smirking at her own daftness.

Falling silent, she watched the few people and taverns they passed, allowing her thoughts to engulf her once again as they continued the leisurely pace. If he didn't want to tell her, that was his decision. He'd never kept anything from her before, and if he chose to, she wanted to trust he had a good reason.

The moonlight danced off the ocean, and she admired the water caustics reflecting off the docks. The walk back took much longer than their venture into town, but she appreciated the time to think. To absorb the information and prepare for what might come next. That she had family was comforting, even if they couldn't follow to Eralas. She'd only have Talon there.

Resisting the urge to glance at the auer beside her during her thoughts, she stuffed her hands into her pockets.

Ever since the night he kissed her, he'd been different. They hadn't repeated the affection; the closest thing was feigned in the streets after overhearing the guards speak of the Berylian Key. Conflict showed on his face whenever she stepped too close or touched his arm. He could have been caught up in the moment that night, trying to prove he was more suave than Jael.

Something, a connection, made her feel closer to Talon. Attracted to him. Yet, she found herself once again questioning if it was just her wish for distraction from Kin.

Her boots echoed over the wooden docks as they made their way towards their ship at the end. Amarie felt comfortable maintaining the silence between her and Talon.

His pace beside her slowed, his boots dragging as he came to a stop, twenty yards from the gangplank they were supposed to cross to finish their journey to Eralas. Flickers of light danced from the lanterns aboard the docked ships. Pale beams from the half-moon shone on Talon's dark hair, making it appear like silver streams falling around his shoulders.

Her steps stilled, and she turned towards him, waiting.

Talon's eyes met hers in the darkness, his jaw tight as he gazed at her. "How are you feeling?" he asked quietly. "With all of this?"

Amarie felt a rush of something akin to resentment flood through her. Why did it matter? Wishing for things to be different wouldn't change anything. The path of her life had never taken her feelings into account, and it wouldn't start now. She gritted her teeth, willing herself to silence the emotions so wholly tainted by everything else.

"I'm fine," she lied, voice void of emotion. She didn't need or want his sympathy. Not right then.

He didn't seem to understand as he reached out to put a hand on her shoulder and stepped closer to her. "Why are you lying?" Talon asked. "You don't need to."

A halfhearted smirk touched her mouth. "What's it matter?"

Talon's eyes narrowed, and he heaved a sigh. "It matters to me," he said. "Are you angry I spoke to your father alone? I merely hoped to spare you from the topic."

"No," she muttered. "You clearly had your reasons. I'm just... exhausted with secrecy." Feeling her eyes sting, she turned and faced the water, clenching her jaw.

"Amarie," he sighed her name, his hand falling from her shoulder. "I don't want to keep secrets from you. I just needed to know if the faction considers Kin a threat. And to... dissuade that notion, if possible."

She took a shaky breath. "And?"

"He listened and said he would consider what I told him. But that was all," Talon said.

"Everyone. Everyone makes all these choices for my life," Amarie whispered. "Will I ever get a say?" She closed her eyes, her hands still firmly in her front pockets as she willed herself to regain control over her emotions.

He allowed her to breathe for a time before his hand closed over her shoulder to turn her towards him and meet her gaze. His hand traced down her arm to her hand, lifting it to his chest where he held it near his heart.

"I *am* sorry," Talon said. "For all you've endured."

Amarie leaned into him. "I don't want you to be sorry," she said quietly. "I don't want your pity; I don't need it."

"Pity is the wrong word for what I feel for you," Talon said. "It's astonishment and respect for what you've overcome. I wish you didn't have to endure it, but I don't pity you. I also find it disappointingly tragic how you have suffered so much in your short life. Yet you have so many, myself included, who claim to be protecting you. All in the name of our love of you."

Her stomach twisted. Love was different to the auer than to humans. The endearment of love was shallow compared to the Aueric word *niané*, which symbolized millennia of commitment. But Talon surely knew what the word would mean to her.

He tucked a strand of her loose hair behind her ear. "I don't mean to confuse you further. I only want to keep you safe. *You.* Not the power you hold. I swore no oath to any faction. I don't know any other way to explain what I feel for you. No one, human or auer, has ever drawn such hope from me."

Amarie studied his face, feeling more overwhelmed than she had before. His vibrant green irises, tinged with the orange of lamp light, offered her no clarity. Absently, she bit her bottom lip, unable to find adequate words to enlighten him on how she felt.

He shook his head. "I'm making this worse, aren't I?" he asked, hardly giving her a moment to catch her breath. His hand came to slowly cup her cheek, caressing over her jaw. "Regret is useless, even amidst the mistakes I've made," Talon ventured. "All life ends, even mine. I refuse to waste one day on regret. I'll always cherish what we have. We've known each other for what most auer would consider a single breath, but my heart is telling me I love you, in a very raw and... human way. Beyond how a friend would. Love. *You*."

The abrupt vulnerability she heard in his tone took her aback. His eyes pleaded with her in a way she wouldn't have expected of him. Not of the confident auer. Before her mind could try to complicate matters further, she acted on instinct and wrapped her hands around the back of his neck. Rising to her toes, she guided his mouth to hers and kissed his bottom lip. Fire threatened to ignite, and she felt his tension dissolve, the warmth of his mouth pressing against hers.

He drew into her, his hand tangling with her hair.

As much as she wished the heat could silence the questions in her heart, her mind flitted to analyze her feelings. *Do I love him?* Was it even possible for her to understand her feelings with everything that had happened in the past month?

Talon drew back as she reluctantly parted from him, his eyes containing the same vulnerability as before.

"Talon, I—"

The sound of rapid footsteps on the dock stole her attention, interrupting all thought.

Deylan ran full speed towards them, and her heart jumped into her throat. Her brother's eyes were wide, and she slid her hands from Talon with a regretful glance.

"Amarie," Deylan huffed out her name, "I'm so glad I found you. There's trouble. Helgath..." He gasped to catch his breath, and Amarie's pulse picked up speed. "Helgath discovered us. I don't know how, but they found us. They took our father for *questioning*," Deylan managed between breaths, hissing the final word.

Her heart plummeted. The torturous methods Helgath used to extract information from prisoners... they weren't known for mercy.

Swallowing hard, she looked at Talon as his hand reached to her wrist. She needed to go but breaking into the barracks was bound to make the auer nervous. But she'd only just gotten her father back, and she wasn't about to lose him.

"I must," she breathed, feeling fear creep into her veins.

Talon nodded. "*We* must," he confirmed, setting his jaw. "Do you know where they've taken him?" he asked, turning to Deylan.

"There are holding cells in the basement of the barracks," Deylan said. "I'm positive that's where he's being held. Amarie," he added, "I didn't want to put you in this position. I'm certain to face the rage of the faction for this, but I can't do this alone. And I'm not ready to lose him."

"Neither am I," she said firmly.

Chapter 19

Earlier that evening...

Kin determined the best use of his time was to follow Trist. He'd received no summons from his Master yet, and he needed to ensure she properly reported Amarie's death. The charade needed to continue for her to be safe. He'd spied on Talon long enough to ensure he intended to follow Kin's instructions to take Amarie to Eralas.

Trist took a meandering path along the coast in the opposite direction Kin expected. The craggy cliffs of Aidensar's border fell into rolling hillsides of Helgath. He'd never known his Master to demand a rendezvous in the aggressive and militaristic rival to Feyor. The coincidence of Trist being at the only stop for Amarie before Eralas made Kin's skin crawl.

The muck of chimney smoke stuck to Kin's feathers as he soared above the uneven rooftops of Rylorn. He'd been in the city only a short while before he heard an unnerving rumor. Trist took an interest in it as well. He followed her as she eavesdropped on the idle conversations of guards, spreading the rumor like wildfire.

Creeping into the realm of shadows above her, Kin observed Trist as she crossed into an empty alleyway, away from the guards she'd spied on. The alley bisected the streets, guiding her towards the barracks. She made it a mere ten paces into the swallowing shadows before she froze, rocking back onto her heels.

Kin sank deeper into the pool of darkness he occupied at the sight of two men flanking Trist at either end of the narrow alley. Their faces hidden by hoods, Kin braced himself to witness their deaths.

Trist would offer no mercy. Towering buildings framed the alley, blocking lingering daylight as the sun dipped towards the horizon, granting Trist plenty to manipulate.

The air around her thrummed as she summoned the Art. Wisps of black danced at her ankles, crawling up her body as the men advanced towards her. They surely saw the shifting shadows yet didn't retreat.

One of them bounced a copper sword in his hand. Runes ran the length of the blade, carved into the soft metal which had no business being forged into a weapon.

The snakes of Trist's Art struck out at the hooded figure who expertly brought the blade to meet them, slashing in a wide arc in front him before raising it to a defensive position parallel to the ground. A pulse of energy exploded. A ripple that began large and faded abruptly as the blade cut through the tendrils. The slashed void ruptured, sending a shiver through the shadow Kin hid within. *Impossible.*

A thin, palpable shield pulsed in the air before the man.

Trist screamed in frustration, willing more dark forms to spring up from the ground at the mouth of the alley. They surged forward like a wave, intent on attacking from behind.

The man turned to face the new threat, his blade cutting through the wall of black like it was a thin, gossamer curtain. But his back was to Trist. A fatal mistake.

Trist drew a blade from beneath her cloak.

Strong hands closed around Trist's body from behind. An arm came up to pull her against his chest and twist her wrist behind her back. The knife clattered to the ground as the second man locked his arm around her neck, closing a copper cuff around her pinned wrist.

A dull hum resounded that Kin could barely make out. A click of metal closing, and Trist's shadows fell like water. Her power dissipated with it, rushing away as she struggled against her captor. Her body could accomplish little without the Art, and the men dragged her off, farther from the bustling marketplace.

Kin faced an unexpected dilemma of two great curiosities. First, the rumor of the Berylian Key within the barracks. But now, there was a pair of men who'd successfully captured a high-ranking Shade with little trouble; she'd become arrogant with Uriel's power. He concluded that the Key would still be there after he finished following to find out more about these men. Perhaps alerting his Master of their existence would aid in returning to Uriel's good graces.

It took focus to maintain Kin's shadowed form, and access within the city was limited. Pests and small household plants suffered. People's energies were out of reach for him, at least at his current rank, and his sources would dwindle if he continued. He pulled himself from the depths of shadow, wriggling into the winged form which would keep him disguised without continued effort.

Trist knew to look for a raven, hopefully these two wouldn't.

The feathered wings and sharp claws felt more natural to him with how often he found himself in the shape. Shaking the last flecks of shadow from his body, he beat his wings against the air, and vanished amidst the smoke.

In an abandoned section of the city, they stopped at a crooked doorway. The men thrust Trist through into the darkness beyond.

Kin turned skyward to make an extra loop through the air before he spotted an entrance for himself. He carefully dove through a broken second story window, wedged open. Landing within the beams of an exposed attic, Kin peered down at the Shade bound to a chair with copper cuffs binding her wrists at her back. A thick strip of leather gagged her mouth, her eyes filled with murder as she glared at the far wall. Her shoulders strained as she pulled at the restraints, but they held strong.

"We should just kill her for what she's done," the younger of the men said, anger in his tone as he turned his back to the room Trist was in. "She's clearly a threat. The council would sanction her death."

Kin hopped closer to the two brown haired men, taking in their features now that their hoods were down.

"Deylan, you think I don't want to? But it would be wiser to use her," the older man growled. His hair was streaked with silver at his temples but cropped short like the younger man.

Deylan scowled and balled his fists, but his shoulders slumped.

The older man shook his head and spoke again. "I know she's a threat," he hissed darkly. "I want to tear every limb from her body for what she did to Amarie."

At the mere mention of her name, Kin tensed, his feathers ruffling as his balance momentarily faltered. He dug in his claws to the soft wood to keep himself upright and swallowed bile rising in his throat.

Kin scuttled a little closer, his feathered chest pressed against the wooden wall, keeping to the shadows as much as he could.

Deylan placed his hand on the older man's shoulder. "You're right, Dad. Amarie is back and we should be smarter about this. Especially with what Collins told me this afternoon," he said, and the older man frowned.

"What do you mean, what Collins told you? What did he tell you?"

Deylan removed his hand from his father's shoulder in what looked like disappointment. "Amarie is here. Collins gave me word of her presence on a ship making port tonight, and we both know she won't stay on the ship. It's only a matter of time before she hears the rumors we started," he explained, and the older man paced.

"The council would have our heads for interfering," he said with a sigh, running a hand through his hair. "They already consider us biased when it comes to the Key. But I can't consider her an object like the rest of the faction. She's my blood! Gods, why must she be as stubborn as her mother."

Kin nearly fell from his narrow perch.

Amarie never spoke in detail about her father beyond that she'd never known him. Now Kin was privy to knowledge he was certain even she didn't have. He felt immensely guilty for overhearing it. His ears dulled to the remainder of their conversation, distracted.

A faction who knew of the Berylian Key. And they sounded capable of watching her without being physically present. It suggested they knew of Kin and his role in Amarie's life, and not just Trist. Surely her father hated him with equaled passion.

Little good could come of Amarie's arrival, and Kin decided to assist in minimizing the damage as much as he could.

The door latch clicked as the men left, tearing Kin back into the present. He and Trist were alone. The opportunity couldn't be passed up, but he tried to think it through before he allowed his baser instinct for revenge to take hold. The deep sea of his rage swallowed all hope for logic.

Trist struggled against her bonds with little success. Her eyes were set in determination as she worked her wrists together where they were bound to the back of her chair. Her movements had grown sluggish, half-hearted.

Kin had witnessed Trist fight without her power before. Such training was required of all Shades. He crept across the beam, idly counting the ways she should have been physically able to break free.

Her sunken eyes stared at nothing, her chest heaving as if each movement exhausted her. Gradually, he saw the glimmer of rage slip from her eyes, overtaken by tiredness.

The war within Kin reached its zenith, and he accepted the satisfaction of watching her struggle. As a fellow servant to Uriel, Kin should have had every instinct to help Trist. Free her. But he loathed her for what she'd done to Amarie. He loathed himself for ever accepting Uriel as his master. He would destroy what he could to fight his master's goal.

Trist proved a future with Amarie was impossible when she channeled their master. She also knew too much already and would remain a pervasive threat to all Kin loved.

Amarie's father had mentioned using her somehow, but Kin doubted he understood exactly what Trist was. How could he know and leave Trist alone? There were too many variables to the situation if she remained alive. She could escape and live, and Kin couldn't tolerate that possibility.

Kin dropped down from the beam with a flutter. As he fell through the air, he pulled on the energies around him, finding plenty of rodent sources to enable his shift to his natural form. His boots hit the ruined floor, and he tossed the edge of his cloak over his shoulder. Shadow dusted through the air like ash, and he tugged his hair before turning towards the helpless Trist.

Relief escaped around the gag in the form of a muffled sigh as her eyes met his, but her brows narrowed as she noticed his fingers wrapping around the hilt of his sword. The familiar rasp of the steel catching on the scabbard reverberated through the room as the weight shifted comfortably into his palm.

Kin advanced as Trist fought against her bonds with new fervor. She glared as he yanked her cloak open and rifled through the pockets. Trist growled, attempting to speak over the gag. He heard what he suspected to be his name, mention of their master, perhaps something about the Key and the shards. But his searching proved futile. No pouch, no shards.

We're too far east for her to have met with Uriel, he thought.

Kin tore the gag, pulling it over her chin, revealing Trist's hard-set lips.

"Stop playing, you idiot, and unbind me," Trist demanded as Kin stepped back.

He narrowed his eyes at her. "Where are the shards you took from her?" he insisted, keeping his voice low and void of emotion.

Surprisingly, she grinned. "Didn't you finish that task already, Kinronsilis?" she purred. "Why would you care?"

Kin's grip tightened on his sword. "I don't have the patience to play this game with you," he grumbled. "Where are they?"

"They won't do her any good now that she's dead." Her melodic voice showed her amusement. "She screamed and fought but begged for death by the time I finally gave it to her."

Kin's hand shot to Trist's neck, feeling her pulse beneath his palm as he squeezed. Her sudden fight to swallow and gasp for breath only urged his grip tighter. He leaned towards her but held firm. "Where are they?" he whispered near her ear.

The gleam of Trist's eyes dulled, and Kin forced himself to loosen his hold. A great wheezing breath flowed through her body, and she coughed as he stepped back. She laughed a horrible croaking sound. "I did my duty," she hissed, her brow twitching with her bitter tone. Rotating her head slowly, she took another breath.

Stepping around her, Kin lowered his sword as he went to confirm she'd received credit for her finished task. Using the tip of his sword, he drew the sleeve of her dress upwards to catch a glance at the foul ink mark. To his surprise, she hadn't gained an additional mark. In fact, she'd lost several, matching her with Kin's current rank.

Kin paused to consider, a smile creeping onto his lips. "It seems our master wasn't satisfied with your performance after all," he mused.

Trist's shoulders tensed, jerking away from him.

Uriel had been told of Amarie's death, and clearly was unhappy with it after feeling her power through his Shade. Trist hadn't thought through the ramifications of destroying such a source of power rather than delivering it.

Amarie would be safe, but a loose end remained.

His mind cursed him with an image of Amarie and her mangled body in his arms as he stepped in front of Trist once more.

Rage roared through his muscles. His knuckles clenched white on the hilt of his sword. With a steady exhale, he thrust the blade forward. Steel tore through her torso. His muscles shook in response to the cry from the Shade's lips, but he pushed deeper, burying the blade to the hilt with a satisfying squelching twist. Hot, slick blood seeped onto his fingertips as he watched Trist's shocked expression fade to nothing. He found a gross comfort in watching her die, knowing she couldn't speak of his disloyalty to their master.

With a jerk, Kin withdrew his blade from her chest and slowly wiped the steel clean on her shoulder. Replacing the blade at his side, he stepped behind her corpse, cleaning his hands on her cloak as he knelt to look at the device securing her wrists together.

Two unpolished copper cuffs, as wide around as his thumb, with a thick bridge of metal between them. A series of runes, angular and sharp, were carved in several rows over the dull surface. Embedded between the runes was a line of small gems.

Reaching out to touch it, he felt the pulse of power within them, buzzing in his ears. He tested a slight surge of his power against them, but nothing happened.

Determined, he ran his fingers over the device, seeking the latch that had to be there. He found multiple small triggers on opposite sides which required both of his hands to activate. The click of release sounded as their weight settled into his palms.

The echo of power vanished. It was silent as if it had never been more than an overly elaborate pair of short manacles.

Slipping the device into his cloak, he stood. The metallic scent of Trist's death burned in his nose as he took in a breath to center his power and retake his raven form.

Amarie was in Rylorn, and he needed to know where. Her father and brother were certain to be interfering in her attempt to follow the rumors of the Berylian Key, so it would spare Kin the trouble.

He wanted to believe it'd be better if he just got out of the way.

His clawed feet shuffled along the rafters until he could step to the windowsill. He peered outside, and his body instantly recoiled as his gaze landed on a familiar figure standing below.

Talon exited the neighboring building and turned back to hold the wooden door open for whoever was behind him. It wasn't hard to guess who, and his heart thudded.

Kin scrambled back into the darkness of the window frame, pressing his bulky raven body as flat as he could. He vaguely heard goodbyes, and he dared a peek out.

They faced the two men, Amarie's father and brother. Satisfied they wouldn't notice, Kin dropped casually from the windowsill, lashing with his wings to climb into the night sky. The wind carried him up, high above the streets of Rylorn and through the hanging clouds of smoke. The sea breeze provided welcome distraction, blowing through his feathers, as he glanced halfheartedly towards the streets below where Amarie embraced her father.

At least it was something to be grateful for. Perhaps this encounter would bring her some peace.

Talon and Amarie turned down the alley that would take them back towards the docks. Watching Amarie walk away made everything in him ache for her. He yearned to bow low before her and beg forgiveness. Beg her to take him back.

Kin observed the city to fight the desire to follow Talon and Amarie again. To the west, the city stretched along the coastline, hugging close to the narrow sand beaches and rippling sea. Lights flickered within most houses, except in this abandoned part of the city. Moonlight glinted on the mix of wood and clay shingles atop homes. The farther the streets spiderwebbed out, the smaller the residences became. The outskirts of Rylorn ended with a tall, daunting wall. Watchtowers balanced precariously on the rim of the
a dim light flickered within, enough for bored soldiers to

Circling around, Kin saw the barracks dominating the eastern side, a defined wall of stone and iron barricading it from the city. Within the dense walls flowed seas of cobblestone courtyards and assembly areas. At each corner stood a proud tower, peppered with glittering narrow balistraria windows. The far south tower was adjacent to the Academy, where users of the Art were taken and 'trained' to serve the Helgathian military.

It was there that Kin noticed something out of place.

A collection of soldiers marched west through the courtyard.

Curiosity and a looming fear pushed Kin closer. He bypassed the marching battalion, swooping towards the base of the south tower, where stone steps rose out of the ground like layers of a cake. At the top stood two decorated officers.

Kin joined a murder of slumbering crows on the wall just close enough for him to listen. The occupants of the sleeping spot gave him a skeptical look, but he skirted far enough away that they wouldn't fuss, and he could listen.

One of the officers, a bear of a man with a wide stance and bulging neck, was red faced. His carefully curled mustache ruffled as he scowled.

A female officer stood next to him, broad enough at the shoulder that Kin thought at first she was another man. Her dark red hair, cropped short, framed a feminine mouth pressed into a hard line as she turned towards the military man. The hem of a long maroon robe brushed her boots.

"What a daft fool! To think he could trick us with a trinket... No one who attempts to pull such a ruse in Helgath shall be tolerated." The deep voice of the burly man grumbled rough with his damaged pride.

"Relax, Admiral, he'll be brought in, and you'll have your chance to remind him of where he is," the woman said. Her gruff voice matched her masculine appearance.

"Oh, I'll remind him," the admiral responded darkly, spitting on the ground. He twisted the toe of his boot on the wet spot and looked back to the woman. "I'm glad you made such good time, Chief Vizier," he said. "To reveal his treachery in time for us to act."

The woman nodded, crossed her arms carefully within her loose sleeves, and looked towards the marching soldiers disappearing from their sight. "Such a matter as this Berylian Key can't afford delay. I look forward to what your men discover. Keep me informed, Admiral," she said briskly. She spun on her heels and made her way back inside the tower.

A brief curse came from the admiral as he watched her go. He glared after the disappearing battalion exiting the west gate, then turned to follow the woman.

Kin's throat seized with a rise of his heart. He felt a deep sense of responsibility to ensure the safety of Amarie's father and brother, who were responsible for the hoax. For Amarie. She'd lost enough family in her life, and he had the power to prevent her from losing more.

Urgency filled his wings, a protesting squawk of annoyance echoing from a crow nearby that nipped at Kin's feet. He didn't have time to waste, fighting against the wind with all his strength to ascend and hurry back to the place he'd last seen Amarie. He didn't have time to worry if she'd still be there when he arrived.

He plunged into the unlit alleyway, entirely unsure of where the guards were. They had a maze of city streets to work their way through. Raven claws scratched at the door he'd seen Talon and Amarie step through moments before, his wings beating before he collected his thoughts enough to try to find a source. Power surged through his blood stream as black flecked from his limbs, and he shook his cloak free of it.

Finding the door unlocked, Kin didn't question his luck as he flung it open, stepping into a small, sparsely furnished space. The bare walls and floor housed only a pair of chairs and a rope ladder leading to an open ceiling hatch. The door on the other side of the room stood ajar, and Kin jogged to it, not bothering to close the door to the alley behind him. He just needed to find Deylan and his father. Tell them they needed to get out.

Both hands on the door frame, Kin leaned into the more furnished space to find it empty. The distant grinding of a latch sounded behind him, a lock gliding into place. Before he could move, a sharp point pressed to his lower back. He slid his empty hands farther up the door frame, holding them up.

"Turn around... slowly." Kin recognized Deylan's voice and heard a second set of footsteps approaching.

"I came to warn you," Kin breathed heavily, realizing how much he'd exhausted himself. He complied to Deylan's demand, keeping his hands raised as he turned to face him.

"*You*," Deylan growled, tossing his sword to his left hand. His now empty right hand closed to a fist, and he hurled it at Kin.

Kin resisted the instinct to defend himself, the blow connecting with his jaw, whipping his head hard to the side.

"Of course, we find another *Shade*," Deylan hissed as Kin stumbled against the door frame.

Kin stretched his jaw, palm touching the area that would surely bruise. *I suppose I deserved that*, he thought.

Deylan stepped forward, lifting his sword again to Kin's chest.

His father spoke calmly with a raised eyebrow. "Where is the other set of cuffs, Deylan?"

Kin sucked in an annoyed breath, lifting his hands in front of him. "You can use the pair in my pocket if it'll help you trust me. A battalion is on its way to arrest you for your Berylian Key hoax."

The two men exchanged a glance, but Deylan didn't lower the sword. The older man stepped forward, and Kin held his ground. The man tore aside Kin's cloak, hand rifling through the pockets to locate the manacles.

"Where did you get these?" the older man growled as the metal clinked together, and he withdrew them.

"From the corpse next door. After I killed her."

Deylan scowled, "Shit," he cursed. He took another step, and Kin felt the blade's tip pierce his shirt.

Kin held his ground. "The Chief Vizier saw right through whatever trinket you gave them. You're wasting time; leave before they find you."

"You expect us to trust a Shade?" Deylan sneered. "We know exactly who you are, Kinronsilis."

"You clearly don't know me well enough," Kin responded, heat in his veins touching his voice.

Deylan's father stepped around Kin, as if sizing him up, before standing beside his son. His dark blue eyes reminded Kin of Amarie's. If this man knew what Trist had done to his daughter, he surely knew what Kin had done as well.

Kin's shoulders tensed, hoping the man would see reason beyond his understandable anger.

"Why did you kill your fellow Shade?" her father asked evenly, with not enough haste.

Kin growled, his gaze darting to Amarie's father. "I did that for me," he said. "And for Amarie. I did what I had to. To protect her. That's why I'm warning you now." He dared a glance at Deylan. "She's lost enough, and I can't watch her lose you too. You need to leave. Now."

They exchanged another glance, and Amarie's father motioned to Deylan. "Go have a look," he instructed.

Deylan hesitated, glaring at Kin and refusing to lower the weapon. Pain pricked as the tip jabbed into his skin.

"Go," his father insisted with a voice that wasn't to be argued with.

Deylan's arm relaxed, the sword dropping from Kin's chest.

"Fine," he said, "but if he kills you, I'm going to have to explain to the faction why *the great Kalpheus* trusted a damn Shade." Deylan sheathed his sword and went to the rope ladder, reaching up to tug it lower before pulling himself towards the roof.

Kin let out a steadying breath, slowly lowering his hands while Kalpheus watched him.

Deylan was almost within reach of the top when something heavy slammed against the locked door with a loud crash. It vibrated the air of the room, and Kin cursed.

Deylan hesitated, his eyes meeting his father's, who spun to face the door, a hand moving to his weapon.

Kin grabbed Kalpheus' shoulder and shoved him towards the rope ladder. They only made it halfway before the door shattered, forcing Kin to raise his arms to protect his eyes from flying splinters.

Soldiers kicked their way through. They charged towards the closest target, Deylan, even though he was halfway up the ladder. A soldier lunged for his heels, reaching to try to pull him down.

Kalpheus leapt to his son's defense, drawing his sword and surging forward.

It left Kin to face a soldier who rightfully perceived him as a threat. Kin withdrew the blade at his right hip with a swift movement.

Chaos erupted. Shouts echoed throughout the room as more guards poured through the door, tripping over one of their own kicked to the ground by Deylan's carefully aimed boot.

Kin grasped for sources to tug on for his Art, but they were scarce. A sword rushed down towards his head, and instinct raising his own to catch it. The vibration of steel added to the din of the room, making it hard to focus on any one sound. He shoved his attacker with all his might into a companion rounding to take a swing at Kalpheus' back.

They stumbled, and one didn't have a chance to recover before

Deylan threw a dagger from the opening above. It sank into the soldier's neck, tainting the air with the scent of death.

A soldier moved to the rope ladder and started to climb only to be yanked down by Kalpheus and thrown to the ground.

In a moment of respite, Kin positioned himself with his back towards Amarie's father, facing the soldiers who were trying to work their way around the edges. "Go," he shouted over his shoulder. "Climb."

As he spoke the words, orders echoed to get forces onto the roof. A soldier had successfully climbed to the roof, fighting Deylan. One side of the ladder went slack.

Kin didn't have time to look up, parrying a sword at his left side. He rotated his hilt to disarm the soldier, and the weapon clattered to the ground beside the rope as it fell. Kin's right hand pulled a dagger from the belt of the off-balance guard and immediately plunged it into the man's side, his body collapsing on top of the ladder that had been their only escape.

"If you want to help," Kalpheus gruffed out as he blocked an attack. "Get my son to safety. I'll hold them off as long as I can."

Kin glanced over his shoulder, recognizing the determination in Kalpheus' eyes as his boot connected with the gut of another attacker. Looking up at the opening, Kin saw Deylan pinned to the roof, struggling against several soldiers.

Another soldier lumbered through the door, a large club bouncing against his palm. There was no winning this situation.

"I'll find you," Kin said as he sought what little energy he could feel around him. His body screamed with exhaustion, but he ignored the pounding in his head as he grasped at the darkness. "Try to stay alive until I do," he said with a hint of a smile.

His gaze locked on the blue eyes just like Amarie's before he tugged on the power within him. He distantly heard a shout, a glint of steel in the corner of his vision as it thrust towards his middle. As shadow paired with his soul, his body dripped into the black at his feet. The blade glided through him as if it pierced nothing but water.

Kin embraced the cold of the darkness as he slithered along the ground. He passed beneath boots of men who danced to avoid the tar-like substance. Kin could have swallowed them whole with enough power, but his focus remained on Deylan. He clawed up the wall and across the ceiling in a sinuous crawl towards the opening.

Once through, he conjured a tendril from the black, grasping at flesh. As if his hand, he gripped the back of a soldier's neck. He threw the man from atop Deylan, and across the rooftop with impossible strength. The soldier tumbled towards the ground with a shout. A sword struck Kin, passed through the shadow that reknit quickly after. A tentacle of his power pulled back on his attackers arms, snapping them from sockets with a satisfying crunch.

Horror coated the face of the last remaining soldier, and Deylan braced a boot against his chest, pushing him off the side of the roof with a grunt. Deylan kicked the hatch shut and jumped to his feet.

Kin reached for him with a stretch of shadow. He often took others into the shadow realm with him, but never while the person was still wholly conscious.

Deylan shirked away before Kin gave him no choice and pulled. He sank into the black pools on the roof, as if swallowed by quicksand. It took all Kin's remaining strength. Deylan struggled against the darkness. It was like they were in a dark room, unable to see each other. Deylan would feel trapped with a constant pressure on his skin and only a vague awareness of what was beyond.

"Stop fighting, you idiot," Kin thought, speaking into the darkness. "I need to get you away from here, and you're making it fucking difficult." He gripped, in a sense, at Deylan's collar, dragging him along the roof to the alley. They crossed desolate streets, avoiding beams of lantern light. Movement felt slower pulling another, even after Amarie's brother ceased his struggle. In the time it took Kin to get Deylan far enough away, the battle within the safehouse had ceased.

He continued through the city until he felt a source of power he could use, drinking it greedily near the water's edge.

Rising from the pool of black, Kin heaved for breath. He expelled Deylan first, who stumbled briefly as his boots caught on the cobblestone. As he manifested, Kin pulled on a handful of his own hair and casted a sideways glance towards the bloated fish bodies floating to the surface of the water beside them.

Deylan pulled from him and glared but made no move to attack Kin.

Kin leaned against the cold stone wall behind him, pressing his head against it to try to fight the nausea. He'd pushed too hard, his body beyond drained from the continuous shifting. "You need to get help," he rasped, swallowing the pain. "This faction of yours. I'll do what I can to find Kalpheus."

Deylan seemed to consider his words for a few breaths before he nodded. "They'll take him to the barracks. I'll see what I can get for help," he said.

"This should go without saying," Kin said calmly, "but don't tell Amarie I'm here."

Deylan eyed him. "I understand," he said with a subtle nod. He hesitated for a moment before he turned and ran back towards town.

Kin watched his back for a moment before he closed his eyes. It was frustrating to be so easily winded, part of what Uriel had taken from him with his 'demotion'. He took the power for granted. He barely felt as if he could be effective without it now, and the more he used it, the more dependent on it he felt.

Now wasn't the time to wish he could rid himself of the addiction. He felt determined to work some good with the power rather than the evil his master wrought. And here, close to the water, there was enough life to replenish himself.

He whispered a silent apology before he reached back into the energy around him. He ate it up, bringing all he could into his soul.

The stench of decay and rot overcame everything else and rose with Kin into the air as he took flight as a raven. His eyes briefly followed Deylan's sprinting form turning towards the docks. Towards Amarie.

Kin didn't have the tongue to curse, nor the time to go after Deylan and berate him for his stupidity of involving her. All he could afford was a glance towards the rolling piers devoid of all but two figures.

Dark auburn hair gleamed a familiar fiery hue in the torch light as Amarie's tied back hair drifted in the night breeze. She stood close to Talon. Too close.

Kin dared notice the embrace, and the placement of a hand at the small of Amarie's back, before he tore his gaze away.

Now wasn't the time. His stomach flopped, but he urged himself that this merely meant his efforts to push her away had worked. He beat his wings harder and flew towards the barracks.

Kin landed in the main courtyard and dissolved himself to shadow. He slunk about until he'd overheard Kalpheus' name and mention of the Berylian Key. Following the directions given by a guard to another, Kin wove through a series of corridors, unseen in the crease where the wall met the floor. Forced to backtrack several times to avoid wards against the Art, he scaled along the side of the building, his shadow form clinging to the stone, to find the right hallway.

A particularly dark block ended with a sealed door, latched from the inside.

Kin seethed ahead, slipping beneath it into the hall lined with narrow barred windows on sturdy doors. Torch light flickered through the only open one, at the end of the hallway on the coastal side. Voices murmured through it. Groans and a sticky dripping that normally wouldn't have affected Kin. His stomach lurched as he flung himself through the shadows, feeling for some of his stored energy as he rounded the corner.

A lean man with gangly limbs leaned with a hand against the edge of a crude table drenched in blood. Kalpheus' broad body lay on top of it, bare from the waist up. He heaved for breath as blood oozed from what his captors had done to him.

The torturer wore a tanned apron, splattered dark with discolorations both new and old from his work. A brazier burned behind him, creating stifling heat in the small room. Iron rods burned red hot, protruding from the coals of the brazier, and a series of chains glowed eerily from where they hung just above. More iron links hung from the rafters above the table, tangled and rusted.

As the man pulled sharply on a chain above, Kalpheus winced as his upper body was wrenched upwards. Manacles locking around his bare wrists forced his spine ramrod straight into a sitting position. Blood streamed down his arms where barbs on the metal bit into his skin. His beaten face already swelled; his beard and hair caked with crimson.

"This'll all end if you just speak," the torturer whispered with a far too sweet tone. "Tell us more about this Berylian Key. Where it really is, perhaps? Or, we can return to discussing your shadowy accomplice. Why don't you tell me about him?" His voice ran thick with saccharine and a purr of satisfaction.

Kalpheus tightened his jaw and hissed as his captor tugged on the chain again, stretching his arms beyond their typical reach.

Kin drifted deeper into the shadows, reaching for the power fueled by his rage. A tangle of guilt mixed with it, and he hoped Kalpheus' torture had not been worse because of his involvement. He saw so much of Amarie in her father's eyes, defiant and strong against any adversary.

Drawing towards the brazier, his shadow danced among the

flickers of firelight at the heels of the torturer, too distracted by his fun to notice. He dared not rely on outside energy; the wards nearby would sense the shift.

Shadows curled up the wall beside the brazier to form his shape, and he silently stepped from it. He reached for the exposed end of the glowing iron resting amongst sizzling embers. Ignoring the pain as it scorched his palm, he drew it from the coals with a bone shuddering scrape.

The torturer spun, his hand releasing the chain holding up Kalpheus, causing his body to collapse onto the table with a brutal exhale.

Kin rammed the red-hot metal through the torturer's gut, his blood hissing. He opened his mouth to scream, but Kin's other hand closed around his throat and slammed the man into the wall from which he'd emerged. The iron rod struck the stone as it tore through the man's spine, the acrid scent of his burning flesh wrinkling Kin's nose. Holding back the attempted screams, Kin watched life leave him.

The torturer's shoulders slumped, eyes fading to nothingness before Kin finally let go of the rod. He flexed his burned fingers as the body crumpled to the floor. He eyed it, using his boot to push the body towards a concave shadow at the base of the wall. An ushering of his will, and a firm kick consumed the corpse in the darkness, swallowed by Kin's power.

"Deylan?" Kalpheus' voice sounded gruff as Kin hurried to remove his bonds. "Is my son alright?"

"He's safe," Kin assured, moving Kalpheus' hands to his sides. At least one shoulder looked dislocated. "We need to get you out of here."

Kalpheus made no effort to rise, blood running from his mouth with a cough. "I don't think that's going to happen," he wheezed.

Kin surveyed his injuries, identifying a grievous wound near

Kalpheus' ribs. Blood rushed from it, and Kin urgently pressed it with his hands to minimize the flow. "I should've gotten here faster," he cursed.

"I was dead the moment they put cuffs on me. Arriving sooner wouldn't have altered my fate. But I do appreciate the brief reprieve you've granted me." Kalpheus' voice was cut off by more coughing.

Kin saw the finality within each rattled breath. A pierced lung would be fatal without an experienced healer. And that was an Art Kin certainly had no skill in.

"You can't die," Kin whined, naively struggling against logic. "Amarie just got you back. She can't lose you again."

"She's strong," Kalpheus managed, the coughing subsiding with a painful looking swallow.

Kin's fingers slipped amongst the hot blood pouring from his side. He held the wound as firmly as he could but drew away a hand to close around Kalpheus' in a reassuring grip.

"I understand why you left her," Kalpheus said. "Even though you love her."

"It seems hardly the time to worry about semantics," Kin said, trying to force a smile. "I love your daughter more than I can possible say aloud. Despite how foolishly I show it."

To his surprise, the man laughed hoarsely, and shook his head. "Foolish. Selfless. You are no Shade, Kin," he said, heaving for a breath.

Kin's chest suddenly tightened. "I wish that were true," he said grimly, trying to swallow the lump forming in his throat. "But I'm cursed and must accept the fate that follows it. She'll be safer without me."

Kalpheus grunted what might have been another laugh and winced before finding his voice. "There's that foolishness you mentioned," he said and squeezed Kin's hand. "Curses can be broken, Son. For the right reasons."

Part of Kin felt like it rattled apart, crumbling in the face of sorrow. Heat stung his eyes. How could he deserve such a familial term from him? "The right reason," Kin echoed, his jaw twitching. "But where do I begin? The addiction is only growing worse."

"You'll find a way. You must. And then tell her how much I love her and wish I could have been there for her," Kalpheus pleaded, voice raising in pitch as the pain wheezed through him.

"I will," Kin promised, failing to think it through. He gripped Kalpheus' hand harder. Blood oozed between Kin's pressed fingers at his side with a new urgency. Life, draining too quickly.

Kalpheus lifted his free hand with visible weakness and touched Kin's wrist straining against the fatal wound. He closed his grip with a subtle nod.

Kin's blurry eyes glinted down before he met Kalpheus' gaze. He heaved a steadying breath and banished his tears with a gulp. "May the goddess Nymaera grant you the peace you've well earned, Kalpheus," Kin whispered. He released the pressure, lifting his fingers from the wound.

"Protect her, and one day, find your way back to her," Kalpheus murmured. Gradually, his breathing slowed, eyes glazing over, relieving him of the pain. His last breath drew deep, then eased from his chest as it fell and never rose again. Hand slacking, his eyes stared blankly into Kin's.

Overwhelming grief rushed through him, unexpected pain in his chest. He laid Kalpheus' hand over his abdomen, cleaning his fingers before he drew his vacant eyes shut.

Kin sucked in a threatening sob as rapid boot steps echoed in the hall behind him. He took a final look at the still face of Amarie's father before pulling shadows towards him. Blackness embraced his body, grief welcoming him.

He pressed himself backwards, slipping away from Kalpheus' body towards the corner. Sliding up the wall to the ceiling, he nestled amongst the rafters. It didn't feel right to leave Kalpheus' broken body on the table. Kin shuddered, his shadow flickering, when Amarie burst into the cell.

Her breath heaved, eyes wide, as she propelled herself to her father.

Kin forced himself to remain perfectly still.

"No!" she yelled as Talon skidded to a stop in the doorway behind her, using the frame to brace himself.

Amarie's hands grappled around the body of her father, searching desperately for a pulse she wouldn't find. Her wild, glassy eyes challenged Kin to forgo remaining hidden. Tears rushed down her cheeks, her eyes bright and rimmed with red.

Her lips parted in a body convulsing sob. "No, no, no," she repeated, a shriek echoing from her lips as she touched Kalpheus' face.

Azure flames erupted in a circle from the floor around her, and Talon stepped back momentarily with a flash of surprise in his eyes.

Kin fought his immediate desire to whisk her from the pain that caused them.

The fire pulsed with radiant blue, dark at its base, and rose to the teal of a perfectly clear ocean. With each breath of Amarie's, each sob, they flickered, spreading outwards like ripples on a lake. The flames spread with another yell of her grief, an explosion that left no time to recoil. They engulfed the entire cell, brushing past Talon's boots and climbing the walls in a blanket of vibrant light. No heat accompanied them when they passed over Kin's shadows.

Kin skulked back as far as he could from the flame, but Talon's eyes had already flitted towards him. His eyes lingered on Kin for a moment, but then turned away.

Amarie lifted her father's head into her arms and clutched him to her chest. Her eyes tightly shut for a breath before they opened. Her hand lunged for her dagger and with amazing speed, Talon caught her wrist before the blade could draw across her own throat. She cried, struggling against the auer's grip as he wrestled the blade from her and threw it skittering across the floor behind them.

"He's still there, he's there, it's not too late. I can bring him back!" she yelled, glaring at Talon.

"Stop," Talon said firmly, pulling her towards him and wrapping an arm around her waist. He held her tightly despite her struggles. "Breathe. You know he wouldn't want you to even if you could."

Kin tensed, his shadow quavering in the corner with the yearning to hold her and tell her the words her father had said.

Her eyes squeezed tight again as more sobs shook her body within Talon's hold. After a few moments, Amarie wretched herself from the auer's arms, falling back to her father's body, and pressed her forehead to his chest as she wept. Her hands gripped his tunic, and Talon rested a hand on her shoulder.

"We need to get out of here. Back to the ship," Talon said with a hoarse voice, but she shrugged his hand off her shoulder.

"I'm not leaving him," she said without lifting her head. "I need to bury him."

Talon gave it a moment as he stared at the back of her head. He glanced in Kin's direction before back to her. He replaced his hand on her again. "We need to go. Your release of energy might have triggered a ward. Your father wouldn't have you die here or be taken by Helgath," Talon urged. "He'd want you safe. And that won't be possible if we don't go *now*."

Amarie raised her head, face stained with blood and tears, and kissed Kalpheus' forehead. "I'm sorry," she whispered to ears that couldn't hear her, lingering near her father's face before she stood straight. The flames around her flickered lower but didn't completely subside as she finally turned and looked at Talon with a single nod.

He took her hand in his, and Talon's muscles tensed in a squeeze. He drew her away from where she stood and towards the door. He stooped to pick up her dagger but didn't give it back. "Come on,"

Talon said softly as the flames sputtered out, and Amarie closed her eyes.

She moved as if each step pained her, and Talon wrapped an arm around her again.

He didn't look back as he led her from the room.

Kin stepped from the shadows towards Kalpheus again as the tattoo on his arm burned. It writhed against his skin, eliciting a hiss from his lips as his bloodied hand dragged red trails across the geometric shapes, scratching at the pain.

Uriel summoned, demanding his immediate return, but Kin had other matters requiring his attention first.

Kin leaned forward, embracing Kalpheus' body against his, moving together into the depths of shadow. He buried the whispers of threats his mind assured for delaying his response to the Master's call. Kin was willing to take the punishment his insolence would earn.

First, he needed to find Deylan. Once he did, they would provide Kalpheus with the proper rites for peace.

Chapter 20

"Let me go!" Amarie shouted, yanking her wrist free of Talon's grasp only to feel his strong arms encircle her waist. "I need to find Deylan!"

In their haste to get to Kalpheus, her brother had taken a different route to cover more ground. She hoped Deylan hadn't also been captured but finding faith in his safety proved difficult. He'd made it clear the faction wouldn't come to their rescue. She needed to find him and tell him about their father. Maybe he could do something?

"Please don't fight me the whole way," Talon begged as he hauled her around towards the ship. "He wouldn't want you putting yourself in danger."

Tears blurred her vision while she struggled against Talon's hold. "I can't leave him there," she sobbed. Her feet lifted from the wooden docks as he resorted to carrying her a few steps. When she relaxed, he set her back down, but she collapsed to her knees. Blue flames erupted out around her, licking at the dock's surface, before quickly snuffing out.

Her head hung forward, hair draping over her shoulder. "Don't make me leave him like that," she pleaded, "*please.*" She couldn't feel the damp wood beneath her knees, the image of Kalpheus on the torturer's table blacking it all out.

"I swore to him I'd protect you," Talon whispered, dropping to a knee. "I can't do that if we're captured ourselves. We have to leave." His empathetic tone did nothing to stifle her pain.

Somehow back on her feet, Amarie turned to bolt back towards the barracks only to have his arms, with a strength beyond human, pull her back to him.

"I'm sorry," he rasped as she cried out with protest. "I'm so sorry."

Agony ripped at her heart for leaving her father's body where it was, broken by the cruelty of Helgath. All to protect her. Always to protect her.

Talon managed to get her aboard the ship and to their room before the sun rose, grief wracking her soul. He cleaned blood from her hands and face as she sat, lethargic, on her bed. The sobs devolved to silent tears, rarely shaking her shoulders as she encouraged internal darkness to bring her respite. Numbness. A mix of denial and emotional withdrawal to grant her sanctuary.

Talon loosened the laces of her boots and tugged them gently from her feet.

She hardly looked at him, her eyes unfocused as they stared at a blank spot on the wall behind him. Images replayed in her mind, scenarios that hadn't come to pass. Ways she could have prevented this from happening, and the last things she'd said to her father. Her last feelings. Those of resentment. Was it possible to have less time with a parent?

She tried to tell herself that things would just go back to how they were before she knew him, but it wasn't so simple. No vague hope remained, no faith he lived. She would never see him again. The finality of the night's events permanently erased any such fantasy.

After tucking her boots beneath her bunk, Talon filled a small tin cup from a pitcher of clean water.

She hadn't even realized he'd left to fetch it.

He leaned over and took her hands, wrapping them around the cup. Holding them there, he shifted to sit cross-legged on the floor in front of her. "Try to drink?" He suggested, nudging her fingers tighter around the cup.

Her gaze lowered to the rippling surface of the water, her mind refusing to register what it was. She blinked and raised the cup to her lips. Wetting her throat with a small sip, a flood of reality hit her again, and she shut her eyes. Tears escaped, and her grip around the cup tightened until her hands shook.

Soft, warm hands closed around hers, taking the cup away. Talon took both her hands in his and raised them to his lips. He brushed her knuckles with a kiss before stroking away her tears.

Amarie's eyes flickered open to finally focus on him, and she eased herself off the bed, her knees hitting the floor in front of Talon. Taking in a breath through her mouth, she blinked back tears as best as she could and tried to reach a place void of feeling within herself.

"This is my fault," she whispered, her head bowing forward.

"No," Talon said, his voice firm. "No," he repeated, softer this time as his hand stroked beneath her chin and urged her to meet his gaze. "This is *not* your fault. You can't blame yourself. Helgath is to blame, not you." His fingers moved along her jaw, eyes searching her face.

She watched him, breath shaky, and shook her head. "Is it my fate, Talon?" she asked with a cringe. "To be on my own?" Her grief weighed heavily on her lungs, making breathing difficult.

His face softened as he brushed a hand over her hair. "I rarely believe fate has such power," Talon said. "I'll be here, at your side, always." He held her hand to his chest, where she felt the steady beating of his heart.

Amarie looked down at her hand, nestled within his, trying to steady her breathing. Something about the way they looked together helped. Something with his grasp, his touch, that helped beyond what she could have anticipated. It made it all seem just a little bit more bearable to know that he was there to help lift her back up.

She craved more of the feeling and looked at him as she rose up on her knees. He seemed to understand, and she crawled onto his lap, seeking his arms as they wrapped around her.

He turned his head, nestling his forehead near hers as her legs folded beneath her.

Amarie found no words, closing her eyes and focusing on his arms and how they felt. The touch became a welcome distraction, his thumbs idly rubbing where his hands held her.

She felt his breath dance against the skin near her temple, in pace with hers.

His previous words of love returned to her mind, and she wondered if this was how that emotion felt. Her fingers tangled absently with the ties of his tunic at his chest, and she breathed in the scent of his skin. He smelled of cedar, fresh touched by the sun after rain. Lifting her chin, she wanted to feel something else. Something good. Her lips tentatively pressed against the soft curve of his neck.

His embrace tightened. The tension faded quickly, and he tilted his head ever so slightly, granting her better access as his breath came out in a soft utterance of surprise mingled with pleasure.

Amarie laced her arms gradually around him, her lips trailing down his jaw in gentle kisses as she shifted herself to face him. She felt the pressure of his hands slipping around her waist, exploring her body with lingering strokes. With her eyes mostly closed, her mouth met his with a sharp inhale of breath through her nose. Her heart thudded in her ears as his lips parted willingly to meet hers.

Fingers tracing the back of his neck, she focused on him. How he felt. Tasted. And how his hands moved against her body. Her pain trickled away, replaced by a need to be close to him, desperate to think of nothing else.

He responded to her tongue in kind as the passion mounted.

Talon intoxicated her, his mouth hot as her hands roamed over his torso. The speed of their passion encouraged her to lose her mind and let everything else fade away. Her fingers dared slip beneath the bottom of his tunic, his skin hot against her touch.

Talon abruptly pulled his lips from hers, leaving the air between them cold. His grip around her softened to nothing so eager as before.

"This isn't the right time." Talon's voice sounded hoarse, and her heart tightened. "It's too fast." His hand touched her hair, but without passion.

She felt reality strive to return, and vulnerability washed over her. She felt exposed on a limb with no safety net. The haze of emotion gradually returned.

Too fast? If it was fast, she didn't need to think.

"Isn't that the point?" she asked unsteadily. "I thought you wanted this." Her whole body felt rigid, not a muscle moving as she tried to understand. He said he loved her, and now he didn't want her?

"You need time to process, and it wouldn't be fair of me to take advantage, regardless of my personal desires," Talon said.

Her hands retracted and gaze faltered as she pushed herself away from him.

Bracing himself briefly on the wall, Talon stood and stepped back.

She pulled her knees to her chest and wrapped her arms around them. She'd never felt so cold, so alone, and now he was leaving too. He didn't even want to be near her. Didn't he just promise he'd always be at her side?

"Go," she managed, feeling her throat tighten as she lowered her forehead into her arms.

"Amarie..." he paused, stepping towards her.

She pulled her knees in closer and shook her head against them. "Get out," she said, voice muffled. Embarrassment overwhelmed her, and he still just hovered. Her voice was growing harder to find as a sob shook her body again.

He hesitated; she saw it in the corner of her vision.

"Leave," she whispered without lifting her face from her arms. Her shoulders vibrated as she tried to contain her Art. She didn't hear him cross the room but felt gentle pressure as he laid a blanket around her shoulders.

"I'll leave," he whispered, sounding far away. "And I'll come check on you in a while."

She felt a distant squeeze at her shoulders and then it disappeared. The door rasped shut behind him.

Amarie shrugged the blanket off and crawled onto the lower bunk as sobs reclaimed her chest. Her pillow muffled her agony, and she curled her knees close to her body. A torturous sleep stole her, riveted with dreams.

When she woke, the room was still empty, but the blanket covered her again, tucked around her. Turning onto her side, her gaze moved over a tray of fruit and bread next to her bed.

She needed something, her body aching and craving a bond. Comfort. She pulled her hair down, running her fingers through it before leaving their room in a daze. Judging by the amount of light coming down the stairs, she guessed it was late afternoon.

The wind of the sea rustled the sails, which she heard from the opening of the stairwell even though she didn't move towards it. The wood rocked beneath her feet, telling her they were back at sea. It granted her some solace, knowing they left Helgath, and what had happened there, behind. But it was hollow comfort.

Instead of climbing the stairs to the deck, she traversed the narrow hallways leading to the cramped cargo hold where Viento was. He already had a fresh bucket of water and feed. Slipping into the stall with her horse, she ran her hand down his black coat before sitting by the narrow gate.

He nickered and pressed his nose against her chest.

Taking a deep breath, she stroked his velvet nose for some time. He huffed when she tickled his whiskers, and she smiled.

"At least I have you," she whispered, feeling her eyes burn again.

Viento snorted and shook his mane, nudging her face with his nose.

Tears escaped her eyes even as she laughed at his antics, and he nickered again. She leaned her head back against the wooden wall and pulled her legs to sit cross-legged with her arms over her middle. The gentle shuffle of hooves and exhale of breath from Viento banished some of the cold.

Amarie remained there, listening to her horse idly munch on oats as long as she could before the rock of the ship threatened to lull her back to sleep. Her eyes closed as she drifted in and out of consciousness. Luckily, her mind spared her of more dreams, too exhausted to bother with cruel manifestations.

When awareness returned, Amarie felt moderately more alert. She rose from her spot and patted her horse's neck before leaving the stall. As she walked, she kept a hand on the wall to counter the lightheadedness. A weight on her chest prevented her from breathing properly. It drove her to emerge above deck, finding the sun gone, stars twinkling in the open sky.

The chill salty breeze of the sea helped clear her mind but encouraged her back below deck towards the cabin she shared with Talon. All was silent in the night, the snores of slumbering sailors echoing through the bowels of the ship. She slipped through the doorway towards her bunk, the dimly burning lantern swinging from the ceiling. The light flickered on Talon's back where he lay on the top bunk. Her stomach tightened, hoping he wouldn't wake at her entry. She watched as his shoulders rose gently with each breath, then crawled onto her bed, burying herself amidst the blankets. Blissful slumber crept over her again.

Distant cries of seagulls woke her, finding the room darker than it'd been before. Daylight seeped through the crack under the door, casting an eerie glow within the room.

Listening, she tried to pick out any evidence that Talon was still in the room. She couldn't avoid him forever, but in that moment, it felt like a priority.

Hearing nothing, she shuffled out of bed and glanced behind her at his empty bunk. The blankets and pillows immaculately arranged. The platter of food had moved, placed in the cubby behind the door with the water pitcher. She absently chose a roll of bread and made her way to the main deck. Her bare feet took her up the additional six stairs to the bow of the ship, the planks warm in the sunlight. If there were other people on deck, she hardly noticed.

Leaning against the rail, she watched the ship crash through waves. Cold sea winds danced across her skin, but only served in freeing her of the grogginess clinging to her thoughts. Pulling her hair up to keep it from being windswept, she tugged the leather band from her wrist and secured it. Letting out a slow exhale, Amarie let her mind wander to her parents. They were together now and imagining the smile Mayen would have for Kalpheus made Amarie's heart soar and tears flood her eyes again. But not all family was lost. She had Deylan now, as well as Ryas. Two brothers she could only hope to see again one day, plus the possibility of more family she wasn't aware of.

Watching the horizon, Amarie focused on the small bit of peace of having met her father.

When Talon assured her Kalpheus' death wasn't her fault, he was mostly right. Regardless of her presence in Rylorn, her father would have been arrested and killed, but she'd never have known.

Closing her eyes, she imagined her father's embrace surrounding her. The warmth of his arms brought a sense of reassurance she'd never known before. She could still feel it if she tried hard enough. With a shiver, she opened her eyes and wished she'd brought her cloak.

Talon would have remembered it and her stomach knotted at the thought of him. Her affection for him felt real, without a doubt, but he'd been right to stop her. Embarrassment hung thick, and she was disappointed in her rash desire to use the auer to forget the events two nights prior. It wasn't fair to Talon, or to herself, and especially not to the man she mourned.

She traced the grain of the banister with her fingertip, humming a tune that flowed with her swirls over the wood. Opening her mouth, she let the first Aueric word of the song come, dissipating over the breeze as quickly as it left her lungs. The sound of her own voice, ebbing with the swelling of the sails and crash of waves brought her solace. She continued through the gentle melody she'd last heard in Eralas. It didn't matter who heard.

Chapter 21

Talon's steps faltered as he crossed onto the main deck of the ship. He carried Amarie's cloak in his hands. Traces of her sweet scent, trapped in the thick material, greeted his nose. He'd seen it bundled on her bunk and suspected she might need it.

When the first melodic note drifted into his ears, he couldn't tell where it came from, and he thought he imagined it. The Aueric words flitted into his consciousness with wonderful nostalgia, as if they embraced him. He urged his lethargic mind to focus on the source, and his eyes found Amarie. He could no longer oblige her desire for him to stay away, and his feet led him to the half set of stairs leading to the upper deck she occupied.

He kept his boots reverentially quiet, unwilling to disturb the beauty of the song caressing his very being. Sailors slowed in their tasks, their eyes following his own towards the wondrous creature who brought such calm with her voice.

Talon's soul stirred, coalescing into a hot flame in his gut as his fingers followed the banister up the stairs towards Amarie. Something about her voice buzzed against his skin. Her tongue so perfectly formed the Aueric words, and her lips uttered them with melodic cadence. It made his knees feel weak and his chest ache.

He recognized the verse signaling the song's end, and it doubled his torment. He closed his eyes, savoring the words with the vibration of her voice, and drew the sea air deep into his lungs.

It took all he could muster to open his eyes again after her voice stopped. He appreciated the way her back gently curved as she leaned against the bow. How a little cluster of her hair defied the rest to loop in lazy windswept patterns on her back. He didn't know how long he stood there enjoying the echoes of the music in his mind and the sight of her before him. His heart swelled in awe at the intoxicating music she created despite all she'd suffered.

Crossing the deck, he made sure to plant his feet particularly hard against the wood so she might hear him. Swallowing, Talon draped her cloak over her shoulders, careful to avoid touching the skin exposed at her neck. He felt tension in her shoulders briefly before he forced himself to release her.

Emotions. Instincts. He was giving them too much power. As an auer, he was supposed to remain in control every moment.

He stepped to the railing beside her, forcing his hands to grip the banister instead of reaching for her. The color had returned to Amarie's cheeks, slightly pink from the cold wind. Her eyes still had vague rims of red, but seemed less dull. She held her body strong.

"You look better," he commented, a hopeful smile on his lips as he turned to her.

She didn't look towards him, staring instead at the twisted grains of the banister.

Is she still angry, he wondered, *or is it something else?*

"I'm sorry," she said, shattering the quiet with a voice barely audible over the wind.

Talon's brow furrowed. "You don't need to apologize," he whispered, turning to lean his hip against the banister. "I should be the one doing so."

Amarie lifted her gaze from the wood. Confusion swirled within the blue depths. "Why would you?"

"For making what you're going through worse," Talon said. "For the part I played in all of it."

He'd made it worse, hadn't he? She'd just needed comfort, but he'd pushed her away. He didn't regret the decision. It was the right one at the time. She'd lost her father and needed time to grieve. But it had certainly made it harder on her, and he could still apologize.

She shook her head with a light huff of breath across her lips, which he found himself looking at. He cursed inwardly at his lack of control, and he forced his eyes away from her mouth.

"You didn't. You didn't make things worse. I did," she said, looking down towards his boots. Her long hair, secured at the back of her head, fell tenderly over her shoulder. Soft waves of dark auburn clung to the collar of her cloak.

"You mean so much more to me than just a distraction. It was wrong of me to try to use you, and I—" She paused, taking a slow inhale. "I'm just sorry, for that. You deserve better," she said, finally lifting her gaze to meet his.

Talon's chest ached. He slid his hand across the banister to touch hers, feeling the lingering cold from the air on her skin, and sought to warm it. "While I may disagree with deserving better," he said, "I appreciate your apology. Even though I don't feel it's warranted."

She returned his smile with an attempted one of her own, followed by an exhale. "I hope you believe me when I say that my affection for you is genuine." She looked down again, biting her lower lip in a habit he was growing accustomed to. "You're more than a distraction." Her eyes returned to his. "Or a replacement."

Her words struck him with more force than he could have expected, his shoulders tightening against his will. While he didn't mind the idea of being a distraction in the right situations, he wanted to be more than that to her. More than a replacement for what she'd lost. A replacement for Kin.

"I don't know how I could've survived all this without you, and I don't want to do something stupid and lose you too," Amarie continued with glassy eyes.

He raised his free hand to touch her chin, urging her head up. Once he met her eyes, he drew the hand over her cheek to brush at the swelling pool beneath her eye. He didn't want her to cry again. Her tears affected him far more than he thought possible; they tore at his soul.

"You haven't lost me," Talon said, squeezing her hand atop the banister. "I'm not going anywhere." He smiled, hoping to evoke a similar emotion from her. "Besides, I hate to point out the obvious, but we're on a ship in the middle of the Dul'Idurr. Few places for me to go," he teased.

Amarie smiled and turned her face into his hand. No longer glassy-eyed, she looked at him with a smirk. "I'm pretty sure Jael would happily stop the ship at the nearest port to get rid of you," she played, but the subject matter made him frown.

"Jael." That was a name he could have kept going without hearing again. He played with the distaste of it on his tongue. "I'm sure he would. He's aware that he has no chance against the charm of an auer such as I." His body demanded to be closer to her, and he obeyed without thinking. The hand caressing her cheek slid down over her shoulder to wrap around her waist.

She stepped closer to him and wrapped her arms around his neck. Her response didn't encourage him to gain control, his grip tightening so he could feel the warmth of her body against his own.

Her face nestled into the side of his neck within the embrace. Her lips curled in the subtle motion of a kiss. It made his heart race.

Talon pressed his lips against her hair, drawing in the smell of it. Sweet with the salt of the sea air. He couldn't help the kiss that formed.

Amarie gradually released him, easing herself back to her heels. Her eyes held a mixture of thoughts, difficult to decipher, but a delicate smile lingered on her face. "Perhaps we could go enjoy the fruit and bread in our luxurious and spacious room?" she suggested.

He admired her spirit; respected and adored it. Drawing his hand down her arm, he found her fingers and intertwined them with his. "I don't know what we'll do with all the extra space for the next few days until we reach Eralas," he said as he walked with her towards the warmth below deck and the promise of sustenance.

He drew their door open and held it from outside their room while he waited for her to go in first.

She gave him a playful scowl, since he'd raced to get to the door before her, but crossed into the room. Unfastening her cloak, she tossed it atop her made bed. She eyed it suspiciously, probably because she hadn't left it that way.

He stepped inside, the tension in her shoulders tempting him to rub it away.

Before he could, she took up the platter and sat on her lower bunk. Tucking her feet up to sit cross-legged, she picked up a piece of melon.

He opted to sit beside her this time and leaned to untie the laces of his boots. "The captain expects about four days before we reach Eralas," Talon said. He used his heels to pop both his boots off, tucking them away beneath the bunk. Turning to sit facing her, he settled his back against the wall, the platter between them.

Her gaze was intent on him. "Are you nervous?" she asked gently, biting into a piece of bread.

"You'll have to be more specific," Talon teased. "I have plenty to be potentially nervous about."

Amarie pushed the platter towards him, and he tore himself a piece of bread. "Well, being stuck on this ship with me for four days *might* feel daunting. Especially while trying so hard to remain controlled." Her tone was coy, and he guessed that she redirected her question away from its original intention.

"It *is* a rather daunting task," Talon said between bites. "I need to maintain appearances, for a certain sailor mentioned earlier. I must also prevent you from understanding just how much you affect me. It would damage my Aueric image."

"That would be disastrous," she agreed with a nod. "Though, if you want my advice, assuming you'd rather keep the truth of your affliction private, encouraging me to spend *more* time with said sailor might be your best bet. Then no one would suspect a thing."

Talon frowned and narrowed his eyes at the suggestion. It was still interesting to feel the tingle the mere suggestion caused in him. A curious and unexpected emotion. "While it may help with one aspect of my image, encouraging such behavior would surely damage another. I can't let the sailor believe that my charm failed to keep you enthralled. I'd rather risk damaging the image of my control. If you're amenable, of course." He took a casual bite of a plum he'd plucked from the plate.

Her smile widened. "I am," she agreed and then paused. "If you wanted to talk about why you're *actually* nervous, you can. You're not the only one good at listening."

Talon couldn't help the small huff of a laugh. It felt silly to avoid talking about it with her, and he shook his head. He took another bite before he set the pit aside on the edge of the platter. "Merely trying to remain realistic," he admitted. His hands twisted against each other. "The Council of Elders made the punishment I'd suffer if I returned to Eralas quite clear. My banishment was a light sentence for the crimes my sister and I stood accused of."

Despite the passage of time, Talon still remembered how cold it felt standing in the center of the Sanctum of Law, drained of his ability for the Art. Goosebumps rose along his arms.

Amarie tilted her head, lips pursed as she picked up an apple and leaned back against the wall at the head of her bed. "I know you must doubt my effectiveness in situations involving the Art," she started, turning the red-skinned fruit with a thoughtful look. "But the reason I spent time in Eralas was because I have no need to fear the Council.

Every auer is connected to the Art in a way that makes them vulnerable to me."

Talon recalled the crumpled body of the grygurr shaman, burned from the inside out.

"I won't let them harm you," she added, raising her gaze to him.

He smiled but shook his head, forcing his back to straighten with a deep breath. "I wouldn't ask that of you," Talon said. "I should face judgement if that's what it comes to. Though I'll do all I can to avoid it. They are still my people, even if they've turned their backs on me. Besides, I wouldn't want you to take on the burden of more death."

Surprisingly, Amarie laughed at him. "I'm not intent on taking innocent lives. I have other tactics, you know," she said as she rolled her eyes at him.

Running his hands through his hair, he pulled out the strap of thin leather and shook it loose. He tucked the tie into his pocket and shifted to find a more comfortable position. "I'm rather curious about these *other* tactics you speak of." He smirked, pulling a knee up towards his chest, the other dangling off the edge of the bunk. "Feminine wiles? Pretty looks?" he teased. "Or did you have something else in mind?"

"Oh, I can be quite convincing," she said, mirroring the smirk.

"Of that, I'm certain," Talon agreed as he leaned back. Silence overtook them for a time, and he considered how effective Amarie could be with proper training in the Art. "When we get settled," he started, "I can begin to help you focus your power."

Amarie bit her lip. "You understand that teaching me is not a safe endeavor?" she asked with an air of hesitation.

He rose his head from the wall, tilting it towards her as his brow furrowed. "I know of the risks of using the Art in Eralas. But I know how to keep the use of destructive Art secret. I did so for many years."

The darkness in her eyes deepened, her full lips pressing harder together. That wasn't the risk she was concerned about.

"Is there more I should be aware of?" he asked.

Amarie took a deep inhale. "There is," she confirmed regretfully. "What happened to the grygurr shaman... I don't want to do that to you. But if I lose control..." Her voice trailed off, and she cringed.

"Ah," he said in realization. He considered the laws of power and energy distribution with the Art. He'd already begun to accept that the Berylian Key's power would not fit neatly within the Laws all young auer were required to study.

"You aren't obligated, of course," she said. "I won't downplay the risk to you. It's a risk I wish I learned an easier way."

Talon caught her inference. It only made him more determined to maintain his offer. "It merely means we'll need to be cautious," he said, refusing to hesitate. "Your concern only further enforces the need for you to learn. Your fear of accessing the Art is what I most desire to help you conquer." He could barely reach her from where he sat but touched the side of her knee. "I know full well that your power could hurt me. And I will maintain an appropriate amount of fear for what could happen. That's what will make this relationship between us work."

"And if I tell you to run, you'll listen?" she asked.

"Absolutely," Talon agreed with a laugh, squeezing her leg. "Without hesitation. I have enough respect after what I've already seen your power do."

Amarie shifted her weight to rock forward onto her knees, lowering the tray of forgotten food to the floor beside the bed. Crawling across the short distance between them, she sat next to him. Leaning on him with her back against the wall, she bent her knees and let them rest on his leg.

His heart thudded as she settled her hand onto his chest. Unable to resist, he instinctively curled his arm around her.

"This relationship you speak of working," she murmured. "You must be speaking of our future teacher and pupil relationship."

Toying, she walked two fingers up his chest towards his collar.

A lump involuntarily formed in his throat as he watched the slow progression up his chest. She had a wonderful ability to make his mind blur and his body forget anything it felt before. Anticipation for her touch grew along with the lingering guilt he'd not fully banished. "That was my original meaning, yes," Talon said as his blood heated. "I wasn't yet aware of another relationship."

Amarie pulled her knees up a little further and traced up his neck to the far side of his jaw, then down around his chin. It felt like she studied him. Her finger brushed across his lower lip.

The rest of the room disappeared as he focused on his breathing and the feeling of her fingertips. His lips parted slightly at her touch.

"I see," she whispered. Her eyes flitted up to his, a smirk playing on her lips. Her hand slipped away from him, removing the tie that held her hair up. "I must have been mistaken then," she added with a playful undertone as he felt her weight shift to sit up from him.

But his pounding heart insisted he stop her, and his arm around her shoulders tightened, keeping her still. The pressure against his embrace lasted only a breath as her smile brightened.

"You're not mistaken," he said, unable to keep his eyes from the shadow on her jaw from the waves of her hair. Everything within him warred, trying to decide what was the right course of action. He wanted her affection. Needed it. Yet, something still nagged the back of his mind. He swatted the thoughts away as his hand traced up the curve of her spine. The strands of her hair fell perfectly between his fingers as he touched the base of her skull.

"You see straight through me, don't you?" he asked. His hand fell gently to the outside of her hip, relishing in her gentle curves.

A flicker of something passed over her face. "These moments of weakness you allow yourself give you away. These moments where you seem the most intent on what you want." Her hand moved up again and touched his face.

238

"You are what weakens me," Talon whispered. Her scent, her touch, drove him to nearly forget it all.

"But there's something else," she murmured thoughtfully. "Something I can't fathom could belong. Guilt? Uncertainty? What is it that holds you captive?"

Her eyes trailed down to his lips as she spoke, and his entire being ached with every word. Her irises were a perfect lapis blue, deep and rich, with a swollen black pupil in the dimness of their cabin. It perfectly reflected the faint glimmers of orange from the lantern flame.

His hand traced the soft curve of her brow, where it came to her temple and followed the luscious draping of her auburn hair. Then the slight roundness of her cheekbone, the red flush of the outside long gone from her pristine skin. His thumb moved across her chin, touching her full pink lips as they parted. Beautiful tortured memories of what those lips had evoked before rose within him. As his thumb traced the soft rosy flesh, the echo of her song buzzed within his mind. His body remembered the way it felt; the fire following the Aueric words. His desire grew like an inferno, threatening to overtake his entire being.

Amarie pressed her palm to his chest, fingers touching the base of his throat. Her lips twitched together in the hint of a kiss on his thumb. "There's no one I'd rather be here with," she whispered. "No one," she repeated adamantly, as if she already knew who his mind would wander to.

It all came back to Kin. Was Talon betraying his friend by giving into his own passions?

A sharp inhale escaped him as he felt the hot warmth of her lips form again against his thumb, with a pleasant flick from the tip of her tongue.

Damn the consequences.

His hand gripped the base of her hair and twisted tighter. He closed the distance between them, pulling her lips to his. As her fingers closed around the collar of his shirt, his tongue hungrily sought hers. Hands moved to her hips to pull her atop him.

Following his urging, she parted her knees to straddle him as his hands massaged the small of her back and up her shoulders. She tasted like the sweetness of apple mixed with fire. Her fingers played along his skin at his neck, sending chills raging through his veins.

Her arms embraced him, and she pulled him with her as she laid back on the bed.

Obediently, he lowered himself atop her supple body, his hips hovering between her thighs. His fingers found the side ties of her corset, hastily freeing the constraint so that his hand could trace the muscles of her abdomen through the thinner material of her shirt.

Amarie sucked in a breath as he bit her lower lip, her back arching. This time, when her fingers touched his bare skin beneath his shirt, he didn't recoil. Instead, he dove into another deep kiss. He felt her bare feet wrap around his legs, heels pressing into his calves as she pulled him against her.

The heat of their touch straightened his spine, pulling him from her lips.

Her hair splayed beautifully atop the pillow behind her head, like a crown of deep red. Lips wet and swollen, her dark blue eyes watched him intently, a hint of a smirk tormenting him as her fingers played at his waist.

Talon tugged the fabric of his tunic free from his breeches. He saw a light in her eyes, an excitement. He teased her, letting the material linger, its hem tickling along his bare skin with the slow lift.

Amarie sat up before him, ripping his shirt impatiently off. She caressed and kissed his bare chest, leaving a hot trail with her lips. Her nails dragged down his abdomen.

The feeling of her mouth made his body howl for more. She was gaining too much control over him. He traced the line of her spine before fingers tangled with her hair, and he tugged her mouth back to his. The soft moan against his lips encouraged him to remove the rest of the clothing on her upper body. With her hands above her head, briefly tangled amongst linen, he took her mouth again. He urged her body back, pinning her hands at the head of the bed. It allowed him freedom from the distraction of her touch, and he traced her body with one hand.

Talon pulled his lips from hers but could not fully part from her skin as his mouth moved along her jaw and down her neck. He savored the taste of her skin, like nothing he could have imagined. His hand cupped her breast, feeling the swell of flesh rise in his palm with each breath as her body arched against him. His mouth dared to venture down her sternum.

A soft moan came from her throat, her heels digging harder into his calves. "Talon," she whispered, voice breathy. She squeezed his hand, forcing his mind to process his own name.

He inhaled against her skin, forcing himself to take a moment before drawing from her, his hands moving away.

Amarie smiled, biting her bottom lip.

He returned to touch her jaw with his index finger, returning the gentle smile. Lowering himself atop her, he brought his lips to hers for a tender kiss.

Too fast, he scolded himself silently. This needed to be slow. Otherwise it was too much like every relationship he'd allowed himself before.

Her arms wrapped around him again, and he pulled away just enough to look into her eyes. Her breath hit the edge of his lip, and his conviction hardened as he carefully lowered himself to her side. A calmness took hold, seeping through his limbs as the adrenaline of passion faded.

She pressed her body against his, nestling her head on his shoulder as her hand caressed his face.

His head turned to kiss her palm before he settled against the pillow, pulling her close. "Sorry," he whispered with a smile as his eyes closed, and he breathed the scent of her hair. "Lost myself a little."

"Mmm," she murmured near his ear. "I like that side of you."

"So, the calm, collected auer isn't your style then? I'll have to remember that," he teased, already feeling his mind fading as his eyes refused to open. "But I want this to be slow. It'll make it better."

She nodded against his skin. "Then, if I remember correctly, this is *my* bed," she pointed out. Her fingertips still traced on his skin, now touching his neck.

He smiled, managing to open his eyes just a slit to look at her smiling face. "Oh?" he responded. "Are you going to banish me back to my own? I'd like to see you wrestle me up there. I'm rather comfortable."

A melodic laugh came to her lips, and her hand slipped from his neck to be around him. "I think I'd prefer you stay right here," she whispered against his chest with a warm exhale that made his skin tingle.

He gently rubbed her bare back, as he let his sleepy eyes close again. "I'd be a fool to argue."

Chapter 22

Amarie's affection for Talon only grew in the blissfully uneventful days at sea. Their desire to take things slow proved to be a struggle, but she tried to enjoy it.

Her mind drifted less and less to Kin, persuading her that moving on might be possible. Time effectively changed the course of her thoughts, and she began to accept the reality that he posed a danger to her. She found herself feeling almost indifferent whenever his name came up, though Talon seemed eager to avoid the subject. She stopped imagining Kin's arms, drowning the memories with new ones of Talon's embrace. His aggressive passion often caught her off guard, but it excited her.

The lazy rock of the sea and fresh air encouraged her to make peace with the events in Rylorn. Grief no longer raged within her, now bundled with the pain she always felt for the rest of her lost family. One day she would join them, but she was in no rush for that day to come or the daughter it required of her.

The danger of their arrival in Eralas brought new nervousness. Standing on the top deck, she took in the view before her as they arrived. Even though she'd seen the sights before, sailing towards the shore of Eralas would never be unimpressive.

No beaches adorned the west side of the island, only rocky crags that stood in defiance to the sea's waves. The black rocks erupted from azure water like parapets of a castle, topped with ancient beech trees.

Different than the trees common in the mainland's forests, these were ancient behemoths that would grow for generations of auer with careful tending. Roots dangled like vines towards the salty sea, creating a thick curtain over the top of the crags where the city of Ny'Thalus was located.

Amarie squinted at the openings on the cliff face, the rock forced to form them by auer Art. The windows, spanning several stories, looked out towards the docks crafted from massive roots of a single giant beech tree. The branches cast an umbrella of shade which the ship drifted within as they neared the shore.

Rock jutted up from the sea to support the dock. As it stretched out over the water, the roots, worn flat, split into an array of moorings. Most ships occupying them were small, single-sailed creations of the auer, meant for journeys around the island rather than the span of ocean towards the mainland. The triangular translucent sails rippled in the sea breeze, shimmering like spiderwebs.

Where the docks met the shore, the roots snaked up the sides of a massive fissure in the cliffside. Its entrance formed a wide inclined path. The long roadway traveled in a straight line to the top of the cliffs. It formed the only passage onto the island from the docks. No merchant carts clogged the road, only people. Auer walked the sloped street casually, treading in and out of doorways and tunnels at its sides. A series of bridges at various heights and angles spanned the fissure like laces of a boot.

Even as Amarie looked at the city, she saw new construction with roots, trees, and rock reforming existing infrastructure. The city breathed with living energies, the sensation of the Art tickling her senses. The wind echoed each breath, rustling the leaves of the towering beech tree above.

Talon shivered beside her as the shadow of Ny'Thalus crossed the deck. They stood together near the gangplank which would be lowered soon. The horses would be retrieved once the ship reached its berth, and the crew secured its ropes.

Talon and Amarie agreed to pass through the city as quickly as possible. There were too many opportunities for Talon to be recognized, even if he'd made attempts to mask his appearance.

The fake aura concealing the energy he normally radiated made Amarie uneasy. He couldn't hide his power entirely, for that would have been even more suspicious. Kalstacia, Talon's eldest sister, was the person he claimed to base his new aura on. He'd told Amarie about her as he crafted the weave of his disguise. He was vague, in his usual charming way, but Amarie could tell Talon held great respect for her.

Built within the weave, which she'd curiously watched him create, Talon made other subtle changes. His hair took on a paler shade, turning to a soft stone grey, common amongst the auer people regardless of their age. His eyes turned to a honey color that didn't suit him.

He gnawed at the inside of his lip as he watched the crew lower the gangplank. Strands of his long hair played along his taut jawline. Tension tainted his entire body, conflicted; an uncertainty whether to feel delighted in seeing Eralas again or fear for what it might hold. The last time he'd seen these docks was when he was forced onto a ship, knowing he'd never see the island again.

It made Amarie's heart ache, and she closed her hand around his.

As they passed through the city streets, Talon stayed a small distance behind Amarie. Just as they'd suspected, she drew most of the attention, keeping the gazes of the people in the streets long enough that they hardly noticed Talon. Amarie was obviously human, with her auburn hair among a sea of monochromatic colors. Her skin was also paler than most auer, who were all richly tanned and dark skinned.

At the city exit, there was no guard station or barracks for the military. The city merely stopped, trickling into the forest beyond. A path cut neatly across the soil, with trees planted uniformly, like statues, marking the way to the capital of Quel'Nian.

Amarie didn't feel a need to look back, able to hear Lynthenai's hoofbeats behind her as they drew further from the city.

Talon came beside her when they were out of sight of Ny'Thalus, with a look of relief and a smile on his lips, shoulders more relaxed. He led the way after that, down the main road until she heard the rush of a river.

Dense canopies let in little light, but glowing orbs nestled in tree branches fashioned specifically to contain them lit the way. A bridge came into view, between the trunks of two massive trees, but Talon turned before they reached it. He steered Lynthenai away from the path, carefully down a steep slope towards the river.

Two streams merged from the north and south to flow west, towards Ny'Thalus. They backtracked down the west arm of the river until it was shallow enough to cross before continuing southeast. The waters were warm, unlike the swollen winter-melt streams on the mainland. Eralas never saw winter, only temperate summers and springs, which Amarie favored.

Night had already fallen when Talon drew Lynthenai to a stop.

Amarie's eyes had adjusted, but Talon blew into his hands to create a glowing ember of light. As the flickering orange flame in the palm of his hand grew and lit his face, she saw the green return to his irises, and his hair shift back to raven black.

With a twist of his fingers, Talon sent the flame from his hand. It fluttered a few paces away, where it hovered as he dismounted.

The trees had shifted to mangled banyan trees. Far larger than on the mainland, natural hollows in the stumps created ample living spaces for wildlife. It was also within the trunks of these trees where many auer made their homes.

The river babbled nearby in the night air. Ferns rustled as Talon's fire caught the gleam of a doe's eyes before she fled into the forest.

Talon stepped silently towards the largest in a clump of banyan trees. Another breath of light came to his fingertips as he leaned around one of the dense root systems to peer into a crevice of the tree. Birds chattered their protest, and he ducked as they fled.

"It'll do," Talon said, turning towards Amarie with a sheepish smile. "If the previous tenants return, I'm certain we can cohabitate until morning. Tomorrow we'll begin your training, and you can help me turn this place into something the two of us can live in."

Morning came with the noisy songs of the birds who'd returned to their nest. Their boisterous chirping announced the slivers of sun forcing their way through the canopy above.

Amarie couldn't help but moan, grumbling against Talon's warm chest as he stirred.

His strong arm wrapped around her shoulder, pulling her close in his new morning ritual. He placed a tender kiss on her temple, fingertips playing with the strands of her hair near her cheek. "I promise I'll relocate our neighbors before tonight," he whispered in her ear with another kiss.

Amarie moaned again, this time a mix of protest and enjoyment. She relaxed her aura, as she'd done a few times before, and let it engulf Talon. It made her feel closer to him, and he breathed deeply in response, her head rising with his chest. She heard his heart pound as he nuzzled against her hair.

Reluctantly, she lifted her head and propped herself up with an elbow to gaze at his face. "Having second thoughts yet?" she asked.

He peeked at her through one half-opened eye, returning her hesitant smirk. "Nope," he confirmed, and let his eye close again. "It should be easier here too. I didn't realize just how much I missed the energies of these forests."

There was something different about Eralas. The air didn't feel the same as it did in the mainland, as if the Art was denser here. Easier to access. She felt its consistent pressure against her skin.

Her smile grew wider. She felt privileged to share the reunion. His face relaxed in a way she hadn't seen before, free of the control he always claimed to have. Even his breath sounded unfettered.

Leaning over him, she kissed his chin, receiving a gentle groan in response. She moved farther to kiss his jaw line. "Shall I let you sleep longer?" she asked playfully, giving him another closer to his ear before finally shifting to sit up.

But he protested, pulling her back down atop him.

She laughed, letting her body settle against his.

"Sleeping wasn't what I thought you were encouraging," he teased as his fingers traced her jaw. He met her lips in prolonged kiss.

Amarie let her hand trail over his neck and down to his chest. Her mouth didn't leave his, renewing the kiss he'd instigated. It caused her heart to float with a lightness uncommon for her.

The birds complained, flapping wings against the branches of the tree, squawking their frustration at the two beings entangled in each other's arms below.

Talon flinched and chuckled as he pulled away. "I think I should move our neighbors *now*. And I might suspect ulterior motives in you. Trying to distract me from beginning your training?"

Amarie scowled, even if he was accurate in her lack of desire to face the day ahead. "Does it matter what my motives are?" she asked and lowered her head just enough to bite his bottom lip.

His body arched beneath hers, another soft sound coming from his throat. "In this case, yes," he said with a poke at her sternum, pushing her up from him.

She pouted. "I'll remember this," she said, and reluctantly rose to her feet.

Walking from under their dwelling, Amarie breathed in the forest air. Anxiety prickled in her stomach. Using her power was something she hadn't done in years, even in the most dire circumstances. Fear of what havoc it could wreak stopped her. And here she was, about to try again, unable to deny the terror it stirred. Grateful Talon couldn't see her face, she rubbed the sleep from her eyes. She focused on quieting her nerves and didn't notice he was behind her until his steady arms encircled her waist. Startled, she flinched, but it dissipated with an exhale, and she leaned against him.

"Still not used to those silent feet of yours," she said, resting her hands on his arms. She felt him smile as he pressed his mouth against the side of her head.

"I'll try to clod around like a clumsy human more often," he whispered. As he spoke, he slid his hands from where they rested on her stomach to take hers. He held her palms against her own abdomen, resting his atop them.

"It starts with breath," he said. "Control of that breath and how deep it falls into you. Just breathe into the power inside you and acknowledge it."

Her breathing came in shaky draws, but she tried to steady it. His gentle inhale and release near her ear provided something for her to match it with. Intentionally touching her power stirred discomfort, but she fought against her instincts and focused on their breathing.

Reaching into the darkest of spaces, Amarie had nothing to guide her. Fear accompanied each metaphorical step. She found the well of energy within her, tepidly touching what was there. A gasp overtook her. The flood of power electrified every nerve, and she shut her eyes, recoiling from the sensation as quickly as she could.

Talon's breath didn't falter, but his grip on her hands tightened. "Tell me," he whispered in her ear, "talk through it as you reach." His breath steadied hers again, his chest gently swelling against her back, and air wisped by her ear. "What do you feel? Do it again."

Fear, she thought. *I'm feeling fear.*

She reached again into the darkness, keeping her eyes closed.

"Breathe," he whispered, ushering another steady inhale.

Had she stopped?

"I'm reaching for it," she whispered.

"Feel your breath drop in," Talon instructed, tapping his fingers against hers. "Feel your breath as it extends and just lightly touches the surface of your power. Don't take it, merely touch and acknowledge its depth." His voice was calm with surprising certainty.

"Is this how you teach all your pupils?" she quipped and felt the hint of a smile against her hair and the smallest variance in his breath. But it quickly restored, and she was immediately distracted when she once again found the pulsing power deep within herself.

Amarie inhaled again, but not as sharply as the last time and forced herself to mentally stay where she was. "I can feel it," she said, trying to maintain control of her breath as she delved deeper into the feeling, exploring rather than grasping.

"Good," he encouraged. "Tell me what it feels like. Only observing it."

She could barely hear him. His words echoed in her mind as if they were her own thoughts. She moved through the power of her Art, enjoying how it pulsed as if it had a life of its own. Ingrained within it was her very soul.

"It feels warm," she started, swallowing back the nerves still tense within her. "It's familiar, comforting, like fresh air or... water?"

"Let us focus on that," Talon said, "but first, let go of your fear. Find it with your breath and let it out with your exhale. It has no place within your power. You don't need it."

Amarie tried to do as told, breathing in deeply and exhaling the clinging trepidation. Her hands relaxed under his, as she swam amongst the depths of her Art. It buzzed against her skin. She could almost taste it, the tang and spark within it.

"I want to hold it," she said.

It wanted to be held and reached for her. It wanted to flow freely in her veins and be a part of her.

"Not yet," Talon instructed firmly, his voice still far away. "Time is necessary. Slow. Wait for the urge to grasp it to pass. Just exist with it."

His breath moved with hers, swelling against the surface of her power, keeping the waters calm. But as still as they were, they were insistent. Magnetic. She felt her heart quicken as she tried to keep it at a distance, but it defied her wishes and encroached closer.

"It's pulling me," she said but kept the instinctual fear at bay. "I have to take it or push it away. I have to."

"It only wants you to think that," Talon said, his hands tightening on hers. "You are in control, not it. Steady yourself. Plant yourself. *Breathe.*" He shifted his breath to match hers to guide it back to slow and steady again.

Amarie used every ounce of self-control to focus on his words, his breathing, and use her will to control the flood from overtaking her. In the calmness, her power surrounded her. She didn't grasp at it but felt it everywhere without holding it at all. Her breathing steadied, and the adrenaline faded.

"It stopped," she whispered. It wafted over her without forcing its way into her veins. "It's just... here. With me."

"Good," Talon said. "Now draw away from it. Place it back where it belongs within you and ride your exhale out and away."

She hesitated, suddenly disliking the idea of leaving the power, tucking it away again. Her brows knitted. "Why?" she asked. "I don't want to. It's here, I can feel it. I want to stay here." Within it, she was safe. So different than what she felt outside of it. No pain. No suffering.

"You can't stay," Talon said, his voice more urgent now as his fingers entwined with hers. "That desire comes from the power, not from you. Be strong, find that separation between it and you. You're powerful enough to go on without it. You don't need it."

His words didn't make sense, and she hesitated still at his instructions. A nagging thought in that back of her mind told her to trust him. She needed to listen. Keeping him safe was more important, and she found the will to push the power away again back to where she found it.

Sealing it off, she opened her eyes, and her breath stilled momentarily as her mind processed where she was and what she was doing. "I'm here," she said, voice clear. "It's gone."

"I know," Talon whispered as he turned her head and laid a long kiss on her temple. "Welcome back," he teased with a squeeze around her middle, still pressed behind her.

"Could you feel it?" she asked, gently squeezing the hand entwined with hers.

"To a point," Talon admitted. "But really, I only get a glance at the surface. Only you will ever be able to sense its true depth. Though we should avoid going that far for at least a couple years," he said in a tone that was both serious and teasing. "You'll need to do this meditation several times a day until you grow used to the contact. And the drive to need it, to take it, starts to fade. Only then will it be safe to try."

Amarie wondered if it was realistic to assume they could stay in Eralas for such a duration. "It'll never be safe," she murmured, "not truly." Memories of exactly how unsafe it could be flooded her mind, but she pushed them back. "I'd like to do it again," she added, leaning back against him just enough to feel the pressure of his body.

"You're right, it'll never really be safe, and that's something you must always remember. Every time anyone uses the Art, they risk taking too much and draining themselves to the point of death. Yours comes with a far greater burden. But you know all this," he said with a sigh. He turned her to face him and took her chin between his fingers, tilting it up. "How about some breakfast before we try again?"

Her hands found his sides, feeling lean muscle beneath his clothing. She nodded, eyes flickering briefly to his mouth. "All right," she conceded. "Breakfast first."

Talon's lips curled into a smile, showing the white of his teeth. "I did mean actual food," he insisted. "Though you seem like you had something else in mind?" He leaned his mouth close to hers, taunting her lips.

She needed no further invitation and pressed her mouth to his. The rhythm of their lips had become a feeling she craved more and more. As she drew away from him, she bit and pulled his lower lip before releasing it. The soft sound that rumbled in his chest made it difficult to maintain her distance.

"I'm sure I'm only able to resist the draw of my power because I'm so practiced resisting something much more tempting," she admitted and traced a finger over his collar.

Talon's breath matched hers now as he drew air in, his chest moving pleasantly beneath her fingertips. "I'm fulfilling my role as teacher then," he said. "Perhaps a little too effectively?"

Amarie grinned and shook her head. "Just effectively enough, I'd say," she said, then added. "I am hungry, though. You know, for food."

"If only life could be sustained on kisses alone." Talon sighed.

Chapter 23

Several times a day over the following week, Talon encouraged Amarie to meditate within her Art. The first few days, it was difficult to find her willpower to retreat from the comforting depths, and he helped to persuade her out. As the days passed, it became easier.

The magnetism lessened. The power allowed her to come and go as she pleased, and she entered it as often as she could. Even once in the middle of the night when she'd woken from a dream. Talon expressed his unhappiness with her about it with his usual frown, and she swore not to do it alone again until he felt she was ready.

When not meditating with her, Talon worked his own Art to construct a dwelling for them to live in. He worked diligently; on several occasions, it wore him out quicker than she would've thought normal for an auer. He tackled the tree in stages, using his power to reshape the natural growth.

The first stage of crafting the tree into their home began with Talon splitting the hollow space in two. A curtain of ivy acted as a privacy screen to the far bedroom, where Talon had fashioned a platform for their bedroll to keep it off the ground, as well as shelves for storage. Above the head of the bed was another thin window, lined with ivy and jasmine flowers.

After a week of laborious work, he claimed to be nearly satisfied with his creation.

Talon rubbed at his temples when Amarie entered their main

living space through the narrow ivy-draped door. He'd manipulated the trunks of the trees into squared walls and a high ceiling. He sat in one of the newly grown chairs, built of roots sprouting from the moss covered floor. The counter along the wall had been there before, but he'd made the addition of a dining table.

Amarie crossed to their kitchen space, lifting a parchment of fruits and some cheese to set it on the table in front of him. She could tell Talon was exhausted just by looking at him. He'd been working all morning on their makeshift home. She'd spent most of the early hours in meditation, but he'd checked on her often. She could stay amongst her power far longer now and still not feel the inclination to grasp it.

Talon insisted it should've taken much longer for her to reach such a point. Lying to her teacher would've been counterproductive, and he was beginning to believe her. She hoped to finally be able to touch it, but Talon would never feel comfortable with that step if he was in a compromised state.

"This place looks wonderful," she said, joining him at the new table. "How are you feeling?" She could help him recover faster if he allowed it, but he'd never accepted before.

"Exhausted," Talon said as he leaned towards the food. "Life-altering energies have always been more difficult for me to control. Makes me a pathetic example of an auer." He smiled.

"I could help you," she offered casually, putting half a cheese slice into her mouth.

Her attempt at keeping the offer light failed, and he narrowed his eyes.

"Perhaps," Talon said, "though it seems like a rather daring idea."

Amarie huffed a laugh and rolled her eyes. "Believe me, it's anything but. I've been doing it for years, mostly to Viento. I can restore your energy without risk. It's really the only aspect of my power I have complete confidence in."

Talon still hesitated. "I think you have ulterior motives again." He pursed his lips, but a vague smile touched the corner of his mouth as he reached for one of the purple berries they had picked together from the forest. He'd said they were his favorite.

"By increasing your endurance and strength?" she scoffed. "Of course not." A smirk played on her lips.

"While those two things may be welcome, especially when considering how I might be able to abuse such things *with* you, I know you well enough to suspect something far more sinister. Involving the Art, perhaps?" he asked.

"I promise, no ulterior motives," she said. She spoke the next part quickly, stringing the words together in the hope he wouldn't pay much attention to them. "But I'd like to actually hold my power today."

"Ah *ha*." Talon pointed an accusatory finger at her, its tip stained with berry juice. "See. I told you." He shook his head and stubbornly crossed his arms. "Taunting me with things like *endurance*."

His tenor voice sent a pleasant feeling down her spine, and she bit her lower lip briefly. Holding out her hand, palm up, she raised an eyebrow. "Would you rather be exhausted, my stubborn auer?" she asked coyly.

He eyed her hand, wrinkling his nose as if afraid it would hurt him if he touched it. "I suppose not. But why do I feel like there are strings attached to this offer?" He mirrored her lip bite purposely, teasing her about her instinctive habit.

"No strings," she chirped and circled the table towards him. "We can discuss the next step of my training once you're feeling better. You can still decline my request."

Talon squinted at her as if he still doubted but finally sighed and shrugged. "Fine, you win," he said, leaning back to let her sit on his lap. "But this doesn't mean you're taking the next step."

"I wouldn't dare assume," she played, tangling her fingers back into his hair. The familiar warmth of his embrace closed around her waist, and she leaned to kiss him.

Her eyes closed as she sought the familiar power she used to nullify other sources of the Art. She severed off a small amount, allowing it to flow through the connection of their lips. This was raw, potent energy and needed no controlling other than how much she let go.

Talon reacted instantly as it rushed into his body. He drew in a sharp inhale through his nose, longer and deeper than the kiss would demand. The hand that had slipped to her thigh tightened, his entire body tensing before rapidly relaxing again. His eyes shot open, and his lips parted from hers. The green in his irises shone brighter, swirling with strength and awareness that had faded in his exhaustion. His face flushed momentarily, as if he'd been sitting in front of a fire.

Pulling her to him, he pressed his lips more firmly to hers. With a single arm around her waist, he lifted her to the table, standing between her knees. His hand played at the skin near her waist.

Amarie wrapped her legs around him, his mouth hot against hers as he pressed against her. The depth of their kisses lingered. She dragged her fingernails through his hair, his touch making her spine tingle. It was hard to remember her initial purpose in getting him to accept the energy transfer. If this continued, their goal of taking things slowly wouldn't last much longer.

As his kisses softened, her mind gradually returned, and she nipped at his lip before pulling away just enough to speak. "I may have won, but I'm pretty certain you didn't lose," she whispered before kissing his upper lip.

He savored her bottom lip with a light flick of his tongue. An inhale took his mouth away from hers as he smiled. "Definitely not," he agreed. "The results of this defeat are acceptable."

"You try my self-control, *auer*," she said affectionately.

His eyes flashed in his desire. "It's my natural charm that you, *human*, cannot resist," he teased.

She shook her head. "I doubt it's merely a trait of your ancestry, considering I spent plenty of time here and this, Talon, I didn't encounter," she said seriously, and then added with playful nibble at his lip. "At least, not to this degree."

Talon hummed in interest at her suggestion, nuzzling his cheek into her hair and moving his lips near her ear. "Interesting," he whispered. "Are you proposing it's something other than my charm?"

"Most definitely," she confirmed, eyes sliding closed as his lips grazed her ear lobe, teeth gently biting.

"And what is that, my *araleinya*?" he asked breathily.

"You," she said, keeping her eyes closed. "You are the something else."

Talon breathed again near her ear, a soft exhale with a low hum. "I apologize," he said, and she could hear the smile in his tone. "I believe it only fair that I try your willpower, since you constantly try mine." He ran his hands down the length of her body, playing at the hems of her clothes.

"I suppose," she agreed, and tilted her head to kiss the side of his neck. "Are you going to fight me so hard next time I offer you energy?" she asked and bit his skin.

He moaned. "I'd be a fool to," he admitted, managing a small laugh. "I could think of many... practical applications to unending energy."

She laughed and moved her lips to his ear. "Are you ready to let me touch it?" she whispered, letting her meaning take an extra moment to sink in.

Talon's body tensed, breath caught in his chest. "I would hope you always feel free to touch," he said but then smiled and moved to take her chin. He held her mouth in front of his, looking at her eyes. "Of course, it depends on *what* it is you're referring to. I suspect my hopes won't match yours."

She met his gaze and grinned. "They do, but at this exact

moment, I'm referring to my Art," she said, legs tightening around him as distracting desires flickered in her mind.

"Really?" he asked slowly, seeming interested at what she implied. He gave her chin a gentle shake. "Perhaps we'll have to explore those alternative desires after you meditate, and I guide you through the next step of using your Art."

She excitedly kissed his upper lip. "Might make it difficult to take things slowly, in that case," she said and unwrapped her legs from him as he stepped back from the table. She slid off it to her feet. "I'll go outside to meditate, and then we can take it a step further?"

He sighed and nodded as he dropped his hand from her face. "I'm right behind you."

Her body still hummed with passion, but she moved away while she could. She slipped outside through the narrow opening within the tree trunk. It was never very bright, but the birds were awake, and the leaves far above her head rustled in the wind. Moving towards the river, which was only thirty yards away, she walked to her favorite spot—a thick carpet of grass nestled into a crescent of roots belonging to a nearby banyan tree.

Amarie sat cross-legged amongst the lush green blades as she usually did. Composing her breath came easier now. As she closed her eyes, she found herself amidst the latent power. It didn't pull at her the way it did the first time she tried. It merely existed all around her, with soft touches to remind her it was there.

She'd learned to remain aware of the surroundings of her physical body while in the trance, and Talon stepped loudly to let her know he was approaching. She smiled as the grass behind her shifted with his approach. The warm pressure of his chest against her back brought a feeling of safety as he embraced her.

"You breathing?" Talon's voice whispered near her ear as his hands pressed against her abdomen.

The play in his voice told her he knew she was, but she drew in an extra deep one just for effect. Her power pulsed with the breath as she let it out, like it too was drawn to Talon's touch.

"Just as I should be," she replied, bringing her hands to rest on top of his.

"How does it feel today?" Talon asked as his breathing matched hers as it always did. Slow, long breaths helped keep her centered even if it wasn't as necessary any more. "Still like water?"

Amarie nodded. "Mhmm. Calm water," she said, squeezing his hands.

"Find a place just outside the water," Talon instructed. "Standing on the shore, looking over it. Where you're not touching it, and it's not touching you."

Amarie took his instruction, removing herself from the depths of power. She imagined herself standing beside the rippling waves of energy somewhere deep within her. It pulsed like ocean waves towards her, but she kept her toes from its reach.

"I'm there," she said.

"Tell me what you feel. Your emotions," he said. "You're anxious." It wasn't a question; he knew what she was feeling but unwilling to admit. "What else?"

Taking a deep breath, she urged herself to relax against him. She had learned many sessions ago that hiding anything from him was fruitless and counterproductive to her learning. "I feel excited," she admitted, "nervous, but I don't feel afraid."

"No fear is good," Talon commented. "But it's important you control all emotion in this moment. Take that excitement and bottle it. The nerves, breathe them out."

Amarie inhaled deeply, their hands rising together. Wrapping the tension in the pit of her stomach with the air, she willed it away with an exhale. Nothing remained but the water and her, standing beside it.

"Reach out your hand," Talon said, taking hold of her wrist. As her hand outstretched in her mind, her physical body followed suit, vaguely aware of him guiding the motion. "Take only the smallest drop from the surface. Feel it between your fingertips, its texture and weight."

Amarie did as instructed. Her hand reached towards the water's surface, pinching a wave between her fingertips. It tickled at first, like a wriggling worm. She drew it back towards her, dropping the dark bubble of liquid into her palm. The energy flopped against her skin, writhing to try to burrow into her palm lines.

"Keep it there, don't let it flow into you. You must control that." His words echoed in her mind.

She drew in a quick breath to prohibit the power from seeping into her skin. It flowed back to seek another entry point, but failed again, rolling towards the center of her palm where it lay dormant.

"It's working," Amarie said, extending her other hand. She poured the energy from one palm to the other in an absent motion she hardly had to think about. It pooled in her cupped hand.

"Draw farther from the rest of the pool," Talon said. "That small amount you have is all you need, carry it away."

Nestling the little bubble of energy between her hands, she held it close to her chest. She imagined stepping away from the beach of her power.

"Good," Talon said, not needing to hear her confirmation.

Staring into the small rippling swirl of power within her palms, she waited for him. This was a point she'd never gotten to before. She'd never held it like this and not been afraid of being swallowed by it all.

"For this, you must focus and keep your mind intent on your singular purpose," Talon instructed as his fingers spread those of her physical body, holding her hands out in front of them.

She nodded, both in her mind and beside his head. Strands of his hair tickled her cheek.

"Water is how you see it and will be the easiest to manifest physically. Not yet, but in a moment, acknowledge the fabric in the air and what it demands you see. That power you hold will be your tool to change it. As it passes from your spiritual self into the physical, you must direct it with your breath to the tips of your fingers." As he described the path the power must take, he traced it with one finger. His hands traveled down her arms and across her palms before returning to her waist. "As it reaches your fingers, imagine it, feel it, press against the fabric and make it become what you see. Water. And force it to obey only you," he said. "Are you ready?"

Nodding, she exhaled. "Ready," she confirmed.

"Don't allow your next breath to touch the pool. Only what you hold. And with your exhale, take it into your being and direct it as I told you," he said.

Bringing a breath to her lungs, she focused on the power she had and as she exhaled, she connected herself back to the physical. Her body buzzed, like a coming thunderstorm. The power stirred within her veins, but it couldn't overtake her control.

Opening her eyes, she saw a pool of water defy nature as it swirled into existence within her palms. It didn't drip or run down her arm but pressed coolly against her skin, distantly feeling wet. She smiled, at ease as she moved it from one palm to the other, aware of the pulse that reverberated like a heartbeat. She'd felt it before but never in such a contained way.

"I can still feel the latent energy in your hands," Talon said as he reached to intertwine his fingers with hers for just a moment. "Use it to shape the water." He guided her empty hand, cupping it over the other. "Control that pulse and tell it to obey your will."

Embracing the flow of energy concealed in her fingertips, Amarie tugged on the threads of the fabric between her palms. The Art allowed her access as she moved her hand away from the puddle of liquid, revealing her creation.

The water, crystal clear, formed a flower. It was one he would recognize as the common stylized depiction of the rare Art-laden flower of Eralas; he had endearingly named her for it. *Araleinya.*

Talon smiled against her hair and kissed behind her ear. "Appropriate," he said as his hands glided down her arms back to her waist. "And beautiful. How do you feel?"

"Calm," she said. "In control."

"That's the most important thing," Talon said.

After he shifted to the grass beside her, she turned to face him. He smiled, eyes bright like the moss on the trees around them. She nestled her palms in her lap, still holding the araleinya bloom.

"It's far too easy for you to be overwhelmed because of the sheer depth. Most people have puddles of power compared to your oceans. An ocean is far more dangerous in its natural state. That's why you must always take small pieces and move it away from the rest. If you go too quickly, try to draw from the entire mass, it will overpower you. It's like opening the gates of a dam. But now you know how to take small parts. And the process will become more natural with practice." He spoke precisely, seeming to want to make it infinitely clear to her.

"I also suspect," he continued, "that over time, your eyes will maintain their usual color instead of this enchanting violet and rosy pink I'd expect in an auer." Talon pinched the bottom of her chin.

She laughed; the Berylian Key's power always surfaced in her eyes first. Her hiding aura usually kept them their natural shade. Something to work on.

"Must I put it away?" she asked, prepared to if he instructed. "Or can I... play, with this?"

His response was a half-smile as his hand passed through the air above where she held her watery creation. With a whisper of power, and a twitch of his fingers, the water froze and dropped into her palm. He took it from her and settled it into the grass beside them.

"You should try again," he said. "You must. And this time, I won't help you. It's time you practice alone. But don't take more than you just did unless I'm with you."

"I'll make another," she said but breathed to control the excitement before it could take hold. She closed her eyes, delving back into her power.

Talon didn't touch her this time, but she sensed him close. She imagined the sound of his breath, unable to hear it over the gurgle of the river and birdsong.

He rose as she reached the edge of her power, imagining it the same as before. The space Talon usually occupied suddenly felt empty. The chatter of the forest faded, but that was to be expected as she focused. Talon was purposely trying to distract her. He'd done so before while she meditated, and she steeled herself to remain focused on her task.

Something unexpected touched her senses a breath later, and it felt like the Art, but not her own. It buzzed somewhere nearby, and the ocean inside her stirred with unease. Before she took a pinch of her power, she stepped back. Dismissing the meditative state, she opened her eyes.

The birds didn't resume their singing like they should have.

Talon stood a few yards in front of her, but his gaze was on something behind her. The expression on his face caused her to tighten her hiding aura, pulling it around her like a dense blanket in a swift movement. In one fluid motion, she stood and turned around.

Blocking the view of the forest stood a formidable formation of auer. There must have been twenty soldiers, and they weren't simple city guards. They stood starkly still as their jewel-like eyes locked on the rejanai behind her.

Her heart thundered as she stepped to the side, placing herself between Talon and those who'd come for him. She shook her head, absently trying to calm the rising adrenaline.

The soldiers didn't move.

Her raw power pulsed at her palm without her fully realizing she'd summoned it.

Talon's hands stilled her when they came to rest heavily on her shoulders. "They don't deserve to die," he whispered, and her throat clenched. "They're merely performing their duty." His voice held a sadness she hadn't heard before.

It made her stomach ache with denial.

"Talon Di'Terian." A commanding female voice sounded as one of the soldiers stepped forward. She was dressed as the others, in silver armor closely fitted to her limbs, the joints covered in a thin, shimmering white material. The high collar, fitted like a choker around her neck, pushed against the underside of her jaw. Her stone-grey hair was looped in secure braids. A cornet with a downturned silver point rested perfectly against her forehead, identifying her as the commander of the brigade. Her ruby eyes were flicked with darker rims, which revealed her age despite the youthful, coffee-colored skin.

"You stand accused," the commander said, "of violating the orders of the Council. You were banished from these lands, and your presence here is inexcusable." Her feet moved silently across the grass, and her hand touched a chakram blade at her side, decorated with scrolling text. "You are to come, peacefully, and face Council Law for your crime, Rejanai, as well as those previously laid upon you." She stopped, her hand still on her weapon, as Talon squeezed Amarie's shoulders before letting go.

He moved to step around her, but she sidestepped again and kept herself in front of him.

"No," Amarie said firmly, eyes locked on the commander. "He's here because I brought him here." Her blood heated with desperation to prevent Talon's suffering.

The commander sneered, looking at Amarie, then at where Talon's hand touched her waist. "It matters not, *human* girl," she spat. "Talon Di'Terian will be held responsible for his defiance of Council Law. Regardless of fault or intention." She took another step forward; the muscles of her arm tensed as fingers closed around her weapon's handle. "Step aside."

"Amarie," Talon pleaded and pressed his hands against her ribs, trying to urge her aside. "Please, don't."

Her panic rose with a deafening pulse in her ears. She'd only be able to prevent this with a great loss of life. But if she couldn't prevent it, then she needed to find another way. "Then you should arrest me as well," she blurted.

The soldiers behind the commander exchanged glances, and Talon's grip tightened to an uncomfortable pressure. But she refused to look at him.

"No," Talon whispered in her ear, but she wouldn't be deterred.

With quick fingers, she yanked the dagger she always kept at her thigh free.

The soldiers instantly tensed, and a series of rasps signaled a collection of weapons being drawn. Their ranks spread a step apart.

The grey-haired commander slid her feet through the dirt to a spread stance as her chakram whipped from her side. She readied it in front of her, eyes on Amarie's dagger.

Talon pulled Amarie back, trying to put her behind him, but she stubbornly planted her feet.

Amarie lifted her empty hand to assure her compliance, quickly flipping the dagger to hold it by the blade, offering the hilt to the commanding officer. "I stole this five years ago. From your armory."

The commander narrowed her crimson eyes but relaxed enough to lower her blade beside her hip. She stepped forward and snatched the hilt, lifting the blade closer to study it.

Talon cursed colorfully in Aueric, the words rolling over his tongue. It drew a glance from the commander before she looked back to the steel, turning it in her hand.

Everyone stood frozen as the commander contemplated. A breath later, the woman spun the blade without warning, slipping it into her belt. It matched her armor in craftsmanship, the hilt dark against it. She eyed Talon over Amarie's shoulder briefly, then took her time in examining Amarie from the ground to her head.

Her jaw tightened before she spoke her order, which rang clear through the air. "Arrest them both."

The story continues in...

UNRAVELING
OF THE SOUL

www.Pantracia.com

A soul can be broken into fragments, but giving them away could cause the rest to unravel.

While continuing the ruse of Amarie's death, Kin suffers at the hands of his master. The path his life must take becomes clear when his mother's life is jeopardized. Ridding himself of the corrupt power in his veins is the only choice he can make. It is no minor task, but he can't let Uriel continue to use him and gain the throne of Feyor.

Confined to restrictive quarters, Talon has nothing to do but dwell on the circumstances of his life and recent actions. Brought before the Elder's Council and isolated from Amarie, he stands accused of crimes, both old and new. He must face the consequences of bringing her to Eralas, and defying his banishment.

After throwing herself to the mercy of the auer, intent on sparing Talon a horrendous fate, Amarie fears nothing can change the outcome of his sentence. In a drastic act, she bargains with the greatest leverage she has and hopes she isn't too late.

Desperation fuels life-altering decisions, placing the future of Pantracia in grave danger. If those who seek to protect it fail... the kingdoms, and life as they know it, will fall to ash and shadow.

Unraveling of the Soul is Part 3 in *The Berylian Key* trilogy, and Book 3 in the *Pantracia Chronicles*.